Robes

Tim O'Leary

All the best

Tim O'Leary

11-25-20

Robes

Copyright ©2020 Tim O'Leary

ISBN: 978-0-9969921-3-8

Published by Tim O'Leary Books
timolearybooks@gmail.com

To order additional copies and/or ebooks (Kindle) of this title, visit www.amazon.com

Other books by Tim O'Leary

The Day Job, 2010

Cover design by Patricia Moffett
Book layout by Robin Wrighton

Printed in the United States of America

For Pat ~
For me, the most important part of
PATIMKERRY and the larger
family we've become.

Author's Note

Writers often thank experts they consulted in the course of a novel's creation. They thank them for the generosity of their time and expertise, and then modestly assert any mistakes in transmitting the shared wisdom to the printed page are entirely of the author's making. I did not consult any experts. I used research, my imagination and life experiences to create the characters, images and incidents depicted on these pages. That, it seems to me, is one of the fine points of a novel – it's fiction – it's not real – it's made up.

To any judges, retired or active, members of the clergy, including cardinals, bishops and monsignors, or any mob bosses who might view these pages, I encourage you to reread the above paragraph before continuing.

A note of thanks to early Massachusetts readers of *Robes*: My wife, Pat, Kerry Crisley of Wakefield, Henry Dane and Rose Cummings of Winthrop, Maura Green of Boston, Janet Fantasia of Reading, and Anthony Gangi of Danvers. Each offered advice, guidance, support and structure to my often unrestrained imagination. They made *Robes* better, and I am grateful.

Thanks to Patricia Moffett, a friend and talented graphic artist, for giving *Robes* a great cover.

Lastly, thanks to my best friend and to a former colleague – both great guys – for allowing me the use of their names to create characters wholly unlike either of them.

Chapter I

On the morning of the last day of his life, the Honorable Robert Charles Bartoni, Justice of the Massachusetts Superior Court, stood bare foot in plaid pajamas in front of the full-length mirror attached to the door of his bedroom closet. He stared at his image, his eyes focused on the growing baldness, made worse by his unkempt bed head. He had awoken early. Unable to recapture sleep, he decided his Saturday morning power walk would be earlier than usual. He reached into the closet and retrieved a pair of sweat pants and a maroon Harvard University wind breaker.

Bartoni enjoyed the limelight. Always available to the media and eager to offer his opinion on whatever had captured their attention, Bartoni was a media star. Two years from the mandatory retirement age for judges, Bartoni dreamed of a second career in television, a legal analyst, perhaps a cable show. He joined a private health club and gym as part of this career plan. He arranged to have the monthly billing sent to a post office box to avoid the curiosity of his wife. By prepaying the annual fee for the box, he avoided further scrutiny. Bartoni was secretly saving for a hair transplant.

He stripped and stepped on a new scale his wife purchased and left in his bedroom. He glanced at the bright red numbers signaling a gain of three pounds since Saturday.

Shit.

He dressed quickly and quietly. He turned off the alarm, set for an hour later. Its sharp buzz cutting through the air might wake his wife across the hall. *Let the bitch sleep,* Bartoni thought.

But the bitch was already up.

Carmela Bartoni sat at the kitchen table, her hair in rollers and covered with a bright blue towel. "Here I was hoping for some peace and quiet," she greeted her husband.

1

"You couldn't sleep?" Bartoni said. "Neither could I." He walked past her, towards the refrigerator, briefly touching her shoulder. Bartoni felt the cringe at his touch.

"Still worried about what you'll do after retirement? Why not travel? Afraid to get too far from the limelight?" She gave out a guttural laugh. Her tone softened. "Keep working on the memoir. Your fans wills buy copies. You should spend more time in your study; get your thoughts on paper."

Get away from me is what you mean, Bartoni thought. Instead he said. "I'm going for a walk. I'll get the papers. You need anything?"

"A life would be nice," she said.

"Jesus," Bartoni muttered. "Give it a rest." He walked towards the back door.

"You've lost your sense of humor," Carmela said without looking up. "Enjoy your walk," she said to the closed door. She stood, stretched her arms, and announced to the empty room, "I have to get ready for a meeting with my foundation."

———

An hour later, Bartoni sat in the swivel chair in his study and watched the dust motes floating in the elongated sphere of mid-April sunlight slanted across his mahogany desk and three newspapers. He poured coffee from a pewter container into a large white cup emblazoned with the seal of Harvard University. He decided against breakfast. "Three fucking pounds since last Saturday," he muttered. The new digital scale angered him. Too precise. Bartoni decided to look for an old-fashioned scale with a stationary needle over a rolling measure wheel. He would bring it to the courthouse and move the weekly weigh-in to Friday afternoon. More visits to the gym were in order. He wrote the word "scale" on a piece of yellow, legal-size paper and tore it from the pad.

These decisions pleased Bartoni. He smiled and added three packets of sugar to his coffee. He walked to the foyer and put the piece of paper into his briefcase. A muted knock on the front door caught his attention.

"Jesus, on a Saturday," Bartoni said. He dropped his cross pen into an outside pocket of the briefcase, unchained and unbolted the door. He forced a smile to greet this unwelcome disturbance and pulled the door back into his foyer. A man in a white shirt, red tie and a dark suit stood on the other side of the screen door. He held a briefcase.

It seemed to Bartoni his features were distorted by the screen. "Whadyawant?" he barked.

The bullet went through the screen and hit Bartoni in the center of his forehead. He stumbled back, knees buckling. A second bullet whispered into his stomach. Bartoni collapsed to the floor, his mouth spewing blood onto the wide oak planks of the foyer floor.

He died with his eyes open.

Chapter 2

I hate running, and I've never experienced a runner's high. The only high I get from running is the exhilaration of stopping. Like when you remove your ski boots after a day of sliding on a mountain with sticks attached to your feet.

I run to stave off the pounds that climb onto my six foot one inch frame whenever I stop running. I can hide two hundred pounds with loose clothing and indirect lighting, but when the scale edges toward 210, I pull out the running shoes. I've been doing this for about twenty years, charting each run, weighing in every Thursday.

A few years ago, I noticed the time it took for the extra pounds to climb aboard whenever I stopped running, had accelerated. What used to take several months, was happening in several weeks. I've been running ever since. If I stop now, the weight would be back before I finished showering.

It was the second Saturday of April, the sky an impossible blue and winter's street litter drying in the warm sun of spring. I was in the third and last mile of my thrice weekly run. The dark green ocean to my right gave a view of Martha's Vineyard, about eight miles across Vineyard Sound. The Island, often shrouded in fog, mist and haze, appeared crisp and new, as if it just erupted from the water.

My wife, Abby, and I moved to Falmouth on Cape Cod two years after my incident with former Massachusetts Governor Thomas Hands. "Incident" might seem too benign to describe my role in exposing a sitting governor as a serial killer, as well as not disclosing who killed him, but it's the word Abby and I use. If he were alive, Governor Hands might suggest a different one.

We sold our colonial home north of Boston and bought a small cape in Falmouth, close enough to hear and smell the ocean, but not to see it. Early morning fog, squawking seagulls and the melodious bark of the passenger ferry's horn entering Falmouth Harbor from Martha's Vineyard, or leaving for the return trip, were frequent and pleasant reminders we were living in a beach town. The one and a half hour bus ride to Boston two days a week for my part-time lobbying job with an environmental advocacy group was a less pleasant reminder.

I lobby because that's what state representatives do when they're no longer state representatives. In my case, I'm no longer a state representative because I went to jail for misusing campaign funds to pay personal expenses like my son's college tuition and the monthly mortgage payments on my house. Since I was an attorney, albeit one with few clients, I was disbarred as a result of the conviction. After serving my time, the name Connor McNeill lost whatever luster it ever had and finding employment became problematic.

I delivered papers for almost a year before I got a part-time contract as a lobbyist for the Clean Environment Campaign. The opportunity was advertised in *The Boston Globe*. I saw it during the ten minute break I took in the predawn hours each day driving around the streets delivering the paper. I got the contract because when I was a state rep, I did a favor for a friend of a friend whose sister's husband was Chairman of the Board of Directors for the Clean Environment Campaign. He never knew me, and I never knew him. When I applied, my friend, who was the first link in the favor chain, made certain the final link knew of my interest and the favor I had done. *Voila* I was hired. Like the sweatshirt reminds us: Life is good.

I chugged up a small incline and a gust of wind blew sand in my direction. I lowered the bill of my green Boston Celtics baseball hat to block it and increased my pace.

Another reason I hate running.

My lobbying contract is only part-time, and I like to eat and live full-time. So, I kept an eye out for opportunities to make money. That's what led to "the incident" with Governor Hands.

A friend hired me to do opposition research on Governor Hands, who was running for re-election. Hands had been a star receiver (with the perfect name for his position) with the New England Patriots in the seventies, well before Tom Brady and Super Bowl victories. A knee injury ended his career. He stayed in the Boston area for the next thirty or so years engaging in a variety of public service activities. Eventually he turned to politics.

An acquaintance from jail hooked me up with a bookie. Before the advent of fantasy football and internet sports betting, bookies were the go to guys to learn about players. I hoped to hear Thomas Hands used performance enhancers or was a womanizer while playing with the Patriots. Anything to dust up the goody two-shoes image he had cultivated for himself after hanging up his jock strap. I wasn't optimistic, but it was a place to start.

The bookie I met used a variety of aliases. I knew him as Freddy. He had a network of older, now retired bookies, as well as others who lived, worked and played on the wrong side of the street. As a result of research, a lot of leg work and enormous luck we developed fairly convincing evidence Hands killed homeless people and prostitutes – folks whose murders would not generate a lot of interest or action – the nights before games played in cities other than Boston.

Killing was his performance enhancer.

We assembled our "evidence" into a binder we called the Victims' Portfolio. I wanted to bring it to the police, but Freddy considered them an occupational hazard he needed to avoid. He left town and agreed I could do whatever I wanted with the information. Before leaving, Freddy gave me a two-headed quarter for luck.

I gave what we had developed to a retired state police office I trusted, even though he was a Hands' supporter. I maintained a low profile as the Massachusetts Attorney General prepared a case against the Governor. The day before Hands was to be indicted, an intruder broke into his Boston Townhouse and killed him. They found a two-headed quarter in the Governor's mouth.

I learned from the chief investigating officer, Anthony Novello, Hands knew of my involvement and had targeted me for one of his next kills. While I told Novello about Freddy, I never disclosed he had given me a two-headed quarter. There's no doubt in my mind Freddy killed Governor Hands. And, I have no doubt if Freddy had not acted when he did, the Governor might well have killed me, and I would not be jogging along Surf Drive in Falmouth.

Maybe "incident" is too benign.

On my right a weathered snow fence ran across dunes with clumps of beach grass sprouting up like cowlicks. Where the fence crossed a narrow footpath to the beach its long, flat pickets had captured a faded Popsicle wrapper, a piece of aluminum foil and some dead leaves. A thirty-something man in a blue windbreaker jogged past me at a hearty clip. He kicked it up to a run and the distance between us grew as if I were planted in the asphalt. Nobody likes a show off.

Governor Hands' death set off a stampede of candidates to succeed the once charismatic, once popular, and once breathing Thomas Hands. The citizens elected Attorney General Paul Francis Concanon as their new Governor.

Concanon benefited from the public's perception it was he who discovered Governor Hands' dark past. As the state's chief law enforcement officer, Concanon had the first press conference, and he held onto the spotlight from the night the story broke to the day he was sworn in as the new governor.

Occasionally, an enterprising reporter or television producer would learn of my involvement and the name, Connor McNeill, would surface in a story which always mentioned I was a state representative, who had gone to jail for misusing campaign funds and was disbarred from the legal profession. There would be another paragraph or two highlighting the irony that it was Concanon, who had prosecuted me. When I was a "rising political star" I looked for my name in the news. Today, I relish my anonymity.

Concanon knew, of course, of my involvement in discovering Hands' secret. After he was elected governor, he offered to expedite a petition I had filed with the state asking permission to do research and paralegal work for a Cape Cod attorney. I filed the petition at the urging of Vinnie Preskin, a Falmouth attorney Abby and I met at a Jimmy Buffett concert. Vinnie recognized me and over five or so margaritas in the parking lot before the concert, he convinced me to accept part-time work in his office. I was convinced after the first margarita, but since they were cold and kept coming, I played hard to get. I liked Vinnie, and I think any attorney who's a Buffett fan and wears a Hawaiian shirt and grass skirt to the concert belongs on the Supreme Court.

I took Governor Concanon up on his offer and my petition was quickly (and quietly) approved. Two weeks later, I began working for Vinnie Preskin, Parrot Head and attorney at law. That was almost eight months ago.

I jogged past a boarded shack, which in two months would be opened. The front side would sell beach parking tickets to Falmouth residents. The back or beach side of the wooden structure would be selling delicious, greasy hamburgers on toasted rolls to the sun worshipers. The thought encouraged me and I kicked the jog up a notch. I enjoy a hamburger or two to celebrate the arrival of summer.

Across the beach parking lot, an elevated lifeguard chair, its iron legs caked with oxidized salt residue, cast a slanted shadow across a dented orange trash barrel that a few weeks ago held winter's last snow.

I rounded a looping corner to the left putting the ocean at my back. Falmouth has sixty-eight miles of coastline, so you're never too far from the water. A pale yellow Cadillac with Florida plates pulled out of a side street in front of me. It drifted to the middle of the road and slowed to what I call a moving stop. A bald head peered over the steering wheel between two hands in the ten before two position. The passenger was a white-haired woman with an active mouth and quiet hands.

The snowbirds have returned, I thought.

Chapter 3

After a shower and shave in our outdoor stall, I put on a bathing suit, a Boston College T-shirt and walked onto our deck. Abby had placed a thermos of coffee and two large cups on a table between two white Adirondack chairs positioned to take advantage of the late morning sun. *The Boston Globe* and the *Herald,* which I had purchased before my run, were stacked on another table. I took a gulp of coffee and grabbed the *Herald.* A minute or two later, I was looking over baseball scores when the storm door opened and Abby's voice preceded her to the deck.

"Hey Connor, somebody killed Bartoni," she said. "Good riddance."

My eyes shot away from the *Herald.* "No shit, what happened?"

"It was just on TV. One of those breaking news bulletins," Abby said. She walked over to one of the chairs and sat down. She wore a faded orange sweat shirt from her days as a lifeguard and tan slacks. "His wife found him on the foyer floor. The front door was open. He'd been shot to death." She took a sip of coffee. "If his wife had been shot, Bartoni would have called the TV stations before an ambulance."

Judge Bartoni had assigned himself the case charging me with perjury and misuse of campaign funds. He was a media hound and expected my case would become a lengthy trial and a media circus. My quick admission of guilt had turned it into a two-day story. The day before my sentencing hearing, my attorney, Carol Bell, submitted a confidential psychiatric report to Bartoni as part of an effort to keep me out of jail. The next morning, huge chunks of the report were in the *Herald.* Carol went ballistic and wrote a scathing letter to Bartoni threatening to file a complaint with Judicial Misconduct Commission.

I didn't care, and I was not surprised when Bartoni imposed the sentence recommended by Concanon. I've always thought he and Concanon had treated me fairly. Abby thought differently. She didn't think I deserved a parade, but she thought the news leak and a year in the can were excessive. Abby's wish for Bartoni was a long life with boils.

"Christ, in his own home," I said. "Wonder if it was a burglary gone wrong."

Abby's large, round, dark hazel eyes peered at me over *The Globe*. "On a Saturday morning?"

"You're right," I said. "A random drive by?"

I got the look again. "In Concord? Shots haven't been fired in Concord since the Revolutionary War."

"You're thinking Bartoni was murdered in broad daylight, on a Saturday morning, in his own house? Pretty bold for a planned murder," I said, pleased with my analysis.

"Maybe whoever did this, didn't care if he got away. Maybe he just wanted to kill the sonofabitch."

"Or she," I countered.

Abby returned to her paper. "I have an alibi."

I stared into the bright spring sky and thought about Bartoni. I felt sad. I could sense Abby watching me.

"Can I ask you something?" she said.

Whenever Abby asks if she can ask, I know she's looking to end the conversation, or at a minimum the subject matter. I smiled. "Sure."

Abby smiled back and a familiar flush washed over me. She tucked a strand of her brown-auburn hair behind her left ear. "Are you going to think and talk about Bartoni the next few hours? Or, can we enjoy this beautiful day, read our papers and maybe hit the Bridge for lunch or an early dinner?"

She was referring to The Flying Bridge, a restaurant on Falmouth Harbor, and one of our favorite haunts.

"Bartoni who?" I said and went back to the *Herald* and baseball scores.

A few minutes later the sun was higher and silence had descended on our deck. I thought about Bartoni. I felt hollow, like my stomach had been carved with a spoon.

Chapter 4

Monday dawned gray and uncertain. A lowering sky hovered over the ocean as I strolled the two miles to the law offices of Vinnie C. Preskin & Associates at the northeast corner of Falmouth Harbor. There were no associates. I didn't count since I was a paralegal. Also, as a disbarred attorney, who would advertise me as an associate? Or, as a paralegal? Perhaps a janitor.

Vinnie practiced law in a rambling, weathered shingled Victorian cape with million dollar views. He could afford it. His practice blended corporate law and tax work, with financial and estate planning. Vinnie's clients were profitable and paid on time. He could also afford it because the property had been in his family for several generations, and, as an only child, he inherited it free from debt.

But not free from dispute.

Vinnie's first cousin (on his mother's side), Robert "Bobby" Morelli, is connected to the Fall River Mob, which is a wholly owned subsidiary of a New Bedford Mob trying to extract itself from the Providence, Rhode Island Mob. When Vinnie's mother died, Bobby produced a letter from her promising him the harbor side Victorian. It was an obvious forgery, but it took Vinnie fifteen months and a ten thousand dollar payout to chase Bobby away and take ownership of the house.

On the two mornings I go into Boston, I get up at four-thirty and take the five-twenty bus to Boston. On my workdays with Vinnie, I sleep in until six. It was almost seven-thirty when I walked through the front door. The unmistakable sound of someone trying to fold a newspaper floated from Vinnie's office.

"Top of the morning to you, Connor McNeill," Vinnie called out.

Vinnie's as Irish as Muhammad Ali, but takes on a brogue

13

whenever he greets or summons me. I stuck my head into his office. "And the rest of the day to yourself, Vincent Preskin."

The Boston Globe was spread across Vinnie's walnut desk. Papers, files and illegible notes on scraps of paper were scattered as if dropped from the ceiling. More stacks of paper and folders occupied the chairs around a cluttered conference table. In the corner behind Vinnie's desk and pointed out the large window to the harbor was a brass telescope, shiny as the day it was purchased. I never saw Vinnie use it. A large black leather bag of golf clubs stood in another corner under a picture of Vinnie and a group of golfers standing behind a mid-size trophy positioned on a table like a center piece. The golf clubs, I knew, were frequently used and bore the markings of an avid golfer, who rarely cleaned his clubs.

Vinnie was fifty-four and joked he would never live to be as old as he looked. Partial to short, thick cigars, his teeth were yellowed like the keys of a neglected piano and framed by a mouth that seemed off-center. He pushed his reading glasses to the top of his head and into a nest of unruly dark brown hair. He pointed to the only chair free of clutter. "Got a minute?"

"Sure," I said and sat. "Whose dime?" I kept meticulous records on my time so Vinnie could bill the correct client. This is something I never did when I practiced law. Probably explains why I never made money. That, and the absence of clients.

"Tell you in a minute," Vinnie said. "You heard about Judge Bartoni?"

"Yeah," I said. "Getting a lot of play. Must kill Bartoni to be missing all this."

"Did you know him?"

"Mostly by reputation," I said. "Friend of mine lobbies for the Judge's Council. I've heard a few stories about Bartoni, his love affairs with himself and the media. The press loved him because he'd talk with them. Bartoni was always good for a quote or a thirty second sound bite. The other judges didn't think much of him. They pretty much considered him an egomaniac, who couldn't be trusted."

Vinnie smiled and nodded. I sensed he knew there was more, so I told him. "Bartoni sentenced me. I think he was fair, and I didn't get his usual harangue even with the television cameras there." Outside the window behind Vinnie's desk, a seagull circled the harbor and came to a fluttering stop on top of a thick piling.

"Wasn't that because Carol Bell threatened to file a complaint against him for leaking information to the *Herald?*"

I felt those words in my stomach and stared at Vinnie. "How'd you know that?"

"Carol's a friend," Vinnie said.

"Is she why I'm working here?"

"Jesus, no, Connor," Vinnie said. He waved his arms as if to dispel the thought. "Carol and I went to law school together. I followed your case because it was front-page news and she was your attorney. I once asked her about Bartoni, what she thought of him. She told me about the leak to the *Herald.*"

"Okay," I said, without enthusiasm. The seagull flew off the piling and coasted toward the Flying Bridge Restaurant on the other side of the harbor.

Vinnie leaned towards me. "Now that Carol's a judge we never see each other. I'd be surprised if she knew you worked here. I hired you as a favor to myself. I needed help. I liked you, a fellow Parrot Head, so I offered you a job. I haven't regretted it since."

"I haven't either," I said. I felt like a fool. Not sure why I reacted the way I did. Why should I care if Carol asked Vinnie to help me? My stomach tightened. "I'm sorry, Vinnie," I said. "Guess Bartoni's murder is stirring up memories I thought were buried."

"Forget it," Vinnie said, with a dismissive wave. A brief smile flashed then disappeared. "But I need your help. Might stir up those memories."

"Got an interest in Bartoni?"

"I got a call last night from Tobias Fisher," Vinnie said.

"Judge Tobias Fisher?"

"The very same," Vinnie said.

Fisher had been appointed to the bench more than forty years ago. He had somehow maneuvered around the mandatory retirement age of seventy and was still hearing cases at the Falmouth District Court on his eightieth birthday. What started as a celebratory story on a judicial octogenarian turned into an expose' on an insider's political clout. The Judge was forced out a few months later, but continued reporting to the court each morning. He kept an office in the building and occasionally sat as a special master in civil hearings. No one seemed to know what to do about him. I think everyone decided it was easier to wait for him to die. He was now ninety-one, still rail-thin and in great health. Fisher became an immoveable fixture with a long memory and hidden connections.

Vinnie fiddled with a pencil, rolling it between his palms. "Judge Fisher told me he and Bartoni had lunch about a month ago, and they were supposed to meet again the day after tomorrow."

"And, Fisher knows the police will see his name in Bartoni's appointment book,' I said. "They'll ask him what the meeting was about. He's smart enough to know they'll see the previous lunch date and ask about that as well."

"And he's smart enough not to lie to police investigating a murder," Vinnie said.

"How are you involved?" I said.

"Judge wants to meet this afternoon. He'll pay me a modest – his word – retainer to create an attorney-client relationship. Then he'll tell me about his conversations with Bartoni, and he wants me to tell him what he should do.

"You might be the first person who's ever done that," I said. Something stirred in me. "No offense Vinnie, but the only experience you have with criminal law is your cousin Bobby. Why'd Fisher call you? You need some quick research?"

Vinnie stared back with eyes like a bright winter day. "Connor, you're the reason Judge Fisher called. He wants to meet with both of us."

Chapter 5

Judge Fisher's office suite at the Falmouth District Court was stashed at the end of a long corridor on the first floor, across from a stairwell to the basement. The lower half of the corridor walls had thin oak wainscoting, which triggered memories of elementary school. The top half was painted a light green with black and white photographs of government and public buildings in Falmouth, including the former arcade/casino at Falmouth Heights.

The court was a political reward to a popular state representative, who voted to increase taxes. Funds were never authorized to build a courthouse so the Falmouth District Court was sited in a National Guard Armory. It wasn't a Quonset hut, but the ambience was more military than jurisprudence.

Vinnie and I arrived five minutes early for the three o'clock appointment. Judge Fisher decided to assert his importance and make us wait. At seventeen past three we were still waiting in a small anteroom on two oak chairs with high rounded backs.

A seventy something woman with white hair, spun as fine as cotton candy, sat behind a metal desk, trying her best to look busy. It wasn't easy. Vinnie and I waited patiently, and I absorbed the silence. No telephones rang, the woman had no papers to shuffle, and no footsteps echoed down or across the corridor. There were no voices from behind the door to the judge's office and neither of the two indicator buttons on the telephone on the receptionist's desk ever blinked. Whatever Fisher was doing in his office, he was doing it by himself, or with a disciple of Marcel Marceau.

At three twenty-five, the door finally opened and a thin hand in a long sleeved white shirt with a shiny red cufflink beckoned us in. The receptionist smiled and remained seated as we rose and walked into Judge Fisher's office.

"Sorry to have kept you waiting," Fisher said. He deposited reading glasses into his shirt pocket. "I was reading the trial transcript of an important case and lost track of time." He extended his hand to Vinnie.

"That's okay, Judge," Vinnie said. "We know you're busy."

I smiled agreement. "Nice to meet you, Judge. I'm Connor McNeill." My hand slid into Fisher's. It was moist and felt as if it had just been pulled from a vat of lanolin.

The judge's desk was positioned near the far corner with the traditional power wall of citations, plaques, pictures and degrees. I thought of the wall behind the desk of the sheriff at the Billerica House of Correction. He had framed drawings of stick figures and the scribbles of his young children. The sheriff's wall was more impressive.

Fisher didn't assume the position of authority behind his desk. Instead, he motioned us to a grouping of two worn faded brown leather chairs and matching sofa, each piece with cracks of age running across its surface. He gestured for us to sit in the chairs while he grabbed the less prestigious corner of the sofa. One point for the judge.

Once we were settled in, Fisher placed an envelope on the glass coffee table in front of the sofa. "That's a check for seventy-five dollars," he said. He smiled and leaned back as if getting out of the way of starving cats diving for a fat fish. When neither of us moved, he pushed it towards Vinnie. "I assume that will cover an hour of your time."

Vinnie smiled. "It would've fifteen years ago, Judge."

Fisher flinched.

Vinnie picked up the envelope. "Just kidding, consider me retained. An attorney-client relationship now exists. It covers Connor as an employee of my office." Vinnie shifted in his chair. "So, what's up?"

"You get right to it," Fisher said.

"Well, we know how busy you are," Vinnie said. "Important case and all."

Fisher looked at me. "Connor, you've had an interesting decade." I didn't know if he was talking about the incident with Hands or the circumstances that brought me before Bartoni. I gave him a neutral smile. It's easier for me to stay out of trouble with my mouth closed.

"The judge smiled back and shifted his weight. He crossed his legs, and the rising trousers exposed white hairless legs thin as pencils. "You know, the last time I saw Judge Bartoni, your name came up."

"Really," I said. "Until Saturday morning, I hadn't thought of Judge Bartoni since the last time I saw him."

Vinnie leaned forward in his chair and said, "Judge, why don't you tell us about the last time you saw Judge Bartoni. By the way, was it here, or someplace else?"

Fisher turned towards Vinnie. "Judge Bartoni, wanted to meet someplace where he wasn't known."

"He actually admitted such a place could exist?" I said.

Fisher laughed. "Judge Bartoni was full of himself, but he wasn't a bad sort. I enjoyed his company. Most people aren't interested in being with someone my age."

Another point for Fisher, I thought. I decided no more fresh remarks about Bartoni. "I'm sorry you've lost your friend," I said.

I sensed Vinnie's glare, although he looked directly at Fisher. "Go on Judge," he said. "Where did you meet?"

Fisher wasn't ready to move at Vinnie's pace. He looked at me. "My God, I've known Judge Bartoni for over forty-five years, going to back to when he was a law student at Harvard." Fisher gave a hard-to-believe shake of the head and smiled. "It's not like we were best friends, but we made an effort to keep in touch. As I said, I met him when he was a student at Harvard Law School. I was the guest lecturer for a class on trial practice and procedure. I had just been appointed a judge, and, frankly, I was nervous as hell." Fisher smiled at the memory. "In any case, the class went well, and a week or so later, I saw young Bartoni observing me at the Wareham District Court. We had lunch and the connection between us was made." Fisher leaned towards me as if to share some profound secret. "We might go a year or even more without seeing each other, but whenever we ran into each other at a conference or whatever, the connection would reignite and we'd be talking our heads off as if we saw each other every day."

"A nice friendship," I said.

Fisher nodded. "I went to his swearing in ceremony when he was appointed judge. Then we lost contact for a good number of years. We'd exchange holiday cards with the typical message of let's get together, but for a long time it never happened. Then, at a judge's conference – must be ten years ago – Bartoni came out of nowhere and gave me a great hug. We sat at the same table for dinner and exchanged war stories, talked politics, that sort of thing. We pledged to make a point of staying in contact, having dinner or lunch two or three times a year." Judge Fisher laughed. "You know, at the time I figured he just wanted to know how I had avoided mandatory retirement. We agreed to get together, and by God we did. And you know the subject of retirement never came up. We would just chat, talk about lawyers, and judges. Who we thought were good and those who weren't." Fisher laughed. "Believe me, we put more in the latter group than the former." His eyes drifted up to the ceiling. "My God, that conference seems like last week and now Robert's gone." Fisher swallowed a sob and looked at me. "He was a good friend, even though we actually knew very little about each other. We were just two guys shooting the shit three or four times a year." Fisher smiled. "When you're my age, it's easy to become isolated. It's one of the reasons I come here every day."

I got a glimpse of Fisher's life and felt bad.

Vinnie's voice slid into my head. "Tell us about the last time you saw Judge Bartoni. Where did you meet?"

"We went to a restaurant in Plymouth. The Sea Spray or Seaside, something like that. A few blocks up from that cage where they keep the rock." He wiggled his fingers as air quotations around the word rock.

I expected Judge Fisher to keep talking but he didn't. It was as if he were testifying or pretending to be answering the questions of an adversary. Answer what is asked -- nothing else.

Vinnie spent less time in court than the Pope. I wasn't sure he picked up on what was happening. "How did he seem to you? What was his demeanor?" He asked.

Judge Fisher smiled. "What I would call anxious, but not nervous." Then he went silent.

While I felt bad Judge Fisher often felt isolated, I wasn't interested in spending the next week with him. "Judge," I said. "Things will go quicker if you just tell us everything. Then Vinnie can tell you what he thinks and what you should do. We can ask questions as you go along if we get confused. That okay with you, Your Honor?"

I got a five hundred watt smile from Fisher. Judges like being called judge, but they love "Your Honor."

"Okay, Connor, let me start at the beginning."

Chapter 6

Judge Fisher pulled an English Oval from his shirt pocket. "I give myself three of these every day. One of the rewards for living into your nineties." Fisher brought the flame of a thin gold lighter to the cigarette. "Either of you mind?"

I quit smoking more than twenty years ago, but I still loved the smell of an unfiltered cigarette. "Just blow a little in my direction."

Fisher tossed the lighter onto the coffee table and inhaled. He expelled the smoke through a satisfied smile. "Two days before St. Patrick's Day, Judge Bartoni called asking if I could meet him for lunch. He told me he had some sensitive matters he wanted to discuss. He was sitting in Cambridge and asked me to pick a restaurant on the South Shore. Someplace convenient for both of us, where we would not be disturbed."

"Why you?" Vinnie said. "I know you were casual friends. Were you also a confidant?"

Vinnie was a guy who couldn't resist asking questions. I wanted Judge Fisher to tell the entire story. You learn more with your mouth closed.

The Judge didn't seem to mind the interruption. He looked at Vinnie. "No, not really. When I was going through that media squabble about my not retiring at seventy, Judge Bartoni sent me a letter expressing support and asked if there was anything he could do to help. He said he had friends who could help. I wrote back thanking him, but I declined his offer."

Fisher leaned towards me. "I said something like save your friends for something important. I was polite, of course, but my God, didn't he realize I had friends as well?" Fisher shook his head at the absurdity. "I had ten years more than any other judge. Why should I embarrass my friends by asking for more? I resigned, and the story went away."

"Tell us about your lunch with Bartoni in Plymouth," Vinnie said.

"Well, as I said, he called me a couple of days before St. Patrick's Day to schedule a lunch, and we ended up meeting on March 19th, I believe. I know it was a Monday. I remember he was fifteen or twenty minutes late," Fisher said. "That was unusual. He was early for everything, even started court on time. I was beginning to think he wouldn't show when he came in like a whirlwind, taking off his coat as he rushed across the dining room my table in the far corner of the room." Fisher smiled at the memory, his cigarette ash growing gray and hooked.

"He say why he was late?" Vinnie asked.

The smile dissolved and Fisher looked at Vinnie with a flat stare. It was the look he might give an attorney who had interrupted the flow of a trial with an irrelevant question. He dropped his cigarette into a large glass ash try on the table. "No, he didn't tell me why he was late. If that were important I'd have told you. What Judge Bartoni did tell me is he suspected one of our illustrious judges was in the process of tampering with a case worth millions of dollars. You want me to talk about that? Or maybe you'd prefer we sit around and speculate why Bartoni was late for lunch? Maybe it was a mistake calling you. A third year law student wouldn't wonder why Bartoni was late." Fisher stared at Vinnie in bewilderment. As if he'd pissed in the punch bowl.

My knee started to ache. I wanted to slap Fisher for the shot he took at Vinnie. Sure, the question wasn't important, but Fisher – like a drill sergeant at Parris Island – enjoyed insulting him in front of an audience. I glanced at Vinnie. He seemed to be studying the empty space on the floor a few feet from his shoes. He stirred and fished the Judge's check from the inside breast pocket of his sports coat and returned it to the precise spot Judge Fisher had placed it earlier.

"Judge, I have clients who pay me more than three hundred dollars an hour to take care of their problems. Most of the time they listen to me. Occasionally they ignore me, but they never insult me. Because once they do, they are not my clients." He pushed the check towards Fisher and stood. "You asked for this meeting. I came out of professional courtesy, and I expected to receive it. I haven't, and I have no interest in staying. Connor is free to stay as long as he wants. But, he's here on your dime, Judge, not mine."

I stood up. Every molecule in my body wanted to hear more about Bartoni and the meeting, but I had to support Vinnie. "Judge, I always go home with the one who brung me." I started towards the door we had entered. I moved slowly. It felt like the dream where you can't walk a straight line, and if you're not careful, you'll go over a cliff or fall off a swaying bridge. Vinnie didn't seem to have any trouble moving. He was almost out the door, when Judge Fisher spoke.

"I'm sorry," he said. "Please stay." He had stood, but then collapsed back to the sofa. Cigarette ashes dotted his silk tie.

Vinnie stepped back into the room and looked at me.

"Your call," I murmured.

Vinnie flashed a wink and brushed past me. "Okay, Judge, let's hear the whole story."

Chapter 7

I sat in the chair I had left a minute ago. Judge Fisher was slumped in the corner of the sofa, his trousers hitched up to his arms pits. Vinnie looked as fresh and sharp as a nun's bib. He picked up the check and returned it to his shirt pocket. "Okay, your Honor, let's get started."

The Judge's dignity and posture resurfaced with the reference to his formal title. He reached for one of the English Ovals in his shirt pocket, appeared to think better of it, and folded his hands in his lap. He turned towards me.

"Connor, before we begin, you should know that Judge Bartoni had some kind words about you. He thought you took your punishment like a man and moved on with your life. Told me he thought about calling you after your involvement with the Governor thing became known, but he wasn't sure how you'd respond." Fisher laughed. "Even admitted he was somewhat afraid to call."

"I wouldn't have shot him," I said. "He'd have gotten an earful if Abby answered the phone."

"Speaking of Judge Bartoni," Vinnie said.

Fisher turned towards Vinnie. "Yes, well I'm not being as circuitous as you might think. Judge Bartoni's remarks about Connor came in the same conversation we had at the Plymouth restaurant."

"Which we're getting to," Vinnie said.

"As I said, he came rushing into the restaurant like a whirlwind and came over to the table. I asked him if anything were wrong, and he held up a finger to hold me off while he gulped down a glass of water. Then without any preliminary greeting or warning of any kind, he told me he might have had stumbled onto a conspiracy to fix a case worth twenty to fifty million dollars. Well, I was shocked and probably said something stupid. One of those mindless remarks you utter when you're taken completely by surprise." The judge looked at me with a smile that begged for agreement.

Outside, the rain that had threatened to appear all day started. Drops of water were plastered against the far window. The room felt stale.

"Go on," Vinnie prodded.

"Judge Bartoni told me he was working late one night at the new courthouse in Boston. Said he was leaving the court from a special exit they set up for judges at the back into a parking lot near Staniford Street. Bartoni told me as he approached his car, he saw a large black sedan heading down Merrimack Street. It caught his eye because it was late – perhaps close to midnight – and it was quiet except for the sound of this car. Bartoni said he saw the Chief Justice of our Supreme Judicial Court, the illustrious Gloria D'Alessandro, in the front passenger seat. The driver was Win Allen. I presume you both know of him?"

"He represented the Archdiocese of Boston in the sexual abuse cases," I said.

"Bartoni say when this was?" Vinnie said

"Said it was a month or so ago," Fisher said. "Those were his words. 'A month or so.' That would make it early to mid-February."

"Was he sure?" Vinnie said. "Couldn't have seen the car for more than a few seconds."

"I asked him that, as well," Fisher said. "Bartoni acknowledged room for error."

I glanced at the rain patterns on the far window and was reminded I didn't have an umbrella. Vinnie's voice brought me back.

"Let's assume it was D'Alessandro and Allen," Vinnie said. "The cases were settled without any appeal to the SJC. Bartoni couldn't hear any conversation they were having. What gave him the idea D'Alessandro bagged a case?"

"He didn't say. And, there was an issue which came before D'Alessandro," Fisher said. "Remember the plaintiffs who were dismissed from the case because the suit was filed after the statute of limitations."

"I'd forgotten that," Vinnie said. "Those plaintiffs argued the abuse they suffered was so horrific, they had repressed the memories of it. So the time period for bringing a lawsuit should not have started, until the memories resurfaced." Vinnie shook his head in bewilderment. "Goddamn church should have paid them something. Instead, everything was kept secret. Fuckin' child molesters in robes and white collars got shuffled around to new parishes and new altar boys."

"Well, in any event," Fisher said, "the trial court wasn't persuaded and approved the church's motion to dismiss those plaintiffs from the suit."

"I don't remember that issue being appealed to the SJC," I said.

Fisher shifted in the leather couch and the muted sound of a fart came out. I couldn't tell if it was gas or his trousers rubbing against leather.

"Your memory fails you, Connor," Fisher said. "The attorney who represented the plaintiffs initially filed an appeal with the appeals court, but the SJC, as they often do on important cases, took the case from the appeals court."

"So, D'Alessandro heard the appeal?" I said.

"Well, there was no hearing or oral arguments," Fisher said. "It was an expedited process. The court gave the parties ten days to file briefs, and there was a period for reply briefs. A few days later, the SJC issued an unsigned single sentence order affirming the trial court." Fisher fidgeted. "You can look it up. *Sheehan versus the Archbishop of Boston.* The vote was five to two."

"When was *Sheehan* decided?" I asked Fisher.

"Early January," Fisher said. "I remember thinking Happy New Year to the church when I learned the plaintiffs had been dismissed from the case."

"There wasn't any great hue and cry against the decision," Vinnie said. "I remember some kind of legislation passed addressing the problem for future plaintiffs."

Fisher nodded. "Judge Bartoni told me he went over to the SJC's clerk's office to examine the papers in the case. I think he was hoping to see how D'Alessandro voted. One of the assistant clerks told him the records were under seal. No review of the papers except by counsel of record and the trial judge."

"That unusual?" I said to Fisher.

"Somewhat, but given the nature of the allegations – sexual abuse of children by Catholic priests, can't say sealing the records was an abuse of discretion."

"So we don't have anything unusual let alone improper," I said.

"Just a five to two vote on a decision that screwed a lot of kids who had already been screwed by priests," Vinnie said.

"The *Sheehan* case saved the church a considerable amount of money," Fisher added.

"Bartoni couldn't hear any conversation between Win Allen and the Chief Justice, I said. "And he doesn't know how she voted on the case. So, why'd he think she bagged the case? Win could've been just driving her from a reception they had attended. Maybe she had car problems, a flat tire or whatever, and he was driving her home."

Fisher gave me a wry smile. "I said all of this to Judge Bartoni. He told me he had sources which encouraged him to keep looking. He also said he trusted his gut and was going to continue to investigate. We scheduled another lunch. Would've been day after tomorrow."

"So it was more than just thinking he saw them in a car together," I said. "Did he tell you his sources or describe them in any way?" I asked Fisher.

Fisher shook his head slowly. "No. I assumed he was referring to a member of the media hoping to stumble on a good story using

Bartoni to do all the work." Fisher smiled at me. "As you know, he had a curious relationship with a number of reporters. He talked with them all the time."

"Do you know if Bartoni had any kind of relationship with the Chief Justice," Vinnie asked Fisher. "I mean did he ever mention meeting her or speaking with her."

"No," Fisher said. "I remember we talked about her when she was nominated to be the CJ. He didn't think much of her. Saw her as an academic with no experience in the trenches."

"Judge, if I brought this kind of flimsy argument to you in a small claims case, you'd throw me out the window," Vinnie said.

Fisher smiled. "I probably would, but this isn't a small claims case and Judge Bartoni is dead." He leaned towards Vinnie. "Bartoni was different and a lot of judges may not have liked him, but he wasn't a fool. He never would have mentioned this to me unless he was sure something was wrong."

"He's right," I said to Vinnie. "This may be nothing, but the smart thing is to let the police decide that."

"Will they ask why I didn't go to them when Bartoni first mentioned his suspicion? I wasn't under any obligation to do so, was I?" Fisher said.

"No," Vinnie said. "You don't go to the police on the basis of someone else's suspicion. Tell them you hadn't given it a thought until you heard about Bartoni's murder."

Judge Fisher turned to me. "Connor, I wanted you here because you know that homicide cop who broke the matter of our former governor being a serial killer."

"Anthony Novello," I said. "I haven't spoken with him in over two years. Besides, Novello is Boston, Suffolk County. Bartoni was killed in Concord, so the Middlesex DA will be handling it with the Concord Police."

Fisher gave me a patient smile. "Novello is now head of the homicide bureau for the attorney general. I can assure you Attorney

General Kevin Flaherty and Anthony Novello will be taking over the investigation of Judge Bartoni's murder. No way is the killing of a judge being left to the Concord keystone cops." His eyes narrowed, and the ambience of judicial authority and confidence asserted itself. "Connor, Novello will remember you, and I want you to set up a meeting with him. I don't want to be dealing with shit kickers in Falmouth or Concord."

Chapter 8

"Did you call Novello?" Abby said. We were in Liam McGuire's Pub on Main Street enjoying tall Jameson and water. Tanqueray and tonic season was almost here, but in an Irish pub, Jameson seemed more appropriate. Besides, water instead of tonic helps reduce caloric intake and is easier than running. Abby suggested I simply switch to water, but I need to stay connected with my Irish heritage.

"I left a message with his office. Said I'd call him first thing tomorrow morning," I said.

"I liked Novello," Abby said. "Trusted him."

"And you thought he was hot," I said.

"I did."

I took a sip of Jameson. "Of course, that's not to say you'd dump me and run off with him," I said.

"In a New York minute," Abby said. She smiled, "The competition will keep you sharp."

"Maybe I should get some handcuffs," I said.

"That would be a start."

"Get you filled up with Jameson and I'll have my way with you when we get home."

"Talk about your New York minute." Abby laughed and lifted her glass in salute.

A waitress waltzed over and placed a small oriental salad with salmon in front of Abby and a large bowl of Guinness Beef Stew for me.

Another reason I have to jog.

The wind drove the rain against the large windows, clouding the image of foot traffic in brightly colored slickers and taut umbrellas. At the entrance, people shuffled as raincoats were removed and hung on a rack of ornate hooks.

Abby picked up her fork. "You're in Boston tomorrow, you could drop by to see him face to face."

"I'll call him first. If he wants to meet I will. But I think he'll just take the information and it'll end there."

"Maybe," Abby said. She poked her salad. "Wonder if he still has the ponytail."

———

He did, and the rest of Novello looked as I remembered him more than two years ago.

We met in front of the large bronze statue of Paul Revere on his horse. It sits at the head of the Paul Revere Mall in the North End. I knew Novello lived somewhere close by. We exchanged pleasantries. I congratulated him on his appointment, and commiserated with his having to work with Attorney General Kevin Flaherty, considered by many a world class asshole. Novello smiled and said he spent most of his time chasing other assholes leaving little time to interact with Flaherty. He knew I had moved to Falmouth, which I found a bit disconcerting, but I decided not to press the issue.

Novello wore an expensive looking double-breasted charcoal suit, white shirt and dark maroon tie. Pierre Cardin. I was in jeans, a faded blue shirt and corduroy sport jacket. Aging graduate lecturer. We sat down on a curved metal bench. Beyond the far end of the mall, the tower of the old north church stood erect and historic.

Anthony Novello was in his mid-forties with a thick, six-foot, muscular body. His long black hair, combed straight back to a small ponytail had the first flecks of gray, as did his goatee. Novello's reputation in closing cases was legendary. He claimed when people lied they gave off an odor he could detect. He was careful, methodical and successful.

"Connor, talk to me."

I told Novello everything Judge Fisher had said, leaving out only the insult he had hurled at Vinnie. I talked about our move to the Cape and my connection to Vinnie Preskin. Novello didn't take any notes, ask questions or offer any comments. For all his face showed, I could have been talking about Einstein's theory of relativity. When I finished he looked at me with the faint hint of a smirk. The diamond earring in his left ear seemed to wink as I waited.

"Am I supposed to be impressed that Fisher wanted to talk with me? I should call the Falmouth PD and ask them to haul his ass over to Concord. I didn't know judges forum shopped. Thought that was just lawyers. And, speaking of lawyers, why'd Fisher have to talk with his lawyer before he'd talk to me?"

"He went to Vinnie to get to me, and hopefully get to with you," I said. "And, please spare me the feigned shock. Everyone forum shops, including cops looking to get warrants. And, everyone knows the AG and the state police will be taking over this case."

"We already have," Novello said. "There'll be a formal announcement later today. "But I like to maintain good relationships with the locals."

"Makes sense," I said. "Look, Fisher's ninety-something and a medium size fish in a pond that's getting smaller. I promised Vinnie I'd call you, and if you want to get a statement from Fisher, he'll drive him to your office. I'd be grateful if you'd humor me on this. Vinnie's been good to me. Frankly, I don't give a shit about Judge Fisher."

Novello stared at me for a few seconds. "Humor *you*," he said. "You withheld information on who killed Governor Hands, and I've let that slide for two years. You think you'd be a paralegal, or whatever you call it, if I had mentioned obstruction of justice to the right people? Vinnie's not the only one who's been good to you."

"Christ, here we go again," I said. "I don't know or care who killed Governor Hands." I lied and hoped I didn't stink. "Don't try to make me spend the rest of my life thinking I owe you something. Call the Falmouth PD, if you want. I don't give a shit. I told Vinnie I'd try to set something up. I didn't promise you'd cooperate." I stood up in frustration and muttered. "Christ, and Abby thinks you're hot."

Novello stood, pulled out a phone and did the mechanics of inputting his password and making a connection. "Ed, get a hold of Attorney Vinnie Preskin in Falmouth. Set up a time for him and Judge Fisher to come by headquarters to give a statement on Bartoni. Make sure it's today and make sure Concord PD is in the loop." He returned the phone to his inside breast pocket. "Okay, I've made you a hero with Vinnie and Judge Fisher."

"Thank you," I said.

"Walk with me," Novello said.

We walked along Hanover Street, seemingly passing a restaurant every few steps. Novello grabbed my arm and we stopped near Mike's Pastry. "Connor, don't insult my intelligence by saying you don't know something about the Hands murder. We both know that bookie character you were working with had something to do with it. I'm letting it slide because he saved us the cost of a long trial and giving Hands three squares the rest of his life."

We started walking. "Mentioning it within a few minutes of seeing me for the first time in two years doesn't seem like letting it slide," I said.

"I like to break balls," Novello said. "You expected a hug?"

We crossed a narrow street, more like an alley. There are few places to park a car in the North End, let alone drive one. It was one of Boston's three original colonial neighborhoods, and cars – like the British Red Coats – were not welcome.

"You're letting it slide because you can't prove I knew anything," I said. "And I'm not admitting to something that would ruin the rest of my life. I haven't seen or heard from Freddy since the day he stuck me with the bill for a breakfast at the Holiday Inn in Somerville." That part was true, and I suspected Novello believed me.

We stepped aside as two girls in blue plaid school uniforms approached. Their lunch boxes collided as they giggled and skipped down the sidewalk and past us.

"Let's leave it at that," Novello said. "Understand that if I ever run across your friend Freddy, or whatever his real name is, he'll wish he had stayed hidden."

"Well, he's still hiding, and I'm not looking," I said.

We walked in silence for several minutes. I've learned that conversations with Novello can take time and do not always follow a straight path. Kind of like walking in the North End.

"Talk to me about Bartoni," Novello said. "He sentenced you, right?"

"Am I a suspect?"

"Don't be a jerk," Novello said, but with a smile.

I smiled back. "I really don't know any more than was in the biographical story in Sunday's *Globe*," I said. "He had a hard ass reputation and a mutual love affair with the media. He loved to grab high profile cases, and I don't think many judges trusted him. But, he was smart, and I read somewhere he'd never been reversed on appeal."

"You have a friend who lobbies for the judges."

"Joe McDonald," I said. "Want to talk with him about Bartoni?"

"And D'Alessandro, and Fisher," Novello said.

"I'll call him right now," I said.

I stopped and pulled out my phone, and in one of life's great rarities, a human voice answered. It was Joe and he agreed to meet with Novello at the Homicide Bureau in one hour. We started walking and passed a comedy club. A window sign declared amateur night every Wednesday. *Laughs and pasta.*

"Anything else?' I said to Novello.

"You have thoughts on this?' Novello stared through me.

"Not really," I said. "I've been focused on setting up the meeting with you to help Vinnie. I haven't given the murder or what Judge Fisher said much thought."

"Well give it some thought," Novello said. "You and that Freddy character put things together a few years ago, so give it some thought."

I'm not good at compliments – probably a lack of practice – so I may have blushed. "Thanks, I will," I said. "You mind sharing your initial reactions?"

"I've read the police reports, and I'm meeting with Mrs. Bartoni later today. No bullet casings were found; the shooter was cool enough to pick them up. No one, not even his wife, who was upstairs, heard anything, so a suppressor was probably used. Has some of the aspects of a professional hit, but it doesn't feel like one."

We went along some pedestrian walkways and Boston City Hall appeared in the near distance.

"Don't remember Bartoni having any mob-related cases," I said. "Most of those are in federal court. Bartoni could be a real ball buster, and enjoyed dishing out stiff sentences. But, it's hard to imagine any defendants he sentenced coming back to kill him."

"Harder than imaging priests, judges and lawyers conspiring to kill him?" Novello said. "Or, a popular governor being a serial killer?"

"When you're right your right," I said. "I should be able to imagine anything."

We were quiet as we walked across City Hall Plaza, dodged the traffic on Cambridge Street and went up the stairs cutting through Center Plaza. We walked around the John Adams Court House, and up to Ashburton Place. We stopped in front of the high-rise state office building, which housed the offices of the Attorney General and the Homicide Bureau.

"This case will bring a lot of heat. But with heat come resources," Novello said. He tugged on the cuffs of his shirt sleeves so that they protruded from his suit coat just so. "The killer knew what he was doing, but so do I. Whoever did this is living on borrowed time."

He said it with the certainty of a prophet.

I saw Novello's attention shift briefly to the State House, perhaps a 100 yards away. He turned back to me and extended his hand. "So Abby thinks I'm hot?" He smiled then said the words I never expected to hear. "Connor, it was good to reconnect. Let's stay in touch."

Chapter 9

Carmela Bartoni was in her mid to late sixties, tall and thin with a regal face white as paper. A long pointed nose seemed to push itself through tight skin that had not yet succumbed to the laws of gravity. Her gray hair was swept up over large ears as to proclaim: So What? She was wearing expensive dark gray wool slacks with a light gray wool sweater. She wore no jewelry, not even a wedding or engagement ring.

Anthony Novello noticed all of this in the first seconds of his greeting, and as she ushered him into the large living room of the Bartoni home in Concord. The room was spacious and furnished with the unmistakable ambience of professional design.

Novello was not impressed by stylish or well decorated homes or by wealth or status. Politicians, lawyers, judges and professional athletes did not impress Novello. Artists, architects, chefs, tradesmen and uniformed cops did. What he did notice about the home was that whatever blood or other fluid stains had existed in the front foyer, where Bartoni had been shot and died less than three days ago, had vanished as if they never existed.

"Would you care for coffee, tea, or perhaps something stronger?" Carmela asked. She sat on one of two mahogany arm chairs positioned on either side of a floral sofa. By assuming this chair, Mrs. Bartoni forced Novello to either sit in the lower sofa position and look up to her with a turned head, or in the matching arm chair at the opposite end of the sofa and then converse from an awkward distance. Novello went to the arm chair, picked it up and repositioned it so that he could face and converse with Mrs. Bartoni from a distance of less than six feet.

"A glass of cold water would be nice," Novello said.

"Perfect," Carmela said. "You'll find a pitcher and glasses on the table in the corner. She waved her hand as a directional guide. "I'd like a glass, as well, if you don't mind."

"Not at all," Novello said. He walked across a deep burgundy oriental carpet onto darkly stained wide plank flooring to a glass table with an ice bucket, crystal glasses and a matching pitcher of water. "Sure you wouldn't prefer coffee?" He said. "I haven't seen the kitchen yet." Carmela's eyes narrowed at his remark. She sat as if painted on the back of her chair. Novello smiled. Time to end the dog sniffing. He poured two glasses and brought them back to the chairs. "I'm sorry for your loss, and I'm grateful you made time to see me." He handed her a cut crystal glass. "You have a beautiful home."

"Thank you. I have only an hour or so, I have a meeting with the funeral director. My husband left detailed instructions as to his funeral. He always enjoyed controlling things." She took a small sip of water. "I think he liked the idea he could control something even after death." Her mouth tightened briefly, accentuating the age lines at the corners.

"When did he make these plans?' Novello asked. "Do you mind if I tape our conversation?" He placed his phone on the coffee table. "I think taking notes is distracting. Makes it difficult to have a conversation." Novello smiled. "Feel free to ask any questions you may have. Now, where were we? Oh yes, your husband's funeral plans. When did he make them?"

Novello's pretending to have forgotten his last question was an effort to take Carmela Bartoni's mind off the phone. He always told people he was questioning that they could also ask questions, but he rarely, if ever, answered any asked.

Mrs. Bartoni reached into a small silk purse and removed an updated and more expensive version of the same phone and placed it beside Novello's. "This will avoid having to send me a transcript of my interview." She emphasized interview and smiled. "I'm sorry, I seem to have forgotten your last question."

Novello nodded a touché to Mrs. Bartoni. "We were discussing your husband's funeral plans. I wanted to know when he made them. If they were recent."

"They were not recent." Mrs. Bartoni said. "Shortly after he was appointed judge, he became something of a celebrity. He was often on TV or quoted in the papers." She waved her hands searching for the right words. Then she shrugged her shoulders in surrender. "Look, you probably already know this, as did everyone who knew Robert. He had a high opinion of himself, and probably thought his death would be an important event." She gave out a quick laugh. "He wanted to be buried in Sleepy Hollow Cemetery. Would have loved to get into Authors' Ridge with Hawthorne and Thoreau." She shook the levity away. "Robert went to the extent of having an invitation list for his funeral. He would revise the plan periodically, but I don't think he expected to be murdered." She shook her head in bewilderment.

"Was your husband a member of any clubs?" Novello said. "Recreational or business? Hobbies?"

"He liked to walk, and he was an avid reader," Mrs. Bartoni said. She seemed embarrassed by her answer. "Robert was a very busy man, and took his responsibilities seriously." She took another sip of water and carefully placed the glass on a small coaster. "Frankly, he didn't leave himself time for casual activities."

"I understand," Novello said. "Who managed the finances of the house?"

"Why is that important? Mrs. Bartoni shifted in the chair. "Never mind. If you have to know, I did. My husband operated off a weekly allowance, which he set for himself, and I paid all the bills."

Novello smiled. "The person who manages the finances of the house is the person who knows more than anyone else. For example, did your husband have a safe deposit box? Perhaps a post office box?"

"No," Mrs. Bartoni said. "Neither of us had a safe deposit box, or a postal box."

"Is there a safe in the home?" Novello said. "Or a strong box or secure place where the Judge might have kept sensitive or important papers."

"No safe or strong box," Mrs. Bartoni said. "Robert kept all of his judicial papers in his study, or at the courthouse. I suppose his filing cabinets were locked, but we considered the house secure. We pay good money for a security system. We considered the house secure." Mrs. Bartoni closed her mouth and bowed her head, apparently aware she had repeated herself.

Novello recognized Mrs. Bartoni was tiring of the interview. "Did the Judge ever receive hate mail, or any form of communication you might describe as threatening?"

"Sure," Mrs. Bartoni said. She smiled. "He kept them and looked at them the same way athletes do their trophies. I don't think Robert considered any of them a real threat. He also got fan mail. He kept those as well." She stared into Novello's eyes. "Somebody from the state police came and took all the letters, his phone, computer, and his electronic gadgets. They were rummaging around his study for more than an hour."

"I know," Novello said with a sympathetic tone. "We appreciate your cooperation and hope to return the computer in a week or so." He leaned towards her. "Do the names Tobias Fisher, Vincent or Vinnie Preskin mean anything to you?"

"Well, I've known of Judge Fisher for almost forever. He's is a retired judge on the Cape somewhere. He and Robert meet – I mean met – for lunch three or four times a year. Not sure I ever met Judge Fisher, although I might have at Robert's swearing in ceremony. Robert enjoyed his company. I think he thought Fisher had a lonely life and felt sorry for him. The other name, Vinnie something, doesn't mean anything to me"

"How about Win Allen or Gloria D'Alessandro?" Novello said.

"Obviously, I know D'Alessandro is the Chief Justice of the Supreme Judicial Court. I don't know her personally. I met her at a reception several years ago. We might have been introduced. I don't know any Win Allen. I don't care to mix in legal circles. When you're married to a judge, you tend to avoid lawyers and find friends with other occupations or accomplishments." She smiled, but there was little warmth behind it.

"Did your husband ever talk about his lunches with Judge Fisher? Where they met? What they talked about, anything like that?" Novello smiled, keeping the conversation light. Nothing of substance here.

"No," Mrs. Bartoni shook her head as reinforcement. "He might mention it was a nice lunch, traffic was tough, or whatever. But never anything more than the briefest of mentions, and never what they talked about."

"Did Robert," Novello's switch to "Robert" was deliberate, "ever talk with you about his current cases, or any projects or research he was working on?"

"Well, it took you long enough to get to it," She smiled, this time with some warmth.

Novello returned the smile. "Carmela, everything we have talked about is important."

"Robert never talked about his cases, even the ones in the news. When he was appointed, he told me he would never discuss his cases with me or with anyone other than court personnel."

"What about any projects or matters he was working on outside of his current cases or courtroom work?'

"He told me several months before he died he was getting close, that's word he used 'close,' on an issue of corruption involving the Catholic Church, specifically, the Archdiocese of Boston. He never mentioned details, and he never mentioned it after his initial comment." She shifted in her chair and leaned towards Novello. "We had an understanding. I didn't intrude on Robert's work, and he didn't intrude on mine." She took another sip of water. "If one of us wanted to talk about what we were doing, the other would listen attentively, and if asked, express an opinion or a suggestion. But I would never push or probe or even comment on what Robert was doing, and he was exactly the same as to whatever I was doing."

"Which was? "Novello said.

"Which was what?"

Novello smiled. "I was wondering what you did."

"Detective, my maiden name is Rothwell, as in Rothwell Industries? Our company was acquired a little over thirty years ago by a tech giant no longer in business." Carmela raised her eyebrows and flashed a quick smile. "Unlike other members of my family, I invested my share of the proceeds wisely, and I haven't worked since. I will do the same with my inheritance. I am what some would call 'very comfortable.'" She gave the self-satisfied smile of a duchess. "I am busy with a number of charities, cultural activities, fund raising efforts; those sorts of things."

Novello nodded and tried to look impressed. "Carmela, other than yourself, was there any person Robert might have confided in or spoken with about this corruption issue he was getting close to?"

"I don't know if he had any friends at the court house, or if he trusted the other judges. If I had to make a guess, and this is a pure guess, it would be Judge Fisher, since he is retired and being on the Cape, he'd be outside the influence of the Archbishop of Boston."

"What about his clerk? Joseph Colby?"

Carmela smiled. "Robert thought Colby was an asshole."

———

Five or so minutes after she guided Novello to the front door, Carmela stood in the doorway to her late husband's study. She looked over to the padded leather chair she paid for, but never sat in. "You pompous asshole," she shouted at the chair. "I can't wait for the stink of you to leave this house."

Carmela walked back to the living room and sat in the chair she had used during Novello's visit. She picked up her phone and played the recording of her interview. She listened intently and silently as the voices echoed in the large room.

———

While Carmela was listening to the recording on her phone, Novello was in traffic on Route 2 heading back to Boston. He listened a second time to his conversation with Carmela Bartoni. Something clicked in his head, like two cogs slotting together. *If she didn't know the name Win Allen, how did she know he was a lawyer?*

Chapter 10

At four o'clock the afternoon Novello interviewed Carmel Bartoni, Ed McGonagle, a balding, six-foot-five former semi-pro baseball player from Jamaica Plain with mischievous eyes and a try-anything-twice attitude, was sitting in a sterile conference room on the eighteenth floor at One Ashburton Place in Boston with Vinnie Preskin and Judge Tobias Fisher. McGonagle was a homicide detective, Anthony Novello's closest friend and second in charge of the Homicide Bureau.

"As I said earlier, I thought I'd be meeting with Detective Novello," Fisher said. "I came all the way up from the Cape, not an insignificant distance, and I expected to be talking with him."

McGonagle continued writing, his long fingers crowding the small spiral notebook. "Imagine how disappointed Captain Novello must be." McGonagle looked at Fisher. "Look, I have your statement. It will be looked into and the Captain will be fully advised. He's interviewing another witness, so you'll have to be satisfied with me."

"Well," Preskin said, as he stood. "It's getting late. I want to get Judge Fisher back to the Cape. Unless, of course, there's something else?"

"Such as?" McGonagle said. "Maybe, why did he need to have an attorney with him today?"

"I'm here as Judge Fisher's friend," Preskin said. "I drove him up from Falmouth."

"A considerable distance, and all of it in traffic," Fisher said.

"The Judge rarely drives, particularly long distances," Preskin said softly. "Judge Fisher has given as full an account as possible. It's past time for us to leave," Preskin said.

"I not sure I like your attitude, Detective McGonagle," Judge Fisher said. "You haven't seemed interested in anything I have to say or even appreciate the fact I came up here to see you."

"I get that at lot," McGonagle said. "Most people are certain they don't like it, so I appreciate your uncertainty." He closed the notebook. "Have a nice trip back to the Cape. I'll be sure to tell the Captain how cooperative you've been and how disappointed you are he wasn't here." He smiled at Judge Fisher. "Hope you can find it in your heart to forgive him."

Judge Fisher started to extend his hand, but drew it back. He turned quickly and walked towards the door. "Let's go Vinnie, the traffic will be a bitch and I've wasted enough time here."

―――

Approximately five miles from where Preskin and Judge Fisher were leaving the meeting with McGonagle, Monsignor Ignatius Paul Roche was fumbling with a decanter of scotch and trying to avoid dropping the file folders and papers tucked under his left arm. "Shit," he muttered when several papers fluttered to the oriental carpet.

"Iggy, let me help you with that," Cardinal Philip Mulcahy said. He struggled from the soft cushioned chair in his private study in the Catholic Chancery Office on Beacon Street. The Chancery Office was in a 4-story brownstone near Massachusetts Avenue, with rear window views of the Charles River. Cardinal Mulcahy had commandeered the building from the Catholic School Office, after a protracted dispute with the then Superintendent of Catholic Schools for the Archdiocese of Boston. The brownstone, the Cardinal thought, was sumptuous and more befitting his station than the other offices available to him.

Mulcahy walked to the ice bucket positioned on a mahogany credenza. He took two Waterford crystal glasses from a drawer and dipped his stubby fingers into the ice bucket.

"Please Your Eminence, I can handle this," Roche said. "You've had a long day." He squatted, squeezing the folder between his thighs and belly and retrieved the papers.

The two men, both in their late fifties, were lifelong friends from the Boston neighborhood of Brighton. The Cardinal's use of the name Iggy, was a throwback to their grammar school graduation, where the boy everyone knew as Paul Roche walked across the stage to the announcement: Ignatius Paul Roche. By the time high school arrived in September, the incident had been forgotten, and Roche was not afflicted with the nickname Iggy. The fact he had sprouted to over six feet and close to two hundred pounds assisted in the development of the mass amnesia. Mulcahy used it as a term of endearment, but only in private.

"We've both had a long day," the Cardinal said. He measured three fingers of scotch into each glass. He left a glass on the credenza for Roche and headed back to his chair. He gazed through the large window, across the Charles, and to the patina green dome of M.I.T.

Roche's knees cracked as he shifted position and rose. He took the glass from the credenza. "Thank you, Your Eminence. It has been an exhausting day."

Cardinal Mulcahy nodded approvingly and resettled himself in the chair. He took a long swallow. "Iggy, God Himself drinks this stuff."

Although from similar backgrounds, they had taken different paths to the priesthood. Roche was a former Navy Seal and living the dream as a golf pro and manager of a small nine-hole course north of Boston. Following a heart attack and an ambulance ride down the ninth-hole fairway, Roche, at forty-seven years of age, found religion and enrolled in St. Pope John XXXIII National Seminary for those with delayed vocations.

Monsignor Roche walked softly over to a chair and sat. He had an affable face creased more by the wrinkles of laughter than age. His brown thinning hair was speckled with gray. His eyes peering through round glasses never left the Cardinal. "Do you think we're nearing the end of this?"

The squawk of a cell phone erupted. "Not a moment's peace anymore." Mulcahy placed his glass on a side table and stood. He fished the phone from his pants. His stomach hung over his belt like a water-filled balloon. "Yes?" He announced into the phone. Mulcahy stared at Roche. "Yes, I can hold for the Attorney General." He covered the mouthpiece with his hand. "This pain in the ass never lets up. Shouldn't have given him this number." Mulcahy's lips pursed as he waited.

Mulcahy's mother had pushed him into the seminary following his high school graduation. She subscribed to the belief the mother of a priest is never denied entrance to heaven. To Mulcahy's great surprise, he enjoyed the rigid structure, the comradery of men, and the complete absence of any need to make decisions. Mulcahy often described the seminary as being a private in the Army, but without any danger.

The Cardinal sat back his chair. "Yes, Mr. Flaherty, what can I do for you?" His eyes drifted back to the glass. "I'm sure that can be arranged, why not call Carolyn Tomei in the morning. She's my executive assistant and can set it up. I don't keep my own calendar. Might take a couple of days. I have a busy schedule. Running around like a Shriners Parade." Mulcahy chuckled into the phone then mouthed "asshole" as he listened. He rolled his eyes. "Fine, call Carolyn in the morning and set up a time. Goodbye Mr. Flaherty." Mulcahy tossed the phone to Roche. "Iggy, please get me a new phone with a new number."

"What does he want? Why are you meeting with him? That sonofabitch leaks everything to *The Globe.*"

"I know, I know," Mulcahy said with a dismissive wave. "When Governor Concanon was AG, we agreed to keep him abreast of the progress we're making on the new rules for handling complaints of sexual abuse. Now that Flaherty is AG, he's looking for ways to look and feel important." He took a swallow and sucked an ice cube into his mouth. "Don't worry about Flaherty, I can handle him. If he were any dumber, someone would have to water him. Twice a week." Mulcahy chuckled and took another sip. "I do worry about *The Globe.* I think somebody wants to win another Pulitzer at our expense." Mulcahy bit into the ice cube.

Following his ordination, Mulcahy rose quickly in the church hierarchy. Using his political skills and Irish wit, he made friends and contacts across Massachusetts. He ingratiated himself with church leadership by volunteering for difficult assignments. He turned around financially troubled parishes, closed inactive churches and opened Catholic schools in poor but growing communities. He became the face of the Boston Archdiocese, and it was not long after his elevation as a Cardinal, that Mulcahy's name was included in any discussion on who could be the first American Pope.

After becoming the Archbishop of Boston, one of Mulcahy's first official acts was to name Ignatius Paul Roche a Monsignor and reassign him from a parish in a quiet Boston suburb to the Catholic Chancery Office. Mulcahy named him Vicar General, an ecclesiastical term for "right hand man."

"Bastards and self-righteous jerks," Roche said. "The church used to be something you couldn't attack every day without consequences."

"We'll get through this, Iggy," Mulcahy said.

"We are nearing the end, aren't we?" McNulty said.

Mulcahy frowned. "I think the worst is past us, thank God. But, there're still cases to settle."

"And the Vatican?" Roche said. The words hung in the air like the smell of wet paint.

Mulcahy shrugged and looked at his glass with annoyance. "Who knows? I think the papal secretariat understands why I had to keep the lid on things. What'd people expect me to do? Put an ad in the parish bulletins announcing we had deviants running around in roman collars and robes? Have them arrested?" He shook his glass and seemed pleased with the sound of the cubes against the crystal. "Iggy, you mind?"

Roche got up and took the Cardinal's glass. He headed towards the credenza. "No one ever mentions the treatment we've provided to those afflicted with," he waved his right hand in search for the correct word. "Whatever their ailment was."

"Well that was your department, Iggy." The Cardinal said. "And believe me, you're lucky nobody talks about or even looks at the amounts we paid for that treatment, or whether it was even effective."

"Everyone screams treatment not jail for drug abusers, drunks and other bums. Why is it different just because the patient wears a roman collar?" Roche said. "We treated a lot of our brethren; that should count for something. All we get is grief and bad press."

"People should just stop talking or writing about the whole mess. Time to move on for God's sake." Mulcahy said.

"You did the best you could, Your Eminence," Roche said.

"Don't placate me, Monsignor. I don't need that." Mulcahy's eyes narrowed. "And, didn't you mean to say – *we* did the best we could?"

Roche stood at the credenza putting fresh ice into the cardinal's glass. He reached for the bottle of scotch, poured a healthy dose and walked over to Cardinal Mulcahy. He smiled and handed him the glass. "Philip, we both did what had to be done."

Chapter II

South Station is one of Boston's grand buildings. The curved brownstone structure runs along Atlantic and Summer Streets. The main entrance, at the streets' intersection, features three two-story arches of stone, glass and steel under a five story portico with a clock second only to London's Big Ben. Inside the Grand Concourse thousands of rail passengers scurry under brick arches, across marble floors, up and down marble steps seemingly oblivious to the ethereal balustrades and vaulted oracles.

Unfortunately for me, I take the bus, which operates from a terminal next door with the charm and charisma of a roadside porta-potty. The buses are clean with friendly drivers and air conditioning and heating systems that sometimes work during the appropriate season. I was sitting in one of those buses waiting for the start of my ninety minute ride home.

We were five minutes from departure. The bus was beginning to fill with the usual suspects. I favor the driver's side of the bus and sit just three rows up from the front. An experienced traveler told me to sit close to the front because as people get on, they always hope to find an empty seat further back. They'll be past you by the time they realize they have to share a seat with another passenger. Since it was still April, the migration of the seasonal commuters to the Cape had not started, and there were plenty of seats.

I adjusted my neck pillow, closed my eyes and felt the lurch of the bus beginning the trip. I heard footsteps coming from the back of the bus and tried to erase them from my subconscious. Usually, I am asleep within minutes of departure. The footsteps got louder and stopped at my seat. The unmistakable sense of nearby movement and the squish of air caused by an ass descending on the seat beside me caused my eyes to open.

"Hello Connor."

I recognized the voice immediately and snapped my body upright. "Hello Freddy," I said. My voice sounded hoarse. There was a metallic taste of fear in my mouth. I tried to control my breathing.

"You don't look surprised to see me," Freddy said.

"Well I am," I said. I tried to laugh, but what came out was somewhere between a cough and a burp. As usual, Freddy was dressed in black. He was still thin. His bad comb-over had been shaved off, revealing a skull that appeared translucent, with the hint of a blueish tone and small veins scattered like markings on a road map. His pock marks were covered by a neat but full beard. The thick glasses had been replaced by fashionable lenses, but his cloudy right eye was there for all to see. "Still going by Freddy? What are you doing here?"

"I'm riding the bus to Falmouth and Woods Hole," he said. "Still using Freddy, at least with you," he added. "Connor, you seem a bit jumpy. Anything to do with your walk with Novello this morning?"

"You're following me?" I said. My voice still felt like it had forgotten how to work.

"Trying to get the lay of the land," Freddy said. "Came back a few weeks ago, and hung out near your office across from the State House. Followed you to South Station enough times to learn what bus you take and that you're only in Boston on Tuesdays and Thursdays. I wanted to reach out to you a few times, but wasn't sure it was fair of me to come back into your life."

"I always wondered where you were or what you were doing," I said. My voice returned to normal. "Christ, the governor's killing was a national story." Freddy seized my arm. I stopped talking.

"This morning, I was sitting on a bench near the State House. "I was waiting for you to come up Bowdoin to your office. Actually thought about reconnecting. Imagine my surprise when I saw you walking along Ashburton Place with Novello. You looked like old friends." Freddy's voice was flat and soulless. He leaned into me and whispered, "What the fuck is going on?"

"I'll tell you all about that walk," I said. "But first you need to know that was the first time I've seen Novello in nearly two years. Second, our meeting had nothing to do with you, or Governor Hands. Third, Novello admitted if you reappeared, you'd regret it."

Freddy smirked. "If he were really interested in finding me, he would have. I always figured the interest in finding me would diminish the more they found out about Governor Hands, and what a piece of shit he was." Freddy scrolled his right forefinger down the beard on his left cheek. A new habit born of the growing a beard. "So, Connor, tell me why you met with Novello and everything you told him."

So I did.

———

A little over an hour later, the skies were dark, the traffic light and the top of the Bourne Bridge expanding over the Cape Cod Canal peaked over an approaching hill.

"Connor, how the fuck do you get into these things?"

"I'm not really into it. Not like with Governor Hands." Freddy's finger went to his lips. I nodded and lowered my voice. "Fisher asked me to get him a meeting with Novello. I was able to do that, and I think that's the end of it."

"But Novello said he wanted to keep in touch. So," he said, infusing the word with syllables. "This isn't over."

"He was just being polite," I said.

"Cops aren't polite," Freddy said. "Firefighters are polite, the Pakistani at the seven eleven is polite. Cops trying to solve a case are not polite. They're relentless."

"But I'm not part of this case," I said.

"You are if I'm the case," Freddy said with urgency. "Novello thinks you know where I am, and thanks to my own dumb ass move, you've seen me. You now know what I look like and that on this date, I was in Massachusetts. He wants to keep in touch with you because he thinks you'll eventually give him information about me."

"You said you didn't think Novello was trying to find you," I said.

"Yeah, but now that you've suddenly dropped in his lap, I'm on his radar screen again. Bartoni may be a different case, but Novello can walk and chew gum. The next time he sees you, one of the first things he'll ask will have something to do with me. Just wait."

"Won't tell him anything," I said with a conviction I wasn't sure was real.

"You'll lie to him?" Freddy asked, skepticism riding on each word. "Accessory after the fact of murder? You want that in your life?"

I paused long enough to confirm Freddy's suspicion. "Look, I don't think Novello will ever reach out to me," I said, rather weakly. "And, I won't reach out to him."

"Forget it," Freddy shook his head. "I own this fuck up. I reached out because I saw you with Novello. What I should have done is go back to where I was, and which I'm am not going to tell you."

"I understand," I said. "Any thoughts on what I told you?" I turned towards the window. Outside, the tall curved steel rods, designed to prevent suicide were zipping by as the bus crossed over the Bourne Bridge.

"Ever wonder why Fisher thought it was so important to speak with Novello?" Freddy said.

"Fisher thinks he's too important to deal with local cops. He wanted to speak with the top dog," I said.

Freddy gave a theatrical sigh and leaned back in his seat. "Fuckin' judges. They get a robe after paying a bunch of money to some politician. As soon as they put it on, they forget how and why they got it. They actually think they earned it because of brilliance and integrity."

"Tell me what you really think," I said.

Freddy turned his body towards me. "Only thing worse than the judge who thinks the robe makes him smart and just, is the priest who puts on a robe and thinks that makes it okay to go out and abuse an altar boy, or protect some other jerk in a robe who did." He said this a bit too loudly. The woman in the aisle seat across from Freddy gave out a disgusted snort.

Freddy rolled his eyes at me and whispered, "Talk about a stick up your ass. She has a whole fuckin' cactus." He paused a moment and went back to his rant. "People need to remember robes don't make anyone holy, smart, or important. All robes do is cover up who's wearing them."

"A truism for the ages," I said with a smile. "Any other thoughts you care to share?"

"That lawyer you're working for, Vinnie Preskin? Freddy said. "Did you know he's related to Bobby Morelli, a jerk off who works for Anthony Bonfiglio? He runs the Fall River and New Bedford Mobs."

"Vinnie told me the whole story," I said. "People are always trying to hurt him because of his cousin. As far as I know, they have nothing to do with each other."

Freddy sighed. "If Vinnie values his law practice, he would hardly admit to a close relationship or any kind of relationship with a guy like Bobby Shits. I know complete assholes who want nothing to do with him."

"Bobby Shits?" I said.

"Bobby wanted to be called Robert. When that didn't work he tried to get people to call him Robbie." Freddy shook his head. "Hated being called Bobby. Eventually, someone figured he was trying to avoid the initials BM. So everyone started calling him Bobby Shits."

"You mobsters are just wild and crazy guys," I said.

Freddy's eyes narrowed. "Bobby works for Anthony Bonfiglio and he's not some wild and crazy guy. You want nothing to do with Bonfiglio."

The bus made the turn into the Falmouth station and stopped. I knew this could be the last time I would see Freddy. He got up and stepped back to let me into the aisle. "Listen," Freddy said. "When Novello asks you if we've had any contact, and he will, don't lie. In forty or so hours, I'll be long gone and his focus will be on Bartoni." He handed me a business card. It had no name or address. Just a phone number. "Don't ever call this," he said. "But, if you get a call or a text from this number, fucking answer or read it."

"Okay," I said. "Take care of yourself." I got off the bus and watched as it left the lot and made the turn towards Woods Hole. I felt a bit sad, but relieved Freddy had told me not to lie to Novello. I also was a bit grateful I had seen him again. It felt like closure.

———

A cold beer, a smile from Abby and the smell of baked chicken greeted me when I came in the door. "You will never guess," I said, "who rode the bus with me tonight."

"You're right," Abby said. "I won't guess, just tell me."

"The hombre known as Freddy," I said.

"Him again? Tell me everything, starting with your meeting with Novello."

So, once again, I did.

Chapter 12

Anthony Novello and Ed McGonagle sat across from each other at a square table in a room adjacent to Novello's office at the Homicide Bureau. Each had a large container of coffee. A box with crumbs and one plain donut sat at the center of the table. McGonagle purchased donuts every Monday and Thursday, part of an ongoing commitment to keeping police traditions alive. To support his friend and second in charge, Novello had allowed the placement of one low-hanging lightbulb with a dark green shade over the table. On his own initiative, Novello purchased a leather sap as a paperweight. Although the room was more often used for meetings than for questioning suspects, it was known to all as the bullpen and a place to get donuts.

"Okay," Novello said. "What do we know?'

McGonagle knew Novello was asking what they could prove or put in an application for a search or arrest warrant. Suspicions or theories would be discussed later. "I.T. confirmed Bartoni's lunch dates with Judge Fisher were in his appointment calendar," McGonagle said. "No reason to suspect the lunch didn't occur, but I've asked our friends in Plymouth to check out the restaurant to see if anyone remembers them, if they have any receipt records, or have them on tape."

"Anything on Bartoni's computer? Novello said.

"Nothing about any investigation he might have been doing." McGonagle said. "I.T. says Bartoni was writing his memoir. They have someone reading it in case it produces fruit, but right now it's only producing yawns." McGonagle took a sip of coffee. "They did a number of word searches on the book, but found nothing on Judge D'Alessandro or Win Allen, or even the Archdiocese of Boston. Same with his computer at the courthouse."

"Interview his clerk, Joe Colby?"

McGonagle nodded. "More interesting, but nothing we can firm up. Colby's been with the Judge a long time. Colby said if Bartoni was doing some kind of an investigation, he'd know about it. But it sounded like he was just spewing some kind of I'm-his-go-to-guy bullshit."

"You tested him?" Novello said.

"Asked him if he knew Mrs. Bartoni's maiden name, and he didn't. That sort of ended his I know everything bullshit," McGonagle said. "To be fair, he was helpful in getting together all of Bartoni's cases going back a few years. I got people going over all that, and we should know later today if we have any possibilities."

"Most of the assholes Bartoni sentenced couldn't make a sandwich. This feels different," Novello said.

"After Colby relaxed and got over his embarrassment, he admitted Bartoni had seemed a bit preoccupied the last several months. He said Bartoni had taken a serious interest in the church sexual abuse cases."

"What kind of serious interest?" Novello said.

"He started clipping stories from *The Globe,* and he copied articles on legal issues in *Lawyer's Weekly.* That's the paper lawyers and judges read at their two martini lunches." McGonagle shrugged. "Colby said Bartoni was making a scrapbook on the case. Bartoni did all the clipping and copying himself. Never asked Colby to help. He told me the one time he volunteered to help one time. Bartoni refused, said it was private. Colby figured Bartoni was planning to write a book on the whole mess." McGonagle took a sip of coffee. "Colby said Bartoni worried about retirement and what came next. He wanted to start a career in TV maybe as a legal commentator. We know he was a media hound. Maybe he wanted to keep that going after he took the robes off. Maybe the next Judge Judy." McGonagle laughed at the thought. "Colby said Bartoni was getting obsessive about his weight and appearance."

"Colby ever mention Win Allen, or Gloria D'Alessandro?" Novello said.

"No," McGonagle said. "And, I didn't mention what Fisher told us."

Novello nodded. "Mrs. Bartoni confirmed her husband's friendship with Fisher. She said they met three or four times a year for lunch. She guessed – and she emphasized it was a guess – that if her husband confided in anyone about what he was working on, it'd be Fisher. She's a strong woman and a bit odd. I think she kept her husband on a short leash. He was a judge and made a decent salary, but he gets a fucking allowance? She made a point of telling me he set the amount, but allowance is what she called it. That hit a nerve with me."

"But, I know what she means," McGonagle said. Liz handles the budget at our house. She pays the bills, and I grab what I need out her purse. When that runs out, I take another trip to her purse. We'd never call it my allowance. It's just how we manage finances."

"She told me her husband said he was working on something big and it involved the Catholic Church. But, it had a rehearsed quality. Didn't feel right."

"No reason for her to lie about that," McGonagle said. He glanced at his notebook and flipped a page. "I.T. checked out Bartoni's emails and social media activity. Nothing there."

Novello shook his head. "She didn't tell me everything, and we're missing something," Novello said. "Crime like this doesn't happen spur of the moment. How did the shooter know the Judge would answer the door? Did the shooter follow him or know his routine? What if Mrs. Bartoni had answered the door? Would she be dead? What if she was the intended victim, and the shooter panicked when the Judge answered the door?"

"That doesn't jive with what Fisher told us," McGonagle said.

"I know," Novello said. "But standing at the front door and blowing a guy's brains out doesn't happen because somebody woke up on the wrong side of the bed. It takes balls and some planning."

"Think it's time to have a chat with Win Allen or D'Alessandro?"

"I'd like to know a lot more before we approach either of them,
Novello said. .

"What's next?" McGonagle said, as he tossed his empty cup into
the wastebasket.

"Let's try to find that fuckin' scrapbook," Novello said.

———

While Novello and McGonagle were discussing scrapbooks,
Monsignor Ignatius Paul Roche was sitting at the desk in his office
on the second floor of the Chancery Office. The pile of papers in
the center of the desk signaled a busy morning. Brightly colored
post-it notes prioritized each packet of paper. Roche was not
concerned with the notes or packets. A large cup of coffee was
carefully positioned on a coaster with the Archdiocesan Seal. Roche
looked out his open door. Carolyn Tomei, Mulcahy's executive
assistant, sat at her desk in the wide corridor outside the Cardinal's
office staring back.

Roche disliked Tomei with her pointed nose and oversized
glasses, which accentuated her bulging eyes. He knew she felt the
same about him. She was the Cardinal's firewall, but Roche was his
best friend, and considered himself exempt from the bureaucratic
hurdles and mazes Tomei constructed and imposed on others.

"Carolyn," Roche called out, "can you come here a minute?"

Tomei held up her phone and showed a what-can-I-do shrug.
She signaled Roche to come to her.

Roche thought a moment, sighed and walked over to her desk.
"Carolyn, Attorney General Flaherty will be calling to set up."

Tomei held up her hand to silence him and spoke into the phone.
"Yes, and please make certain it's wheat bread, not toasted, and the
mayo is thinly spread. His Eminence is very particular about his
tuna salad sandwiches." She paused and then, "thank you, someone
will be by to pick it up at eleven-thirty." She looked up at Monsignor
Roche and smiled. "Yes Monsignor, how I can I help you?"

"Attorney General Flaherty's office will be calling this morning to set up a meeting with the Cardinal. I want you to delay the meeting a week to ten days, and let me know once the day and time are set. Philip, wants me to attend." Roche enjoyed watching Tomei flinch whenever he used Mulcahy's Christian name.

"They already called and the meeting's been set," Tomei said. "No one told me you were to be included or that I should stall things." She smiled, insincerity oozing from her thin lips "Maybe if you arrived earlier, we could have avoided any confusion."

"Never mind, just give me the date and time of the meeting," Roche said.

"I'll get it to you, once I have been able to tell his Eminence. "He's on a conference call with the Office of the Papal Secretariat. He didn't mention the call to you? I guess not." Another thin insincere smile.

"Of course, he did," Roche stammered, barely able to contain his anger. "I don't discuss my conversations with Philip with anyone. Not even you." He turned and walked toward his office. When he was ten or so feet from her desk. He turned. "Enjoy your tuna salad sandwich, Carolyn. Didn't His Eminence tell you he's allergic to mayonnaise? I guess not."

Roche went back to his office. He fished a cell phone from his trouser pocket, pushed in a password then the number. "The Cardinal has a meeting scheduled with the Attorney General. I'll have the details by the end of the day." He terminated the call. Roche tried to sip his coffee, but was careless and burnt his lip. "Shit," he muttered, as he rushed the cup back to the coaster, causing a small splash of the liquid on some papers on his desk. "Jesus H. Christopher Christ."

———

At three-thirty that afternoon, Novello sat at his desk reading the inventory list of items removed from Judge Bartoni's home and courthouse office. His eyes skipped over those he knew were being examined by the technical people: the computers, phone, and tablets.

He focused on item nine, a leather brief case. The absence of any listing of its contents made Novello suspicious. Someone had been careless. If the briefcase had been empty, that should have been noted. Otherwise, any of its contents should have been itemized. Novello suspected the briefcase had contained something someone had decided was not important and neglected to list it. "Nobody carries an empty briefcase," Novello said. He rose from his chair and headed over to the temporary inventory room established for the Bartoni case.

The briefcase was slumped against the leg of a table, its soft brown leather faded from age and use. The shoulder strap bore the creases and grooves of heavy use. Novello picked it up. It had the softness and flexibility of an old wallet. He examined the evidence tag attached to the shoulder strap, and learned State Trooper Douglas Tanner removed the briefcase from the foyer of the home on the day the Judge was shot. Novello signed and dated an inventory slip indicating he was removing the briefcase. He put the slip in a basket and carried the briefcase to his office.

Back at his desk, Novello examined the two outside pockets of the briefcase and found a silver cross pen. He opened a drawer of his desk and pulled a set of tweezers. He lifted the pen out of the outside pocket and placed it in a plastic bag. He dated and signed the bag and set it aside. He opened the briefcase. A single sheet of yellow legal size paper curled into itself rested at the bottom. Novello used the tweezer to remove the paper and placed it on his desk. He examined the rest of the briefcase and found nothing else. The paper had the single word "scale." Novello stared at the word for several seconds. He felt the smile developing on his face and took out his phone. "Ed, need you in my office ASAP."

———

Less than three minutes later, McGonagle and Novello were staring at the sheet of paper, which was now in a plastic bag dated and signed by Novello.

"Scale?" McGonagle said, "Colby said Bartoni was getting obsessive about his weight and appearance. I think the Judge planned on buying a scale, and this is a reminder for him to do it when he got to work."

"That'd be my guess, as well," Novello said. "But why wait until you got back to work? Why not simply go out on a Saturday and buy a scale?"

"Because he wanted it for his courthouse office?" McGonagle said. "His house must have had a scale, but he wanted one in his chambers." McGonagle looked at Novello. "You're a few steps ahead of me, aren't you? What's going on?"

"I think the Judge was obsessive about his weight, and wanted to track it in his chambers, away from the prying eyes of his wife. Anyone who tracks his weight eventually does one of two things, maybe both. He begins a diet and…"

"He joins a health club," McGonagle said.

"Which has showers and lockers, where the Judge could keep his scrapbook."

"Carmela never mentioned any health clubs," McGonagle said. "None of the financial records we've seen show payments for a health club."

"I don't think Carmela knew about this," Novello said. "This was something the Judge wanted to do, and he didn't want anyone to know. I need you to get folks calling every gym, health club or weight loss clinic to see if Bartoni was listed as a member. Start close to the courthouse and work out from there."

"On it," McGonagle said. He started to rise.

"One other thing," Novello said. "Find out who Douglas Tanner is, and make sure he gets a good share of the leg work on this. That idiot tagged the briefcase and never listed its contents."

Chapter 13

The days passed slowly and the nights seemed longer. It had been seven days since I rode the bus with Freddy, or spoken with Novello. Other than telling me how angry Judge Fisher was that he wasn't interviewed by Novello, Vinnie had moved onto the legal issues that paid the bills. He warned me Fisher might call looking for more favors. Vinnie told me to tell Fisher to call him. He told me to stress there would be no more seventy-five dollar retainer checks.

Fisher never called; neither did Novello. I felt like the punch line of an old joke. I never told Vinnie about the sudden appearance of Freddy, or even that somebody I called Freddy existed. Other than Abby, no one knew Freddy had reappeared and then vanished like a puff of smoke.

Judge Bartoni got the funeral of his dreams. The first several rows of St. Bernard Church in Concord were occupied by dignitaries, including Governor Concanon, Attorney General Kevin Flaherty, Chief Justice Gloria D'Alessandro, and dozens of judges, wearing dark suits and somber looks. Vinnie told me Judge Fisher did not attend. He later admitted the Judge had asked him for a ride, and he had declined. "I am not Uber," Vinnie declared to me. I suspect he used a softer tone with Judge Fisher.

It was Wednesday afternoon. The day carried the false promise of sun behind a flat gray sky. Dusk was descending and the waters of Falmouth Harbor were choppy, as though anxious for night. Vinnie left in the late morning for a business meeting, and I did not expect him back. The fact he had stuffed his golf clubs into the trunk of his Lexus provided an important clue.

I had just finished the paper work for a commercial closing Vinnie would cover tomorrow. My cell buzzed and I saw the number Freddy has given me before he got off the bus. I answered. "Hello, this is Connor McNeill."

Freddy voice came through as if he were in the next room. "Why was it so important for Fisher to speak to Novello?"

Before I could answer, he terminated the call and silence filled my ear.

———

Attorney General Kevin Flaherty, his six-two frame stiff under a faultless dark blue suit, sat erect in a cushioned chair with ornate carved wood arms. His pale blue eyes peered through silver glasses to the darkening view of the Charles River. Flaherty glanced at his watch. Eight minutes early for his five o'clock meeting with Cardinal Philip Mulcahy.

Outwardly, Flaherty exuded the confidence of a man who couldn't remember the last time he had second-guessed himself. But it was a practiced aura, developed over years of fighting the demons of doubt and low self-esteem. *How should I greet him?* Flaherty wondered to himself. *Your Eminence? Cardinal Mulcahy? Christ, do I have to kiss his ring? Do they still do that?* Flaherty tried to remember the name of his local parish in Dedham, a way to open the conversation. He drew a blank and felt a bead of perspiration roll into the small of his back.

Flaherty had been an unknown state representative and one of a handful of Democrats who had supported Republican Thomas Hands for governor. When the incumbent district attorney died in office, Flaherty agreed to Hands' request that he become a Republican, and, in return, was appointed to fill the remaining six months of the unexpired term. This infuriated Democrats, who took to calling him Gypo after the notorious Irish traitor and informer, Gypo Nolan. The Republicans shunned him as well, calling him an opportunist unwilling to wait his turn. But the political move made Flaherty the incumbent, and he easily secured election to a full term as district attorney.

Flaherty sat in the chair and absorbed the silence. So different from the energy and noise of his office. Phones ringing, harried lawyers, busy secretaries, intercoms beeping and buzzing like pinball ball machines. Here, it was the hushed silence of unfettered power emanating from the closed doors around him. He took another look at his watch. Two minutes before five.

The death and disgrace of Governor Hands had created another opportunity for Flaherty. He and Attorney General Paul Concanon received media attention and plaudits as both claimed credit in the investigation of Governor Hands and the revelation he was a serial killer. Concanon was elected as the new Governor and Flaherty became Attorney General.

"Mr. Attorney General," Cardinal Mulcahy said with practiced enthusiasm, as he emerged from his office and extended his hand. "So good to see you. I hope I haven't kept you waiting." His hand was in the traditional position for a handshake, not palm down to encourage a kiss of his ring.

"You're right on time, Your Eminence,' Flaherty said, surprising himself as how easily the formal greeting came from his mouth.

"I have asked Monsignor Roche to join us," Mulcahy said. "I hope you don't mind," He guided Flaherty into his wood paneled office, where Roche was seated.

"Not at all," Flaherty said. He stuck out his hand. "Monsignor, I'm Kevin Flaherty."

"Nice to meet you Kevin," Roche said. He extended his hand, but it seemed to Flaherty it was neither sincere nor insincere. Just part of an opening ritual.

The three men sat in comfortable leather chairs positioned to provide views of the Charles River. Just three guys shooting the breeze, dressed in dark suits, two with Roman collars, one with a red power tie. Silence briefly claimed the room.

"Forgive me Kevin," Mulcahy said. "What kind of host am I? Can I get you anything? Coffee, ice water, something stronger?"

"I'm fine, Your Eminence," Flaherty said. "I'm grateful you could make time for me." *C'mon Flaherty, you're the Attorney General. Act like it. You could have made them come to you.*

"Well, I always make time for my friends," Mulcahy said. "Particularly, those with subpoena powers." He flashed the great smile simultaneously with Roche's loud laughter.

"Glad you think of me as a friend," Flaherty said. "I want to be. I think it would be helpful if we could tell the media that, at my urging, the new rules and procedures for reporting future complaints of child abuse are going into effect immediately."

"We don't expect any future complaints," Roche said.

"No one does," Flaherty said around a smile. "But, we all agreed given the lack of clarity and, frankly, the inconsistencies that occurred in the past, we need clear procedures and expectations, for what will happen if any future complaint is lodged." *That was good, firm, with the right tone. Keep it up.*

"We know mistakes were made in the past," Roche said. "We get reminded of them every day."

Mulcahy reached over and touched Roche's arm. He smiled at Flaherty. "Kevin, you have to understand Monsignor Roche feels passionately about this. No one was angrier at or more disappointed in the church's hierarchy than the Monsignor. He and I are both committed to making certain we, and the good people we serve, never have to endure an ordeal like this again."

"And, I appreciate your sentiment," Flaherty said. "But unless you put these regulations into effect and change how the Church responds to future complaints, the Monsignor's anger and disappointment should be directed at you and not the oblique Church hierarchy."

"Now just a minute," Roche said, his face turning red. "Don't even think about turning us against each other like some cheap interrogation trick. His Eminence cannot initiate the new regulations until he receives approval from the Vatican. You should be directing your remarks and facile threats to Rome instead of at us. We're trying our best to help, but there are limits on what we can do." Roche shifted in his seat and took a deep breath. "You may think all Cardinal Mulcahy has to do is snap his fingers and these regulations take effect, but that's your naiveté getting in the way of reality. The Cardinal answers to the Pope. We need Vatican approval, no matter how much you want to believe otherwise."

Horse shit, Flaherty thought. "I am the Attorney General of the Commonwealth of Massachusetts not Rome. It was children living in Massachusetts not Rome, who were abused by your priests. I am not going to wait for some bureaucrat in a robe and collar to sign off on these regulations. If the Cardinal can't get this done, I'll ask the Massachusetts Legislature to make these proposed rules the law of the Commonwealth."

"The Pope is not a bureaucrat," Roche shouted. "Who the hell do think you are coming here and threatening us? Governor Concanon understood it would take time. We are doing all we can to get the Vatican to act, but matters such as these take time."

"Which you have run out of," Flaherty said. *Christ, hope they don't call my bluff. Take forever to get the Legislature to act.*

Mulcahy closed his eyes in thought. He opened them as if to pronounce an eleventh commandment. "Please, please, we are all friends trying to do the right thing as quickly as possible. Let's not allow the stress of our responsibilities to drive a wedge between us. Kevin, I am disappointed it has taken this long, and I wish I could tell you approval is coming soon, but I do not know. What I do know, is that I will not lie to you, a friend."

"I'm grateful for your friendship and your honesty," Flaherty said. *Steady, don't cave.* Flaherty turned towards Monsignor Roche. "And I appreciate your sincerity, and I apologize for my bureaucrat in a robe reference. I meant no disrespect to His Holiness."

Roche nodded and said. "Thank you."

Now stick it to them. "You have to answer to the Vatican, I have to answer to my constituents, and to the families of those who have been injured. These folks have little regard or sympathy for the burdens of the church hierarchy, or the need for Vatican approval. As far as these families are concerned, the Vatican was part of the cover up." Flaherty held his hands up to stop the expected interruption. "Forget the past, for a moment, and focus on the future. These families rightly believe the church failed them and their children. What we – all of us – need is for them to believe that this will not happen again. Implementation of these new regulations will go a long way towards convincing them of that.

"You're right, Kevin," Mulcahy said softly. "It has taken too long for us to get papal authority for these new rules. It's unfair to expect you to wait any longer."

"Your Eminence," Monsignor Roche interrupted with a cautionary tone.

"How about this?" Mulcahy paused a moment then slapped his thigh as an exclamation point. "You can tell the media, you expressed your impatience, we went back and forth a bit, but in the end I agreed to implement the new rules as temporary, pending Vatican approval, which I am certain will come. The rules will take effect immediately and become permanent once approved." Mulcahy nodded, as if realizing the brilliance of his decision. "And, I have agreed you can suggest changes, which I will also implement as temporary, pending Vatican approval." Mulcahy flashed his great smile. The one that ended many disputes and closed even more deals.

Flaherty nodded. "I know Governor Concanon, when he was attorney general reviewed the proposed rules and was satisfied, but I appreciate your giving me the same opportunity."

"Well then, it's settled," Mulcahy said slapping both knees in delight. "Let's have a drink to celebrate and seal the deal, so to speak. Mulcahy started the slow rise from his chair.

"I have another matter I'd like to discuss," Flaherty said. "It's related and won't take long." *Nice work, catch them by surprise, Inspector Colombo.*

"And what might that be, Kevin?" Mulcahy said.

"Well, as you know, when he was attorney general, Governor Concanon wrote an exhaustive report on this issue: 'The Sexual Abuse of Children in the Roman Catholic Archdiocese of Boston.'" *Let's remind these nice people what we're really talking about.*

"We're familiar with the report," Roche said. "What seemed to go unnoticed was Concanon's conclusion not to charge the Archdiocese or its senior managers with any crimes under Massachusetts law. That was, it seems to me, an exoneration of sorts. But all any one focused on were the names of the priests charged and the number of victims."

Flaherty held up his hand. "Filing of criminal charges carries a heavy burden of proof. Concanon said the evidence was not sufficient to sustain that burden. He also said the mistreatment of children was so massive and so prolonged that it bordered on the unbelievable." *Make them sweat, Flaherty. Who's in control now?*

Mulcahy had had enough, "You said you had a question."

No more Kevin? Flaherty smiled. "Concanon's report stated there were three psychiatric institutions that were used most often for evaluation and treatment, and they were all affiliated with the Catholic Church."

"Yes," Roche interrupted. "St. Luke Institute in Maryland, Southdown Institute in Ontario, and the House of Affirmation in Whitinsville, Massachusetts. All fully accredited and fine institutions."

"Monsignor has been our point person on treatment programs and getting help for those who needed it," Mulcahy said. "As I said earlier, he is passionate on the subject."

"Well, I'm glad he's here," Flaherty said. He shifted his gaze to Roche. "I'm interested in the fourth institution used, which is not affiliated with the Church."

"The Institute for Recovery, Independence and Self-Empowerment," Roche said. "The acronym is I. RISE. It's in New Bedford. Does very good work; came highly recommended. And, I should add, does its good work for considerably less than the other three."

"That's nice," Flaherty said. "My Division of Public Charities has no records of I. RISE. With the exception of those affiliated with the Church, we register all non-profits, as you may know. Since I. RISE is not affiliated with the Church, I don't understand why it isn't registered with us."

"Because it's a for-profit corporation," Roche said with a shadow of sarcasm. "Many health providers are now for-profit organizations. I suppose to avoid the over regulation that comes with being a non-profit."

Fuck, should have known that. "Well then, that explains it," Flaherty said.

"So, we are done?" Mulcahy struggled from the chair. The offer of a drink long forgotten. "It was good of you to join us. I'll get the word out to all the parishes about the new temporary rules."

"And, that these rules specify the need for detailed quarterly progress reports to be filed with my office," Flaherty said. "It will be important to start collecting data."

"We're familiar with the rules. We wrote most of them," Roche said, as he ushered Flaherty from the room.

———

Attorney General Kevin Flaherty walked to his car parked on Beacon Street. He was very pleased with himself, and he imagined the press release that would go out tomorrow, as he slid into his car. Perhaps a press conference, the next day. *So, I.RISE is for profit?* He thought. *Time to catch up with Novello. I want information on I.RISE.* He jockeyed the car from its parking space and headed towards Kenmore Square. *Maybe I should use a driver. Traffic's a bitch.*

———

"Well, that went well, I think," Mulcahy said to Monsignor Roche. The two men were back in the comfortable chairs each with a crystal glass of ice and the Scotch that God himself drank.

"He not as dumb, as we were led to believe," Roche said.

"Nonsense," Mulcahy said. "Up until that business about Concanon's report, we were right on script. We played him like a fiddle. A fuckin' Stradivarius."

———

Abby and I were in bed, doing what people do when they've been married over thirty years. Watching TV. "You're sure the call came from Freddy," Abby said.

"I know his voice, and it was the number he gave me. What I don't know is why he thinks it was a big deal that Fisher wanted to talk with Novello. Fisher thought he had important information on a murder case. He's a judge, a big shot. Not hard to figure he would want to talk with the top dog and not some cop in Falmouth or Concord. What's the big deal? I think Freddy is playing games with me."

"Has he ever done anything but play games?' Abby said.

"Well, he killed Governor Hands," I said. "I think that qualifies as more than playing games."

"Even then he left a two-headed quarter in Hands' mouth," Abby said. "You know he did that so we'd know it was him, who done Hands in. It was still a game for Freddy."

"So why the call?" I said

"I think Freddy wants you to think about it, and not simply assume everything's as it appears to be."

"I have thought about it," I said. "I think Freddy's just playing games." The phone rang as I was reaching to turn out the light.

Abby groaned. "If this is a robo call on cruise travel, I want Freddy to blow up their goddamn boat."

"I think they call it a ship," I said. I reached for the land line phone on my night stand. Abby and I are probably the only people on Cape Cod with cell phones and a land line. Suspenders and belt.

It was Novello. "Can you meet me tomorrow morning at eight in front of the Park Street entrance at Boston Common?"

"Sure, what's this about?"

The dial tone hummed in my ear.

"Novello and Freddy are men of few words," I said to Abby.

Chapter 14

I came down Park Street from my office on Bowdoin, carrying two large cups of coffee. As I passed the Paulist Center, I gazed through the black iron fence along the Boston Common. Novello was in front of the two squat kiosks that provide entrance and exit to Park Street Station. His back was still to me, as I crossed the expansive concrete area in front of the station. Several vendors had started opening their wagons to offer T-shirts, jewelry and leather goods. Pigeons scurried about hunting for anything a commuter might drop. In a couple of hours, they would multiply by the hundreds to gather up popcorn dropped by folks who amuse themselves by feeding what a former New York City mayor once called rats with wings.

I was about fifteen feet away when Novello turned, holding two large coffees. He wore a dark double-breasted suit with a pale blue shirt and maroon tie. I had donned my formal wear of Khakis, blue shirt and blazer, no tie. We shifted over to a small wall to place and then exchange the cups we each bought for the other.

"Is this great minds think alike, or fools seldom differ?" I said, as we turned and walked along a path parallel to Tremont Street.

"Connor, I need you to do some research for me and no one can know what it is, or that it's for me. Can you do that?"

"I'm fine," I said. "And how are you?"

Novello stopped and turned to me. "Connor, whether or not I have time for niceties depends your answer to my question."

"Nobody, except for Abby," I said. "I tell her everything."

Novello nodded. "And she tells nobody."

"Then the answer is yes," I said.

"Good, Novello said. He smiled, and kicked at a pigeon. "So how you've been?"

———

Gloria D'Alessandro, Chief Justice of the Massachusetts Supreme Judicial Court rode alone in a private elevator reserved for the justices and anyone accompanying a justice.

D'Alessandro was fifty-three, attractive, and well aware the impact her beauty, intelligence and position had on her colleagues, attorneys, adversaries and friends. She had long reddish brown hair, styled and colored each month. Striking green eyes were the centerpiece of a face that projected intellect and humor not vacuous beauty. She exercised daily and approached her diet with the resolve of a Hindu penitent.

D'Alessandro had been the surprise pick of Governor Thomas Hands to fill the vacancy caused by the retirement of her predecessor. Since most of her legal career had been as corporate counsel to Boston University, she was a stranger to judges, most trial lawyers and the courtroom. But, she was well known and respected by the two largest bar associations in Massachusetts, where she had volunteered and had served on numerous boards and committees. Her looks and availability made her a media star and her nomination, while criticized by judges, was quickly approved.

D'Alessandro gazed at her reflection against the brass doors as soft chimes signaled each passing floor. She saw herself split as the doors opened to a small reception area with plush red carpeting and no furniture. A tasteful brass plaque reading: No Admittance, was affixed to a door on the far wall across from the elevator.

A somber, sixty-something man with gray hair in a military brush cut approached D'Alessandro. He bowed slightly, "Madam Chief Justice."

"Good morning, Edward. Is there something you need?" D'Alessandro said.

Edward Cummings, the Reporter of Decisions for the Court and its chief records clerk, stepped to D'Alessandro's side and walked with her over to the far door. "Madam Chief Justice," he whispered in a deep voice intoned with the wisdom of the ages, "I have been informed we will soon receive a grand jury subpoena for all of our records, including briefs, internal memoranda, judicial minutes, notes and votes of the justices in the matter of *Sheehan versus the Archbishop of Boston*."

———

Novello and I continued walking parallel to Tremont Street.

"Yesterday afternoon, Kevin Flaherty had a meeting with Cardinal Mulcahy and a Monsignor Roche," Novello said. He took a careful sip of coffee. He dropped one of his cups into a black iron basket. "You brought better coffee."

"Flaherty met with the Cardinal about Bartoni?" I was incredulous.

"No," Novello said. "The Archdiocese signed an agreement with Concanon when he was AG, promising it would develop new rules and procedures for dealing with abuse complaints against priests or church personnel. Part of the agreement was the AG and local police would be notified whenever a complaint was made. The Church also promised to file periodic progress reports tracking those complaints and a bunch of other things. The new rules haven't been implemented. Meeting was about that."

We passed a large black iron fountain surrounded by benches and iron litter barrels. The fountain was either broken or still off from the winter. As a result, it attracted little attention. The benches were empty save for the occasional piece of litter a steady but mild breeze carried from somewhere else. Boston Common was America's oldest park, and parts of it were showing its age.

"We've learned from a source other than Fisher that Bartoni had taken a special interest in the church abuse cases. He may have been making notes and keeping a scrapbook on the case." Novello stopped to sip more coffee. I joined him. It was a pain in the ass holding two cups, but I couldn't bring myself to throw one away. The day was still young.

Novello started walking. "We've gone through his computers, his home, his office at the courthouse, but haven't found any such book or even notes on any investigation he may have been doing. We're chasing shadows. We thought he might have a locker at a health club, but nothing so far."

"Bartoni wouldn't join just any health club. He's not one to mingle or sweat with the riff raff," I said. "He might use the facilities at Harvard University, or a place like the University Club of Boston, or maybe the Jefferson Street Gymnasium."

Novello stopped and stared at me in a way that asked for more information. "I know Bartoni went to Harvard Law," I said. "He might have joined an alumni group or program where he can use the facilities at the gym and have a locker," I said. "Just a thought."

"A good one," Novello said. "We should have thought of that. Tell me about the other places you mentioned."

"University Club of Boston," I said. "It's on Stuart Street. It's a private club with a pool and a gym. Bartoni would like that kind of place even more than a Harvard gym, where he might have to interact with a student. The Jefferson Street Gym is less upscale. It's small, doesn't have a pool, but it has exercise equipment and lockers."

"Thanks, that's helpful."

"Does Flaherty know about what Judge Fisher said?" I took another sip of coffee.

"I told him last night, after he got back." Novello stopped and looked at me. "Frankly, I should have told him much sooner, but once you give information to anyone in the AG's office, it begins to leak, and I didn't want that." Novello shrugged. "But, Flaherty's the boss, and if we're to work together, I can't keep him in the dark on big things. Besides I couldn't trust Judge Fisher to keep his mouth shut."

"Will Flaherty keep his closed?" I said.

We turned onto a path headed towards the glistening gold dome of the State House. Novello took a quick left and we headed towards the far corner of the Common, where Pope John Paul II had celebrated mass in a pouring rain storm during his first visit to the United States.

"Flaherty's not the asshole he's reputed to be." Novello nodded over his right shoulder towards the State House. "I know the folks in that building don't trust or respect him, but that's a plus in my book."

I gave up walking with two cups and placed one on a bench with peeling and splintered green wooden slats. We walked in silence along a path towards a large bandstand often used as the meeting spot for protest rallies. I read somewhere it was built on the site once used for public hangings. "What was Flaherty's reaction to what Fisher said?"

"Let's sit for a minute," Novello said.

We parked ourselves on a bench about thirty yards from the bandstand.

"Connor, let's be clear on something," Novello said. "I'm not going to tell you what was said in my conversations with Flaherty or anyone else."

"I know that," I said, a bit too quickly. "I just want to help, if I can. Tell me about the research."

"I'll get to that," Novello said. "The fact you asked me to tell you Flaherty's reaction to what Fisher said, is an indication you've forgotten your role in all this." He took a long sip of coffee."

I felt my face flush. "I know that," I said. "This is a murder investigation. I get it. No more questions from me" I remembered a stern faced nun in the 2nd grade once reprimanded me for talking in class. I thought the nun was mean, and stuck my tongue out at her when she turned her back. I'm older and like Novello, so I gave him a solemn nod with no tongue.

"I'm going to tell you Flaherty's reaction, but not because you asked me, Novello said. Whenever I tell you something on this case, it's because I decided to tell you not because you asked me to tell you. We clear?'

"Clear," I said.

"Flaherty said he would get one of his ongoing grand juries to issue a subpoena asking the Supreme Judicial Court to turn over all of its records on the *Sheehan* case. It could be served as early as today."

"Holy shit," I said. "That should shake things up.

"It's going to throw some shit at a very large fan," Novello said.

"How do I fit in? What's the research you want?"

"It has nothing to do with the Bartoni murder," Novello said. "Flaherty asked me to get some information on a treatment program called I.RISE. That an acronym, I've already forgotten the actual name. It's in New Bedford. I figured you've done corporate records and title searches. Seems to be important to Flaherty so I'd like to get him something soon. Don't want him thinking I've ignored his request. I can't have my usual people working on this now, particularly with subpoenas going out." Novello shook his head. "Flaherty runs probably the largest law firm in the state and he says he didn't want to use any of his people."

"So that leaves me," I said. "Should I be flattered?"

Novello ignored the question. "One more thing about Flaherty," he said. "When he was talking about his meeting with the Archdiocese, and I was telling him about Judge Fisher, he never hesitated in talking about a grand jury subpoena. Lot of prosecutors who would have ducked that fight."

"You're right," I said. "Case seems a bit thin to go after the Supreme Judicial Court with a subpoena."

"I said that to him," Novello said. "Know what Flaherty said to me? 'Hell, if you're skating on thin ice, you might as well dance.' Not sure what the fuck that means, but it tells me he isn't afraid of a fight, or to use his authority."

I laughed. "Doesn't sound like the Gypo Nolan Flaherty I remember."

"And another thing," Novello said. He seemed to be enjoying his defense of Flaherty. "He didn't appear to have been awed by the Cardinal. In the course of our conversation, he referred to the Cardinal as a bullshit artist, and Monsignor Whatshisname as an asshole."

"He'll be excommunicated if he says that to one more person," I said.

Novello got up from the bench. "Whatever you may think of him, last night our Mr. Flaherty grew a pair."

Chapter 15

"This is an outrageous overreach and you know it," Chief Justice D'Alessandro told Attorney General Kevin Flaherty in a tone a few decibels shy of a shout. "A simple phone call to me, and I would have quietly provided you most of what some piece of shit subpoena demands. And, there wouldn't have been any leaks."

She really is attractive, Flaherty thought. "No leaks so far," is what he said.

"How the hell do you think I knew about the subpoena before it was served?"

"Leaks go to the media," Flaherty said. "What you got was a heads up. Let's calm down and talk this through." *Let her know shouting won't work. Nice clothes, she's quite a presence.*

The two were sitting in D'Alessandro's chambers at the court house. It was nine-thirty. An angry phone call to Flaherty within minutes of her conversation with Edward Cummings, had resulted in an agreement to meet. Flaherty would come to her since his appearance in the John Adams Court House would not attract attention. It was a short walk, and she agreed to allow him access to the private elevator as further protection against media.

"Why didn't you go to Win Allen, the attorney for the Archdiocese? He'd give you copies of the briefs," D'Alessandro said.

Can't believe she mentioned Win Allen. "I suppose that wouldn't have been a violation of the order sealing the records," Flaherty said. "But Win wouldn't know how the justices voted. Would he?" *Would he, Gloria? Huh?*

"Kevin," D'Alessandro said in a softer tone, "what the fuck is going on? The *Sheehan* case was a routine appeal of a trial court's decision to drop a number of plaintiffs because of the statute of limitations. The plaintiffs appealed and we issued an unsigned order denying the appeal. The vote was five in favor of dismissal and two opposed." D'Alessandro shook her head, giving her an unkempt yet stylish look. "Kevin, I thought we had a good relationship." She paused and ran her fingers through her hair. "To be blindsided like this is, frankly, beyond the pale."

Oooh, it's Kevin now. "Madam Chief Justice," Flaherty said. "First of all, you weren't blindsided. I'm in your chambers, and we're talking about a subpoena that hasn't been served. Truth be told one hasn't been issued. There are no reporters calling you or TV cameras chasing you. You either have a low threshold of what constitutes being blindsided, or you've never been blindsided. Let's turn down the drama and resolve our differences."

"You haven't told me what's going on," D'Alessandro said. She brought up a whisk of her sultry look, then the briefest vision of a tongue at the corner of her mouth.

Nice try, Gloria. "We're investigating a matter and the issue of the appeal in the *Sheehan* case came up," Flaherty said. "I have an aggressive investigator, and the requested subpoena may have been overly broad."

"What is the matter you're investigating?" D'Alessandro said.

"I'm not telling you that," Flaherty said. "Grand juries operate in secret."

"Well, I'm not going to give you internal court memoranda, judicial notes, or how the justices voted. We have our secrets, as well," D'Alessandro said. "You want to fight with me in court? There is not a judge in this state who would require us to turn over confidential notes, or anything that invades our deliberative processes."

"That's true," Flaherty said. "But court fights are not secret. Those TV cameras and reporters you're so worried about will ask me why we want those records, and they'll ask you about the public's right to know and what are you afraid of?" Flaherty smiled. "Or, I can file a motion to unseal the records and at least get all the briefs and orders. Of course, that would also draw the attention of the media."

D'Alessandro's face squinted in thought. "Look, I'll get you all the briefs, and a summary of any draft orders. My memory is there weren't any." D'Alessandro blew air from her mouth in a loud sigh. "I'll tell you how each of the justices voted, but I can't give you our internal memos or notes. I'd lose whatever respect my colleagues have for me. I simply can't do it." The victim card, the last one in her deck.

Flaherty got up from his seat. "Okay, if you get me that information by five this afternoon, I'll hold off the subpoena for now." He headed to the door and turned back. "You want to tell me how you voted on the appeal, or make me wait until this afternoon?"

"I voted to hear the appeal, D'Alessandro said. "I was one of the two justices who voted against the Archdiocese and in favor of the plaintiffs."

———

"She voted with the plaintiffs," Flaherty said to Novello, about twenty minutes after his meeting with D'Alessandro. The two were at the conference table in Flaherty's private office on the 18th floor of One Ashburton Place. Views of the State House and the Charles River, winding its way towards Watertown, framed Flaherty's empty desk.

"Not what I expected, Novello said.

"When she gave in on telling me how the justices voted, I figured she must have voted no," Flaherty said. "Doesn't mean she didn't bag the case. Once she knew there were enough votes to deny the appeal, she could have put herself on the other side as additional protection."

Novello nodded. "Be nice to know how the deliberations proceeded."

"We were never going to get the internal memoranda or judicial notes," Flaherty said. "No court would ever order disclosure of those." He shrugged. "We might learn something if there were any draft orders, but I'm not optimistic." Flaherty smiled at Novello. "By the way, you should know that I blamed my overzealous investigator on the subpoena. Somebody had to be the bad cop."

"Happy to oblige," Novello said. "She as good looking as her press pictures appear?"

"Yeah, for sure," Flaherty said. "And she uses it, believe me. That lady exudes sex. Turns it on and off like a light."

"Yet you were able to resist her charms and the temptations of sin," Novello said. "Good for you."

"Indeed, I summoned up my moral character and fiber and resist I did," Flaherty said.

"Your fine Catholic upbringing stood you well?"

"That and the fact I'm as gay as a French horn," Flaherty said.

———

Winfield "Win" Allen was divorced, fifty-seven, handsome and rich. His great grandfather had come to America with just the clothes on his back and two suitcases, each with two million dollars in cash. He was a partner at Spencer and Joyce, a boutique law firm of three litigators, three paralegals, five private investigators and one harried but efficient office manager. With annual billings in excess of twelve million, all were well paid. The firm, housed in a large brownstone on Marlborough Street in Boston, specialized in insurance defense work, patent litigation and sophisticated commercial mergers and transactions. Win had inherited the building from his father and used the fifth floor penthouse as his residence.

While Novello and Flaherty were discussing Gloria D'Alessandro in Flaherty's office, Win was less than three miles away, sitting near an open window smoking a menthol cigarette. He was watching a sliver of sunshine that had slanted in through the skylight and across the curvature of the Chief Justice's naked behind, as she lay sprawled across the large bed in his penthouse apartment.

D'Alessandro stirred and woke up. She looked over to Win. "What time is it?"

"Twelve forty-five," Win said. He dropped the cigarette into a small jar of water he had placed on the outside ledge, "You have plenty of time for a shower. I'll get you back to the court house before two." He smiled. "Glad to see you're not overly concerned about what Flaherty told you."

D'Alessandro rolled over, dropping her feet to the floor. She sat on the bed's edge looking over to the frosted glass door to the bath. "He won't learn anything from what I agreed to give him," D'Alessandro said. "The real question is what is he investigating and how did the *Sheehan* case come into it."

"Smart to vote against me on the appeal," Win said.

"If Novello is as smart as people say, that won't fool him," D'Alessandro said. "I can't figure out how the hell our names got dragged into whatever he's investigating."

"You told me this Novello was the head of the Homicide Bureau," Win said. "Christ, hope I'm not caught up in a fucking homicide investigation."

"You're not, and it's we. Remember?" D'Alessandro said. "Just stick to the script when you're interviewed. They'll do us separately, so stick to the script and we'll both be fine."

"I asked a friend at the Archdiocese. Flaherty met with the Cardinal, but it was routine and had nothing to do with *Sheehan*. I know nobody knows about us or the help you've provided. No worries there," he said a bit too joyously.

"Well, somebody knows something," D'Alessandro snapped. "That fuckin' subpoena didn't come out of thin air." She padded over to the bathroom and slammed the frosted door behind her.

———

An hour later, D'Alessandro, a large scarf covering her head, exited discretely from Win Allen's car at the corner of Charles and Beacon Streets. A brisk walk up Beacon, past the State House and to the John Adams Courthouse would take her about twenty minutes. Win drove up Beacon, past D'Alessandro. He did not wave or offer any acknowledgment. D'Alessandro, eyes forward, did not see Win's car as it passed. Nor did she notice the dark gray Toyota two vehicles behind Win. She had not noticed it when she exited her taxi a few doors down from Win's townhouse on Marlborough Street, about two hours earlier. The Toyota was there when she walked to the rear of Win's townhouse to take the private elevator to his penthouse. And, the Chief Justice and Win had failed to notice it following them from Marlborough Street to the corner of Charles and Beacon.

Inside the Toyota with an expensive camera and telescopic lens, note pads, and a baloney and cheese sandwich on the passenger seat, with a large coffee in the cup holder, was Ed McGonagle. "Gotcha," he said with a broad smile as he followed Win up Beacon Street.

Chapter 16

The State House was quiet and my quarterly lobbying report completed and mailed to the Secretary of State by twelve-thirty. I decided to enjoy the warm late April afternoon and take an early bus to Falmouth. My conversation with Novello that morning replayed in my head. I was thrilled to be part of something, even if it wasn't the murder investigation.

By two-thirty I was making the less than three mile drive from the Falmouth Bus Station to my home. Several merchants stood outside their shops on Main Street cleaning and scraping the dust and peeling paint of winter and replacing it with the glossy, pristine white of summer. In a few weeks, the summer job applications for life guards, wait staff and traffic control personnel (AKA rent-a-cops) would start arriving.

I turned off Main at King Street, past the auto repair and lube shop that kept our aging cars running. I passed the new fire station on the right, and several new houses on the left, which had replaced one of Abby's favorite haunts – a large barn full of used furniture, odd signs and memorabilia from years past. Its loss was made easier because the developer had built modest Cape style homes with cedar shake shingles, already turning gray from the sun and winter chill. Our home was on a horseshoe street running off King, then back onto it near its intersection with Clinton Avenue. Clinton Avenue was only a block or so from the beach. The million dollar homes started there. The eight houses on our horseshoe hamlet were all small capes built on small lots. We breathed the same air, walked the same sand and swam in the same ocean as the millionaires about two hundred yards away. I'm sure it pissed them off.

When we arrived two years ago, Abby planted a shrub of beach roses at the end of our driveway and in front of a small white corner fence. The shrub thrived in Falmouth's salty air and heavy morning dew. It soon grew over the fence and began to encroach on the driveway. I offered to uproot the damn thing and bring it to the dump. But, the summer roses were attractive and Abby doesn't give up easily. So, once a week during the growing season, which for this shrub seemed to be year round, Abby trimmed it. This is what she was doing when I turned into the driveway. She was wearing a faded blue Brandeis University sweat shirt and cutoff jeans. The flecks of white paint on the shorts told me she had touched up the corner fence.

She greeted me with a look of surprise, which morphed into a wide grin, then a quizzical twist of her face.

I got out of the car. "Let's get inside before your husband shows up."

"He'll be here in ten minutes," Abby said. "Plenty of time, for you."

"This is my reward for coming home early?" I said.

She gave me a hug. "This is a nice surprise. I want to hear what Novello wanted, and it's not too soon for a couple of perfect T&Ts on the deck."

We keep a bottle of Tanqueray Gin in our freezer, along with tonic water frozen in ice cube trays. With a perfect T&T, the gin pours out of the bottle like syrup and into a frosted glass with ice cubes of frozen tonic water. The drink never waters down, as the cubes melt. Abby made the drinks while I changed into Bermuda shorts and a green golf shirt.

Abby was on our deck, which had been enlarged by the previous owner to run from behind the attached garage along about half of the backside of the house. It reduced the mowing of grass to a fifteen minute activity, and was large enough to provide areas of sun and shade throughout the day. On weekends after four o'clock, the deck is a neighborhood gathering spot for those without plans. Everyone brings beer or wine, or whatever to put on ice, their own food for the grill, and Jimmy Buffet, Eagles or other CDs for an old player, with a shuffle play function, stationed in the garage with outside speakers to the deck.

Abby had elected shade, and I joined her at a white table where two perfect T&Ts had been placed on either side of a bowl of white cheddar popcorn.

"Life is good," I said as I sat. "How'd your day go?"

Abby brushed a thick strand of auburn-brown hair to behind her left ear. The first flecks of gray reminded me how long we've been together. We met at a college party in Boston. It used to embarrass me to admit after meeting her, I never dated anyone else. Now I brag it's evidence of good judgment. "Got everything done I needed, and I picked up some work from Blue Cross," Abby said. She did consulting work for several health organizations and insurers. She was a registered nurse with a master's degree in biology, and had carved out an area of expertise in Medicare auditing and claims billings that I could never understand or explain. But it allowed her to work from home and she made more money in three days than I did in five. She also made perfect T&Ts.

"Nice," I said. "So I can retire?"

"If you find a place to live." We toasted our glasses. "So tell me about your meeting with Novello."

Abby rarely interrupts a story with questions or commentary. She quietly took short-hand notes and listened intently while I told her my entire conversation with Novello. It took me thirty minutes, and when I finished I got up to make myself another drink. Abby's glass was nearly full.

"Why does the first T&T always taste better than the second?" I said, when I returned.

"Drinks taste better when someone else makes them," Abby said. "Have you started researching I.RISE?" She took a small sip of her drink. "Wasn't that a Maya Angelou poem? Pretty pretentious for a program treating pedophile priests."

"I had the same thought, so I Goggled Angelou. Her poem was

Still *I RISE*. Pretty close. I think they stole it from the poem then created a name to fit the acronym. Institute for Recovery, Independence and Self-Empowerment. Even more pretentious."

"Find out anything about them?" Abby said.

I fished a reporter's notebook from my back pocket. "I went on the Internet and printed out a list of the board of directors. Names didn't mean anything to me, but it'll be in the packet I give to Novello. I also printed out an annual report with a listing of the major funders, but I haven't studied it. The clinical director is a Nelson Decker, Ph.D." I flipped a page in the notebook and snagged more popcorn. "According to their website, I.RISE was established in 1987, primarily for the treatment of alcohol and substance use disorders. It's mostly day treatment, but a small residential program was established in the late nineties. I think it was six beds, then expanded to ten in 2005." I looked at Abby. A signal to see if she had any questions.

"Licensed?"

"I called the lobbyist at Public Health, a guy I served with. He checked, and told me in confidence that I.RISE is fully licensed with no current or past complaints. He told me Nelson Decker is licensed with no past or current complaints. Facility has a residential license for ten adult beds, and has several licenses for day treatment programs in alcohol abuse, substance use disorders, something called self-awareness skills and psychiatric assessment and treatment."

"He gave you a lot of information. Novello should be pleased," Abby said.

"This is just surface stuff," I said. "Tomorrow, I'll do a title search and find out who owns the land where I.RISE operates. Then, I'll research the owner.

"It won't be I.RISE?"

"Probably not," I said. "My guess is the property will be owned by a realty trust, with some obscure company named as the trustee. I.RISE probably rents the space from the trust."

"What about the owners or beneficiaries of the trust?' Abby said.

"The beneficiaries don't have to be named. One of the advantages of the realty trust is the privacy it gives the owner or multiple owners of property."

"So why bother with the title search?"

"Might get lucky," I said. 'Maybe it's not in trust. I have to check. Even knowing it's a trust and a dead end is better than not knowing. And, I want to get Novello as much information as I can."

"I can check with some of my contacts," Abby said. "I doubt if I.RISE has any Medicare eligible patients."

"Gives a whole new meaning to I.RISE," I said.

Abby laughed. "Well, they also have alcohol and drug abusers, so they may be part of the Mass Health network. I'll check."

"Great," I said. "I'd like to get something to Novello ASAP.

"What's next?'

"Tomorrow, I'll ask Vinnie for the day off, find out who owns the property where I.RISE operates and later we can drive to New Bedford and see this place." I said. "I'd like to take a look and go from there."

"Hope it's sunny," Abby said. "I'll find us a waterfront restaurant for lunch."

Chapter 17

Ed McGonagle, Anthony Novello and Attorney General Kevin Flaherty hovered on one side of the conference table in Flaherty's office on the 18th floor of One Ashburton Place. Eight color pictures of Chief Justice D'Alessandro were spread on the table, along with four pictures of Win Allen and D'Alessandro walking together from his townhouse on Marlborough Street to his car. Off to the side was a picture of D'Alessandro exiting Allen's vehicle with a large scarf covering her head.

"I was tailing Win Allen and parked on Marlborough Street," McGonagle said. "All of a sudden a cab pulls up and out jumps the Chief Justice. I grabbed the camera and shot away. This is her passing the front entrance and now walking down a side alley to the rear of Win's building." McGonagle's fingers danced across the pictures in tune with his narrative. "By the way is Win short for something?'

"Winfield," Novello said. "Sounds like a cologne."

"How long she inside? Flaherty asked.

"About an hour and a half," McGonagle said. "No way of knowing how long Winfield was inside. The building, I mean."

Flaherty shook his head. "Novello warned me about you."

McGonagle smiled and pointed to a picture. "Look at her hair when she's getting out of the cab." His finger moved to another picture. "Now look at it as she's walking with Winfield to his car."

"Looks like she took a shower," Novello said. "Hair's wet."

"You don't suppose Win is an attorney and a hair dresser," Flaherty said.

"Yeah, Novello warned me about *you*," McGonagle said.

Flaherty laughed and sat down. "Okay, let's sit down and figure out what we got here. Win and the CJ had some afternoon delight. Doesn't mean there was a payoff."

McGonagle walked to the other side of the table and sat. Novello drifted over to the large windows facing west. Outside, the glare of a lowering sun slowed the early rush hour drivers on Storrow Drive heading west. He turned back to the group. "The pictures confirm some of what Fisher told us. We now know D'Alessandro and Win Allen are more than legal colleagues."

"Should have recused herself from the appeal," Flaherty said. "Not a crime, unless money was exchanged, but it could force her to resign or get her impeached."

"Buy some leverage with that," McGonagle said.

"Fisher says Bartoni thinks he saw them riding together in a car. Yet he started calling it corruption and a bag job," Flaherty said. "What did he know that we don't?"

McGonagle flipped a few pages in his notebook. "Fisher says Bartoni told him he had other sources, but never revealed them or whatever information he might have uncovered. Fisher said the 'big reveal' was to happen at their next lunch, which was scheduled for the Wednesday following the Saturday Bartoni was killed."

Novello walked to the table and sat in a chair beside McGonagle and across from Flaherty. "Bartoni's wife says her husband told her he was working on something big that involved the Catholic Church." He looked at Flaherty. "You're right, the question is how could Bartoni know all this? He saw them in a car. So What? Even if he saw these fuckin' pictures, he couldn't know D'Alessandro was bagging a case. We're missing something."

"Did the subpoena produce anything?" McGonagle said.

"Not a lot," Flaherty said. "But something."

"Let's hear it," Novello said.

"This is technical with a lot of legalese," Flaherty said.

"Just talk slow," McGonagle said.

"Okay," Flaherty said. "The appeal was all about the statute of limitations, the time period for bringing a law suit after the occurrence of an event."

"Okay, you can talk faster than that," Novello smiled.

"Like the sell date on a can of tuna fish," McGonagle said. He picked up a pencil. "How do you spell statute?"

"No more straight man," Flaherty said. "The plaintiffs argued the abuse they suffered was so horrific their memories of it had been repressed. So the clock shouldn't have started until the memories were restored. How can you bring a suit about something you can't remember?"

"And the church's position?" Novello said. He felt the onset of a caffeine withdrawal headache. His eyes searched the office for coffee, or a Coke. Nothing. The muted sounds of telephones ringing, which had filtered into the room, sounded like maracas.

"The Archdiocese had three arguments," Flaherty said. "One, the concept of repressed memory was not established science and shouldn't be recognized by the Court. Two, if new rules for repressed memory cases were to be established, it was up to the legislature to do it, not the courts. Three, assuming the Court could establish new statute of limitation rules for repressed memory, those rules would only apply in future cases, where the alleged abused happened after the date of the new rules."

"I get it," McGonagle said. "One, we didn't abuse altar boys. Two, if we did, they don't remember, so no harm no foul. And three, you should only punish us for the ones we might molest in the future. Assuming, of course, they remember it. Do I have this right?"

"Sure you don't have a law degree?" Flaherty said.

"So, no surprises with the briefs," Novello said. "Did we learn anything we didn't already know?"

"The first briefs that were filed by the plaintiffs and the Archdiocese were pretty much confined to the arguments I outlined," Flaherty said. "Frankly, both sides of the case were well represented."

"That's a relief," McGonagle said. "Hate to think our Chief Justice is getting shagged by a legal hack."

"I mentioned it because the church had a strong legal position that was well presented." Flaherty said. A hint of exasperation hung in the air. "They didn't need to have the case bagged in order to win. It cuts against our theory of what's going on."

"You said earlier we learned something," Novello said. "What?"

"The Court gave both sides ten days to file supplemental briefs to respond to anything in the other side's brief that they hadn't anticipated." Flaherty's phone buzzed. He stood and glanced at it. "Sorry, I have to take this. I'll be right back."

When he was gone, Novello turned to McGonagle. "I don't think this is what Bartoni was investigating. We're missing something." He pulled out his phone, briefly stared at the screen, and returned it to his inside suit pocket. He looked at McGonagle. "Another thing. You might want to ease up on the wise cracks. This is Flaherty's biggest case since becoming AG."

McGonagle fiddled with a pen, wearing an abstract expression, as if he had left the room. "You got it." He looked up. "You want a coffee?"

"It's that obvious?" Novello said.

McGonagle smiled and nodded. He got up and left.

Flaherty re-entered. "That was the Governor. Wanted to know if we made any progress. He calls couple times a week."

"What's his interest?' Novello said.

"He and Bartoni were friends," Flaherty said. "Said they go back to when the Governor was District Attorney." Flaherty smiled in thought. "You know, Concanon and I are kind of on the same career path. District Attorney Concanon, District Attorney Flaherty, Attorney General Concanon, Attorney General Flaherty. Who knows? Governor Flaherty has a nice ring to it."

McGonagle came into the office followed by a twenty-something man holding a tray with a pot of coffee, three cups, a creamer and scattered packages of sugar. He placed the tray in the middle of the table and left.

"I miss anything?" McGonagle said.

"Bartoni and Governor Concanon were friends," Novello said. "Apparently for a long time."

"Would have been nice to know about the friendship," McGonagle said. He turned to Novello. "Mrs. Bartoni mention that to you?"

Novello looked at McGonagle and briefly shook his head. He poured a cup of coffee. "Forget what I said earlier about wisecracks." He turned towards Flaherty. "Tell us what we learned from the supplemental brief."

Flaherty nodded. "Win Allen raised an issue in his brief that had not been mentioned by the plaintiffs."

"Which was?" Novello said.

"He argued against the SJC sending the case back to the trial court for a hearing on whether or not repressed memory had gained acceptance by the scientific community in Massachusetts."

"You think the CJ tipped him off that some of the brethren were considering doing that?" Novello said.

Flaherty shrugged. "All of a sudden Win's arguing against doing something no one has suggested doing? Add that to what we now know about the Chief Justice and Win Allen." He let his words lie on the table.

Novello nodded. "D'Alessandro told Win some of the justices were thinking of avoiding a decision on the *Sheehan* case by sending it back for this additional hearing. That would have been a partial victory for the plaintiffs and a loss for the church."

"Exactly," Flaherty said. "Sending the case back for more hearings might have been a compromise offered by one of the justices. A lot of horse trading goes on in the deliberations of an important case."

"Do you know if repressed memory has been accepted by the scientific community in Massachusetts?" McGonagle said.

"I've been told yes," Flaherty said. "But some would disagree."

"You can find someone who'll say the earth is flat," McGonagle said. "But if the hearing judge concluded repressed memory was real science – like climate change – that would have been a big victory for the altar boys."

"Right," Flaherty said.

"This is starting to make sense," Novello said. "Still hard to see this leading up to the murder of Bartoni. Something's fucked up."

"Interview D'Alessandro and Allen," Flaherty said. "Find out."

Novello nodded. "Ed, you take the lawyer, I'll take the judge."

"You've always been partial to redheads," McGonagle said.

The three rose from the table. Novello and McGonagle drifted towards the door. Flaherty touched Novello's shoulder. "Have you had a chance to get someone to check up on I.RISE?"

Novello turned. "I have a good man on it. I'll check to see where he's at."

Chapter 18

Abby and I spend a lot of time in an upstairs room we use as a combination office and TV den. She has a desk and I a table, each with a computer and printer. There are two oak filing cabinets commandeered from my law practice.

The den section of the room includes a small refrigerator with sodas, ice tea and ice cube trays of frozen tonic water for perfect T&Ts. Two recliners face a large flat screen TV the previous owner had mounted and never bothered to move. He left the recliners because after some second floor remodeling, you'd need a chain saw to get them out the door. We are the only people who use or even see the room.

Abby's work area is well organized, not a scrap of paper out of place. The sole wall decoration is a bulletin board to her left with a dry board To Do List that seems always to have items crossed off or checked. The wall closest to my work area is adorned with framed coasters from bars visited across Massachusetts, New England, Ireland and parts of Spain. More cluttered than her space. Like the Louvre is more cluttered than a hospital corridor.

I was seated at my table preparing to do a title search on the address for I. RISE. I could do routine title searches because when I practiced law, I spent time on divorce cases at the Middlesex Probate Court in Cambridge. The Registry of Deeds is in the same building, so colleagues often asked me to get a copy of a deed, a mortgage or to update a title search. Before the Internet, title examiners physically searched records, going through stacks of large books with dusty canvass-like covers. These tomes each weighed close to five pounds. The older record books were in seven foot high steel bookcases on a section of the second floor, which encircled the entire room.

Title examiners rarely wore white shirts or blouses since carrying the record books from the bookcases to their desk dirtied the sleeves. Most of the men wore short-sleeved darkly colored shirts.

The Internet changed everything. Computer terminals replaced many books and clean modular stations were scattered among the long oak tables with carved initials and other etchings. Today, many parts of a title search can be done from home, where you can wear a white shirt or no clothes at all.

I elected to wear clothes.

I knew I.RISE was created in 1987 and its business address was in New Bedford, which is part of Bristol County. All of Bristol County's title records going back to the mid-fifties have been computerized and put on-line. A few clicks on my computer confirmed what I had suspected. Title to the land and building was in a realty trust with the clever name: EZ DUZ IT Realty Trust. It had been purchased in 1987 for $425,000.

Easy Does It is a popular slogan in the recovery community. I figured the creators of the trust used the phonetic spelling to avoid any copyright problems or confusion with an existing corporate name. Additional clicks told me there was no mortgage on the property. It had been a cash purchase. Nice for someone.

I spent the next several minutes learning nothing about the EZ DUZ IT Realty trust, which is the point of a realty trust. Secrecy and privacy. If I could ever discover the beneficiary of the trust, I assumed it would be a Limited Liability Corporation.

Think of it this way, Jane and John Doe own property for investment. They put the title in a realty trust, so no one sees their names as the owners. Who wants tenants or contractors calling them? The trust gives them privacy. Then, to give themselves some liability protection Jane and John Doe can create a Limited Liability Corporation, which they own, to be the beneficiary of the trust. The combination gives them privacy and protection.

I knew LLCs were registered with the Secretary of State. I could go on-line and learn everything. But, that requires knowing the name of the LLC. If the beneficiary of the EZ DUZ IT Realty Trust was an LLC, only the trustee and the creator of the trust would know the name.

I printed out the terms of terms of the trust, which were pretty standard. Vinnie does a lot of commercial transactions, so I recognized the boiler plate language. A company called Realty Trustees, Inc. was the named trustee of EZ DUZ IT. I could do a search of corporate records and find out its board of directors and corporate officers, but that probably wouldn't tell me anything. You'd lose the secrecy if you made the trustee a person or organization connected to you. But knowing is better than not knowing, so that search would come later. I took a sip of my coffee. It was getting close to room temperature.

I looked further and saw a notice of a ten-year lease was recorded on the property by I.RISE in 1988. Notices of the renewal of that lease were filed in 1998, 2008, and 2018. The actual lease was not recorded, but the notice said it was available for inspection at I.RISE.

I checked to see if either I.RISE or EZ DUZ IT had purchased property in Bristol County after 1987. Neither had. I exited out of the Bristol County records and searched the tax records of New Bedford. The most recent assessment of the land was for over a million and the owner was listed as EZ DUZ IT Realty Trust. Someone has invested wisely.

I took a sip of coffee. It was cold. Time for another cup, and that required a trip downstairs to the kitchen. *Maybe we should put a coffee pot up here.*

Chapter 19

"Should I be lawyering up?" D'Alessandro said to Novello, who sat across from her at a small table at the Café Fleuri in the Langham Hotel. It was nine o'clock and the early power breakfast crowd was thinning out. The meeting had been set up the day before, shortly after the gathering in Attorney General Flaherty's office where Novello and McGonagle had seen the pictures of D'Alessandro and Win Allen.

"That's up to you," Novello said. "But if he comes, Win Allen pays his own tab."

D'Alessandro frowned. "Win's not my attorney, he's currently my lover."

A waiter, quiet as a cat on a rug, came to the table and placed a bowl of Greek yogurt and seasonal berries before the Chief Justice. With a modest flair of elegance, he placed a plate of two poached eggs resting on griddled corned beef and red onion hash before Novello. His last maneuver was to slide a plate of sliced wheat toast to the center of the table.

As the waiter retreated, D'Alessandro said, "Does it shock you to hear me say that?"

Novello shook his head. "Not much shocks or surprises me." He used a corner of the sliced toast to scoop some hash and egg yolk into his mouth. He brought the crisp white cloth napkin to his lips. "I mentioned Win's name, you instinctively recognized I knew about your relationship and decided not to complicate things by lying. Smart."

"There is nothing for me to lie about," D'Alessandro said. She balanced a single berry on her folk and put it in her mouth. "Win and I are both adults, both single and our relationship began after *Sheehan versus the Archdiocese of Boston.*"

"Of course it did," Novello said. "So tell me, when, where and how did you two love birds meet? Who else was there? Was it a blind date?"

"None of your business," D'Alessandro said. "I don't have to explain myself to you."

"Too personal?" Novello said. "Then tell me if the two of you ever went out in a public setting, maybe a restaurant, a wedding reception, you can just get me the names of people who saw you. Maybe you could get me the name of anyone who knew you were dating, were meeting socially, or, to use your words, had become lovers." He took a large forkful of hash.

"I'm not going to do that," D'Alessandro said. "You can either take my word for it, or shove the whole matter up your ass."

Novello stared at her. "I have a third alternative. You and Win can tell it all, under oath, to a grand jury." He slid his fork into the hash.

D'Alessandro leaned into Novello. "I'll be polite and smile in this nice restaurant." She smiled and hissed, "Don't you threaten me. I'm not someone you can intimidate or push around. I can destroy you with a phone call. If you ever insinuate to anyone that I have done anything improper, I'll have your balls cut off so fast, you won't know it 'til your morning piss. Do. Not. Fuck. With. Me." She stood and threw her napkin on the table.

Ever the gentleman, Novello rose as the Chief Justice hurried out of the café.

———

"So Winfield, when did you and Chief Justice D'Alessandro become an item?" McGonagle asked. The two men sat at a table in the Fill-A-Buster, a small Greek breakfast and lunch restaurant on Bowdoin Street, across from the side entrance to the State House. The early breakfast and coffee crowd had left, and the three owners, all in white shirts, trousers and long white aprons were preparing for the heavy lunch crowd of legislators, staffers and lobbyists who filled the place each day. Most received their large portioned meals over the counter and in white Styrofoam containers to be taken elsewhere. Eight pale yellow Formica tables were continually filled from eleven-thirty to three o'clock each afternoon.

"Call me Win, and may I ask what business is it of yours when Gloria and I became lovers?"

"You don't deny a relationship?" McGonagle said.

"Why would I? The Chief Justice and I are both adults, single and our relationship began after the *Sheehan versus Archdioceses of Boston* case." Win Allen sipped his tea and smiled. Not a care in the world.

"So tell me, Winfield, when did it start? You must have told friends. Give me a few people who can testify under oath as to when the two of you began seeing each other."

"This isn't seventh grade, Detective," Win said. "I'm not telling you anything. You can either take my word for it, or go to hell." He drank the remainder of his tea and walked out the door.

McGonagle remained seated. He ordered another coffee.

———

At ten thirty, Novello and McGonagle sat in the bullpen on the eighteenth floor of One Ashburton Place, less than 800 feet from the Fill-A-Buster. They had exchanged notes on their meetings with D'Alessandro and Win Allen.

"Didn't hide the fact they scripted their responses," McGonagle said. "Seemed to enjoy it. Who the hell uses 'lovers' to describe a relationship?"

Novello nodded. "They talked and decided not to say anything more than it all started sometime after the case was decided. They're wiseasses, but smart. Knew enough not to lie about anything we can prove to be a lie. Avoided any specifics, and stuck to the lie everything started after the case was decided. I'm sure they were incredibly discreet, avoided places where people would know one or both of them, and kept their mouths shut. Won't be easy to prove it started earlier."

"I'll get the registration numbers on their cars and get some people to check the Easy Pass records at the Turnpike Authority," McGonagle said. "Who knows, we may get lucky and find both plates using the exit to East Bumfuck on the same date and time. You're sure they're lying?"

"They're lying," Novello said. "I'm sure of that." He stood up and began pacing the room. "Look, if the relationship really started after the *Sheehan* case, we'd have known about it. These are two powerful people; someone would have noticed them somewhere, snapped a picture, and it would be in one of those celebrity columns, or on somebody's website. The mistake they made was being too discreet. They kept it hidden for so long, they got used to being discreet. Don't be surprised if we suddenly see them in a celebrity column."

McGonagle looked through his notebook. "The statute of limitations issue was decided in favor of the church on January third," he said. "According to Judge Fisher, Bartoni said he saw D'Alessandro and Win Allen in a car late one night in mid-February. Let's call it Valentine's Day; about six weeks after the SJC ruled in favor of the church. And, now Winfield getting afternoon quickies in his penthouse playpen? Quick work even for a rich white guy with perfect teeth."

"Still not sure this has anything to do with Bartoni's death," Novello said. Doesn't feel right. We're missing something."

A phone buzzed. Novello retrieved it from the suit jacket hung on the back of a chair. "What's up?" He listened. "Good work, we'll get on it." Novello smiled and looked at McGonagle. "Bartoni had a membership at the Jefferson Street Gym, one of the places Connor McNeill mentioned to me. And he had a locker." Novello drifted over to the conference table and sat down. "We need a search warrant or Mrs. Bartoni with us before the Gym will open the locker."

"Not unreasonable, McGonagle said. "You want to involve Mrs. Bartoni or ask Flaherty to get us a warrant?"

"We may not have enough for a search warrant, but I'd rather not involve Mrs. Bartoni or even tell her about the locker unless we have to," Novello said. "Let's start with Flaherty. If we can't get a warrant, we'll go to Mrs. Bartoni."

"Hope we find more than a sweaty jock strap," McGonagle said.

Chapter 20

I made a cup of coffee and called Vinnie to tell him I'd like the day off. I described in detail where in the clutter that was his office he could find the completed research and paper work on the matters he left on my To Do list. He took longer than usual to agree, and I began to worry my plans for the day were about to change. "If this doesn't work for you, I can come in," I said

"No, that's okay," Vinnie said. "No problem, Connor. Closing up early myself. Meeting someone for golf. I was just checking the calendar. Have a great day and weekend. See you Monday, or whenever."

I spent the next hour on the research I was doing for Novello. The EZ DUZ IT Realty Trust was basic and offered no surprises. I researched Realty Trustees, Inc. It was, as I suspected, a company that served as a trustee of numerous trusts. It also owned several commercial properties. An Internet visit to the Massachusetts Secretary of State revealed the names of its officers and treasurer. Most people just look at a company's website to find out its leadership team. However, if it's a corporation, the names of its principal officers and treasurer are required to be filed and updated each year with the secretary of state. A corporation's website could list the Three Stooges and Barack Obama as its principal officers. A quick search through the Secretary of State's website provides more accurate information.

My attention turned to the research I had collected on I.RISE. It had a nine member board of directors and a leadership team. Everyone was a stranger to me. The names matched those listed with the Secretary of State. At the Secretary of State's Office, I checked to find the original incorporators of I.RISE. More strangers.

I prepared a brief note to Novello explaining realty trusts, LLCs and the paperwork I had accumulated. I told him nothing appeared irregular, but recommended he have someone check out the incorporators, board of directors, and the listing of corporate supporters and sponsors provided in the Annual Report I had printed from the I.RISE Website. Neither the Catholic Church nor the Archdiocese of Boston was listed as a corporate supporter or sponsor. Not surprising. Getting paid for treating and hiding pedophile priests is not something any company would highlight.

Another page in the Annual Report purported to list Major Funding Sources & Expenses:

Revenues:	Grants, Donations, Contracts &	
	Third Party Payers	$9,000,000
Expenses:	Personnel, Contracts, Occupancy &	
	Community Giving	$6,000,000

I wondered how much of the $9 million had come from the Church, and how much of that from the Sunday collection boxes across the Archdiocese of Boston. I attend mass once or twice a week at the Paulist Center in Boston, but never on Sundays. Wasn't a matter of principle, just a matter of wanting sleep. It had been decades since I dropped something into a Sunday collection basket so I doubted if any of the nine million had come from me. Didn't make me feel any better.

I called out to Abby, "We should head out to New Bedford in an hour or so. You find a place for lunch?"

Abby came into the den and went over to her desk. She turned her chair to face me. "So Sherlock, you have a plan?" She said. "I mean after we have lunch."

"We'll find I.RISE," I said. "I'm hoping to get a feel for the place, its clientele." I shrugged. "Not much of a plan, but I do want to see the place. You have any thoughts?"

"I think we should go inside. Pretend to be looking for help for a troubled family member. We should get some program brochures, ask to speak with someone to answer questions about waiting lists, referral requirements, costs, insurance, and other things. Maybe we can get a tour of the facility."

"Or, we could do that," I said.

We both laughed.

"You'll have to forego T&Ts at lunch," Abby said. "Unless you want to be the troubled family member?"

"Let's eat after we see I.RISE," I said.

"Or, we could do that," Abby said.

———

It didn't take long to find I.RISE, which was housed in a building at the intersection of two cobblestone streets, a short distance from the Whaling Museum. It was a beautiful cement structure, its body a faded taupe, with large windows, framed by cream colored blocks. The windows themselves were wooden twelve over twelve double framed painted a dark green. The top floor had half-moon windows peering out from under an overhanging slate roof with an aged green patina.

We parked in a lot behind the building. A dark green wooden sign with gold lettering announced it was for guests and employees of I.RISE. The building was on a hill, so the rear view exposed a basement or lower level and a door. Another dark green wooden sign on the door displayed a gold arrow pointing to our left and the word Entrance. I pulled on the door. Locked.

We walked around to the entrance, a dark green door recessed under a cement arch. Painted in script along the rim of the arch were the words: "Protect this house and all who enter." Another gold lettered sign read: I.RISE. There was no doorbell or knocker, so I pulled the door open. Abby and I stepped inside.

Chapter 21

We stepped into a wide corridor with light oak floors and wainscoting extending half way up the white plastered walls. To our right was a large room with brightly colored Native American rugs on the floor and on the white walls. Recessed lights along with the windows created an open and inviting area. There were comfortable looking dark oak or walnut mission styled chairs scattered throughout the room, each upholstered in Native American design. A floor to ceiling bookcase covered the far wall. It was filled with books, magazines and artifacts, which, like the rugs and upholstery, were Native American. "Must be the reading room," I whispered to Abby.

"And, a place for support group meetings," Abby whispered back.

I could see perhaps 20 feet away, the corridor would bring us to another open area with a large oak partners' desk turned to face us. A brass reception sign was centered on the desk. I dropped into a baseball catcher's stance. The knee hole provided a clear view through the desk to a dust free fireplace on the far wall. I got up stifling the groan that usually follows that kind of exertion. A low, wide phone system, probably with multiple lines, was at one corner of the desk. A banker's lamp with a yellow glass shade was positioned at the other corner. Two wooded chairs, facing the desk were on either side of the knee hole.

Since there was no one at the desk, we continued our slow journey down the corridor. A closed door on our left had a plate with the words Executive Director.

"Quiet as a tomb," Abby said. "Where the hell is everybody? TGIF started yesterday?"

I looked at the pictures on the corridor walls. There was an old – or a reproduction of an old – navigation map of New Bedford

Harbor. A smaller frame had a quotation from Herman Melville's *Moby Dick,* describing New Bedford as, "The dearest place to live in all New England."

"Ever read Moby Dick?" I whispered.

"In high school," she said. "Don't remember much beyond the white whale."

"I remember the movie," I said. "My mother had a crush on Gregory Peck. Think she saw it five or six times."

Just as we arrived at the reception area, a door I hadn't noticed opened. A tall thin woman in her sixties, her dyed mahogany hair tied in a bun, entered and smiled at us. "Welcome to I.RISE. I'm Phyllis, how can I help you?" She sat in her chair and with a sweeping gesture invited us to sit. Over her shoulder and above the fireplace a large wooden sign painted a distressed white with faded black lettering read: "Welcome to I.RISE, where recovery begins and YOU are the most important member of your treatment team."

"Hi," Abby said. "I'm Amy Coumounduros this is my husband Pete. We're interested in learning more about your programs." Abby did a theatrical pause and looked down to her hands. "We have an adult son, he's twenty-three, an alcohol and drug abuser. After a number of years, he has finally asked us for help. This time we believe him."

I sat silent in my chair, trying to quell any look of surprise. In truth, our son Cade was twenty-six, a college graduate with two children, a happy marriage and a good job. I never thought of myself as Greek, and hoped nobody asked me to spell Coumounduros.

"Well that's an important first step," Phyllis said. "Tell me, how did you hear about us?"

"Our son lives with us in Falmouth," Abby said. She gave an exasperated shake of her head. "Well, only recently, has he come home to us. For a few years, we weren't sure where he was." Abby shifted her hand towards me, a signal to join her in the performance. I grabbed her hand to show comfort and support.

"He would prefer to get treatment somewhere other than Falmouth, or even the Cape," I said. "We did some research and came across I.RISE."

"What's your son's name?" Phyllis asked me.

"Brandon," Abby said with no hesitation. "I think he's serious this time about getting help. So, we'd like to get some information we can share with him when we get home. Is there someone we can speak with today?"

"You didn't make an appointment?' Phyllis said with a raised eyebrow.

"No, we didn't," Abby said, with a hint of annoyance. "We know since he is an adult, Brandon is the one who needs to reach out and make the appointment for an initial intake. Our being in New Bedford today was spur of the moment, so we thought we'd come by for general information to share with him. If that requires an appointment we'll simply leave and I'll ask Brandon to give you a call next week." She started to rise.

"No, no, no," Phyllis said. "Please wait a minute. I can get you several brochures." She opened a desk drawer then appeared to think better of it. "Let me see if I can track down our executive director to meet with you." She scurried through the door from which she had emerged.

"Well played," I said. "Coumounduros?"

"I almost said Gregory and Elizabeth Peck," Abby said.

————

A few minutes later, Abby and I were in the office of Susan Landry, the Executive Director of I.RISE. Susan was attractive, in her mid-forties, with prematurely gray hair cut short to frame an open, honest face. She wore round rim less glasses, which gave her a professorial look. I imagined her twenty years earlier. A disheveled social worker with a mountain of student debt, a dented Volvo with a hundred twenty-five thousand miles and an inside smelling like a Taco Bell burrito. She sat at an oak table desk, which provided me a look at her fine legs. Several degrees, certificates and plaques were arranged in a cluster on a white plastered wall across the room from her desk. Abby and I sat in comfortable mission styled upholstered chairs. The chairs and the scatter rugs in her office, like the others we had seen, were Native American design. I wondered if Sitting Bull had a seat on the I.RISE Board of Directors.

Susan told us she had been executive director for the past nine years. She provided a quick history of I.RISE, which we already knew, but sat through as attentive and inquiring parents might be expected to do. I.RISE was established in 1987 to address the needs of those convicted of operating under the influence of alcohol. In Massachusetts, first time OUI offenders could avoid jail and long-term license suspension if they attended a six-week program of classroom instruction on the evils of alcohol and driving. In 1987, the courses cost approximately eight hundred dollars. Today, it's more like twenty-five hundred dollars. A second OUI offense can require an inpatient stay running in excess of five thousand dollars.

"Where do you get most of your OUI referrals?" I asked.

"Well, New Bedford, of course," Landry said. "And we receive a large number from Falmouth and the upper Cape."

"By the way," I said. "This is a beautiful old building. I.RISE own it?"

"Yes, Landry said. "We're very fortunate to be in this location. We're close to everything."

"Seems pretty quiet today," Abby said. "That because it's Friday?"

Landry smiled. "The OUI classes are at night, since most of our clients in those programs have jobs. Upstairs, there are several group meetings in progress." She smiled a little harder. "But you're right, Fridays are less hectic than other days. Gives all of us a chance to catch a breath."

Covering the entire wall behind her was a custom made floor to ceiling white bookcase, which appeared to have been carefully filled by a professional designer. Books were neatly divided by artifacts, photographs and other items in a way that suggested they were moved only for dusting.

Susan looked towards me. "Tell me about Brandon."

Suddenly, the door opened and a tall man with frizzy brown hair that covered both ears, but not much of his thin pointed head, stepped in. He had a wimpy brown moustache, thick brown glasses, and a serious pot belly. "Excuse me, Susan. I didn't know you were tied up."

Susan stood. "Dr. Decker, please come in. Let me introduce you to Peter and Amy Coumounduros. They're interested in our services for their son." Susan turned towards us. "This is Dr. Nelson Decker, our clinical director and chief medical officer.

I stood and reached for his hand. He seemed stuck half way between the hall and Susan's office. He stretched out his hand. His fingers looked long as pencils.

"Nice to meet you both," Decker said in a voice that oozed uncertainty or perhaps extreme shyness. His head shifted towards Susan. "I'll come back at a better time." He closed her door.

I returned to my chair. "Where were we?" I said.

Susan appeared unfazed by the interruption. "I asked you to tell me about Brandon."

"He's twenty-three," Abby said. "He's been abusing drugs and alcohol since he was fifteen, maybe even younger. Until recently, he was in complete denial. He dropped out or was thrown out of high school. Lived on the streets off and on for over two years." Abby took a deep breath, as if trying to control her emotions.

"The good news is he's looking for help," Landry said, inserting hope into the discussion. "Wanting help is key. Any idea why suddenly now?"

"Not sure," I said. "There wasn't an intervention we know of. I think Brandon saw his friends, or those who used to be his friends, with good jobs, getting married, having children. Maybe he finally took stock in his life, and decided he needed help." I wanted to look at Abby. "Ta-Dah!"

"Brandon's very lucky to have loving and supportive parents like you. Many of our clients don't have supports outside this building." She looked at us. "Brandon ever have a psychological or psychiatric assessment? It's not uncommon to find an underlying emotional disorder in people with alcohol and substance use disorders."

"Not to our knowledge," I said. "But, it wouldn't surprise me if Brandon was bi-polar. Could you arrange an assessment?"

Landry nodded enthusiastically. "We can do that. We can care for all his needs. At I.RISE we use a holistic approach. The first step in an intake and assessment. If we think he should undergo a psychiatric evaluation, we will arrange that. Once we have the information we need, our team will sit down with Brandon and develop a treatment plan that best meets his needs. And, I should Brandon has to agree to everything we propose, and we will let him know he has the right to say no to all or any part of the treatment plan we propose to him." Susan leaned back in her chair and smiled.

It was, I thought, a practiced spiel. Effective, but one said so many times, there was nothing behind it, like the smile you give the waiter who brings the rolls. I also thought it was time to move away from the fictional Brandon and closer to the pedophile priests. "I read you have a small residential program," I said. "Can you tell us about that?"

Landry gave the practiced smile. "Do you think Brandon needs residential services?"

I returned the smile. "I don't know, but if he does, do you have a bed available?"

"We have a small ten bed program that is housed on the top floor," Landry said. It's at full capacity now." She sighed. "There are a lot of damaged people in our world. If Brandon needs residential services, we have what we call contracted services throughout the area. Brandon would receive his services here, but live at a residential program run by one of our community partners."

Abby took a more direct approach. "I know you treat or have treated a number of priests referred from the Archdiocese of Boston," she said delicately.

"They are not treated here," Landry said with more emphasis than required. "We have almost nothing to do with that population. They are with one of our community partners. Brandon will not have any interaction with them, whether he is a day client or in a residential program," Landry said. "We are very firm about that." Then, as though fearing she had been too harsh, she added, "It's not that we lack empathy or compassion for the men, it's just our treatment protocols require they have no interaction with our other clients."

Abby flashed a smile that indicated relief and complete satisfaction with Landry's answer. "Let's talk finances." She looked at her watch. "You have been very generous with your time. I don't want to keep you from the start of your weekend, so we can be brief. Do you take insurance?'

"I assume Brandon is eligible for Mass Health. They will cover a certain amount of services such as group therapy, employment searches and training. Insurance does not cover our self-empowerment programs or much of our residential services should they be required. But, why don't we wait until we do a complete assessment," Landry said. "Then we can address the cost and insurance coverage for the various aspects of Brandon's treatment plan."

"We are not without means," Abby said. "We will cover whatever Brandon needs, with or without help from the insurance company. Do you have information on rates you can provide us?"

"Certainly," Landry said. She pulled open a drawer in the middle of her table desk and handed a single page to Abby.

Abby briefly glanced at it. "$4,800 per month for residential," she said, as if it were just $48. "That include meals and services, or just the bed?"

"It includes some, but not all services," Landry said. "It's not just a bed. It's a supportive and empowering environment. As I said earlier, we use a holistic approach." She shook her head. "But let's get through the intake and assessments before we worry about the costs."

"Oh, I'm not worried," Abby said. "We want the very best for Brandon, and we are willing to pay for it."

Susan Landry's smile lite up her office.

———

We left I.RISE about 2PM. Landry accompanied us to the front door. We passed a framed black and white photograph of eight or so white males standing behind a large ribbon. The man in the center held a pair of oversized scissors. The rest had goofy grins.

"Opening day, 1987," Susan said. "Well before my time."

I looked at the faces of the men. One of them looked familiar. I had seen him somewhere. Something in me stirred, like the unsettled feeling of a forgotten dream. I tried to retrieve it, but nothing came forth. Abby was behind me, and I instinctively knew she was watching me stare at the picture. I turned and headed towards the door. Abby stayed back to let Susan and me move ahead. By the time we reached the front door, Abby had taken out her phone and snapped a picture of the photograph. She caught up with me, and we said goodbye to a still smiling Susan Landry and stepped outside.

I took Abby's hand as we headed to the parking lot. "Nice work getting a picture of that photograph." We continued walking along the side of the building to the parking lot. "I'm glad Novello wasn't here," I said. "The stink of our lies would have made him sick."

Abby squeezed my hand. "First thing we need to do is apologize to Cade, for all the horrible things we said about him."

"As well as his new surname," I said. "Hope he realizes how lucky he is to have loving and supportive parents like us."

Abby laughed. "What'd you think of Dr. Decker?

I thought he was strange," I said. "I shouldn't be too harsh. Maybe he has some sort of disability."

"His belly tells me he has a liver dysfunction from too much booze. But, I suppose you should expect recovering alcoholics in a place like this."

"You deserve an Academy Award," I said. "You notice she lied about I.RISE owning the property?"

"I did," Abby said. "But you'd expect her, or anyone else there, to say that rather than getting into a discussion about trusts and LLCs."

"I agree, but, we learned something else that Novello or Flaherty might think is important."

We had turned the corner of the building and were close to our car. "You mean the Archdiocese is paying I.RISE maybe $4,800 a month for services that someone else provides?" Abby said. "A community partner? Bullshit. It's probably a cheap hotel or motel for seventy bucks a night. Maybe less."

"You really didn't need me here today. Did you?" I said.

"Well, I hate to eat alone," Abby said. "And, admit it, you enjoyed the view of her legs."

———

Archie sat in an upholstered wing back chair alone in a room cluttered with bulky furniture, pictures and wallpaper yellowed by dust, smoke and time. Two large mahogany bookcases its shelves stuffed with pictures, old books, and paperbacks, covered most of the north wall. Tall narrow windows provided cloudy views of dusk beginning its decent on a yard that was more mud than grass. He was in his private place. A safe place to think and to plot. No one knew about it and no one ever would.

His burner phone rang. He kept it on the table beside his chair. Other than himself, only two people knew the number, which changed every month. They were instructed only to call from a burner.

Archie picked up before the second ring. "Yes?" He sat motionless in the chair, his eyes fixed on a spot only he knew. Close to a minute passed. "That was smart," Archie said. "When are you meeting?" Another pause, then, "Don't panic. "Go over tomorrow, bring the necessary papers and remove everything. We'll meet Sunday morning. Early, say seven o'clock, the usual spot. Bring everything with you. We'll look it over and either destroy it, or bring it back. Relax, it's not a problem."

Archie looked at the phone in his hand, as if seeing it for the first time. He returned it to his ear and listened. "I said it's not a problem. Is there anything else?" Archie waited a beat. "Good." He hung up.

He opened the drawer in the desk by his chair and removed a well-oiled gun. He placed it in his lap and softly rubbed it with his hand. A minute or so later, he reached into the drawer and removed a silencer. It was a Coeur d'Alene, its blue finish gleamed in the late afternoon light of the window. Archie enjoyed the weight of the instrument, its substance. He fastened it to the gun and shifted the weapon to his shooting hand. Archie closed his eyes.

The world around him vanished.

Chapter 22

The last Saturday in April held the promise of May without the raw bark of March: bright sunshine, a China blue sky and no winds. A perfect day for golf, which is what Abby and I were doing. We were approaching the eighteenth hole at the Paul Harney Golf Course in Falmouth, when Abby's cell phone buzzed.

When we golf, Abby and I play best ball. Whoever hits the better shot, the other player (often me) brings his ball to that ball. Both players hit from that spot and the process repeats itself for eighteen holes. Abby is a good – not great – golfer. I am a fair – not good – golfer. Best ball lowers the score, quickens the game and gets us to our ultimate destination, the Flying Bridge Restaurant on Falmouth Harbor, before the harbor side tables are taken.

I watched Abby struggle to find her phone in the myriad of pockets, slots and zippered compartment of her golf bag. "A place for everything and everything in its place," I said to her raised middle finger.

"This better not be a robo," she said. She found the phone rubbed the screen, and it came to life. "Hello." She paused, a quizzical look took over her face. "Oh hi, how are you? Connor's right here, but his phone is at home." She laughed. "On weekends, they're not on speaking terms. Want to talk with him?" I stepped towards her, but Abby raised her hand like a crossing guard. "Lots of good stuff," she said to the phone. "We're on the 18th green. We can be there by 12:30, she said. "Does that work for you?" Another pause, and "Okay, see you at the Bridge."

Abby put the phone away and retrieved a club from her bag.

"Who's that?" I said, immediately regretting the question. I knew she was drawing things out for suspense. I played along and took a nine iron from my bag.

Abby took two practice swings and hit a soft pitch shot, the ball rolling to a stop about four inches from the pin.

"Nice," I said. I skipped any pre-shot routine and sculled my shot into a green side bunker. I consoled myself with the memory it had been my drive that placed us within forty feet of the green. "A birdie on the last hole. Finish her off, my dear," I said. I used a rake to drag my ball out of the bunker as Abby tapped in her putt.

"Who we meeting at the Bridge?" I said.

"Captain Anthony Novello's treating us to lunch. He wants to know if we've learned anything about I.RISE."

"Good thing we spent last night putting it together," I said. "Twelve-thirty gives us time to print it up, and still get a table on the harbor. Does he know how to get to the Bridge?"

"He's a detective," Abby said. "He'll figure it out."

We organized our golf clubs and placed the bags in the back of our Ford Escape. As we drove out of the parking lot, a thought occurred to me.

"How the hell Novello get your number?"

————

Anthony Novello stood at a harbor-side table on the outside deck, as we approached him at The Flying Bridge. His sunglasses propped on his dark hair and a broad smile crossed his face as he greeted Abby with his eyes. Novello was wearing an off-white linen sports jacket, brown slacks, tasseled loafers without socks and a dark green golf shirt. I think he spent more money and thought on his outfit for the day than I had on mine the past month.

"Abby, great to see you again," Novello extended his arms towards her for a quick embrace.

Abby obliged, and offered, "You look wonderful."

"You as well," Novello said. He extended a hand to me. "Connor, I can see why you moved here. Beautiful."

We sat across from each other. I had a large envelope of papers on I.RISE in my lap. In the distance the Island Queen, the passenger ferry to Martha's Vineyard, approached the harbor. In less than three minutes it would pass and back into its pier diagonally across the harbor from us and less than fifty yards from Vinnie Preskin's law office.

A waiter appeared at our table. He placed a steamed roll in front of each of us and asked our drink orders. I ordered a frosted mug of draft beer, Abby selected unsweetened ice tea, and Novello ordered a glass of pinot noir.

"How'd you play?" Novello said. "I know I caught you on the golf course.

"Not bad," I said. "We play best ball, so we can usually hover around par. Today, we were one under." I dropped the large envelope of paper on the table. "Here's probably more than you ever wanted to know about I.RISE."

"Information is power," Novello said. "You can never have too much." He took the envelope from the table and placed it on the empty chair beside him. "Thanks. Feels like a lot of work. I'll read it tonight. Right now, I'm more interested in hearing any thoughts you might have. But first, I need to thank you."

He was interrupted by the waiter with our drinks, who asked if we had any questions on the menu. Novello said, "Not yet, check with us later." He raised his wine glass. "Cheers. Here's to us; the hell with everyone else."

"Sure you're not Irish?" I said.

"Maybe a speck or two on my mother's side," Novello said. "But mostly I am what I appear to be. Italian. Where were we?"

"You were about to thank Connor for something," Abby said.

"I was and I will," Novello said. "Turns out Judge Bartoni had joined the Jefferson Street Gym, one of the two you suggested during our walk at Boston Common. And, he had a locker."

"Nice," I said.

"Anything in it?" Abby said.

Novello looked at me. "I know you tell Abby everything, and that's fine. But did you forget to tell her about asking questions, or that I will tell you only what I decide to tell you, not because you asked a question?"

Abby tapped Novello's wine glass with her knife. "I'm right here. Don't talk about me as if I were five miles away."

Novello saluted her with his glass. "You're right. I'm sorry." He put the glass down without taking a sip. "Abby, it's important to the way I approach a case that I not reveal everything to anyone. It's easier for me to do that if the people I'm with do not ask questions. It's not a lack of trust or respect, although it is with some of the folks I deal with, but not with you or Connor. It's just the way I work. I'm sorry, I know I can be rigid, but it's the only way I know how to work."

Abby met his stare and I felt the birth of tension across the table. "Well, I'm glad Connor's suggestion worked out for you." She put a little oomph into my name.

"Actually, we don't know what's in the locker," Novello said. "We asked Kevin Flaherty – he's the Attorney General."

"I know who he is," Abby said.

Novello smiled. The contest was on. "We asked Flaherty if he could get us a search warrant, but he didn't want to bother even friendly judges with that kind of a request, since the Club said it would open it if requested by Mrs. Bartoni." Novello took a sip of his wine. He patted his lips with a small white napkin. "Yesterday, one of my officers called Mrs. Bartoni, told her everything. He asked if she could meet me at the Gym. She told him she was going away for the weekend, and would meet me at the Gym on Monday at ten o'clock."

"And that annoyed you," Abby said. "Your officer gave out more information than needed." Abby smiled. "Just a comment, not a question."

Novello laughed and the tension seemed to fade. "Very perceptive, Abby. I am more than annoyed. I'm pissed. I didn't want Mrs.

Bartoni to know we had found a locker. I didn't want her setting the day and time to meet at the Gym. I hardly know the woman or the relationship she had with her husband. It's never helpful to give out information, and you should never provide it before you absolutely have to. My officer did both, and he should know better."

"Speaking of providing information," I said. "Here comes our waiter."

———

During the meal, I explained what I learned from my title search. Abby and I decided she, as the health expert, should do most of the talking about our meeting with Susan Landry, the Executive Director of I.RISE. Novello listened intently, took a few notes but did not ask any questions. When we finished, I said, "Questions?"

Novello smiled. "That was good work. Thanks. You said you had a list of I. RISE's donors and board of directors in this envelope?"

"It's in there," I said. "Names didn't mean anything to either of us, but I'm sure you have access to a larger data bank."

To my left the Island Queen chugged by on its trip to Martha's Vineyard. The passengers on the top deck waved to nobody and to everybody. I've never understood why people on boats wave to those on shore.

"I hadn't expected you to visit the place, but I'm glad you did," Novello said. "Tell me what you think of the off-site treatment plan for the priests referred by the Archdiocese? Forty-eight hundred a month?"

Novello was looking at Abby, so she responded. "That's the residential rate, so I suspect that's what the church is paying. My gut tells me it's a scam. I think I.RISE is warehousing priests in cheap hotels, maybe giving them some walking around money and a group therapy session every other day or week. They collect almost five thousand a month per priest. Eventually, I.RISE proclaims them cured, or whatever, and the dioceses moves them to another parish in another state."

"Beautiful and cynical," Novello said. "How could they pull that off?"

"If no one is checking, doing audits or program evaluations, it's easy," Abby said.

She shifted in her chair. "If health insurers were paying the bills, they'd check closely and frequently to make sure what is being billed is being done. They have sophisticated algorithms to determine what services should be required, how long treatment should last and a bunch of other stuff to make sure they are not overpaying. Every patient gets tracked, the services received, and the expected end date for those services."

Novello nodded. "No insurance company ever went broke paying for covered services."

Abby laughed. "Right. And they know how to control what they pay for."

"Health insurers are not involved?" Novello said.

"Not with these priests," Abby said. "The Catholic Church is footing the bill, and I doubt they have a clue as to what is going on at I.RISE."

"Probably think an algorithm is a pagan ritual," I said. I wanted to remind them I was still there.

"I'll need to see how many priests have been referred to I.RISE," Novello said. "We need to know how much money is involved. Hard to believe you could pull off a scam as simple as this for any period of time."

"Unless," Abby and I said together. Last night's work on the report we prepared for Novello had jelled our thinking.

"Go on," Novello said.

"What if someone in the Church's hierarchy is in on it," I said. "Think about it. They're so busy covering up what the priests have done, and covering up the cover up, they don't have time or the inclination to bean count the costs of treatment."

"And, remember this," Abby said. "The forty-eight hundred fee is probably consistent with what the church is paying to the other treatment facilities it uses. The difference here is we think the services are not being performed."

"Flaherty told me when he met with Cardinal Mulcahy, the Cardinal had brought a Monsignor Roche into the meeting, Novello said. "Mulcahy said Roche was in charge of or oversaw the treatment of these priests."

"Somebody you might want to talk to," Abby said. "Just a comment."

"You're never going to let that go, are you?" Novello said around a laugh.

"Not in your lifetime," I said.

———

An hour later, our table was cluttered with a bucket of the empty shells of steamers, a wine glass, a beer mug, its frost having dripped and darkened the white table cloth, three plates of crumbs with a scattering of uneaten fried calamari, crumpled napkins and two tall thin glasses containing lime slices and the pale end of melting Tanqueray and tonics.

Novello picked up the envelope I had given him. "Connor, when are you next in Boston"

"Tuesday," I said.

"I'm going to schedule a meeting with this Monsignor Roche. I'd like you and Abby to come. I'll tell him you're working at the AG's Office on a research project or some such bullshit. You can ask questions, but don't be accusatory. I want him to think it's all routine." He turned towards Abby. "This work for you?"

"Long as I get to ask questions," Abby said. "Speaking of which, may I ask you a question? Understanding of course, you do not have to answer it."

"Sure," Novello said. He signaled the waiter for coffee. "Two regular one decaf," he said, He turned his gaze to Abby. "Go ahead."

Abby took out her phone and showed Novello the picture she had taken of the picture in the hallway at I.RISE. "We were told by Susan Landry that this was taken on opening day in 1987. Recognize anyone?"

Novello took the phone from Abby and squinted at it. "No, I don't. Should I?"

"No," Abby said. "We didn't either." She pointed at one of the men. "Connor thought he had seen this guy somewhere, but couldn't place it. Probably not important," she said, doubt hanging on every word.

The waiter set down the coffee and present a bill. Novello dropped a black American Express card on the bill without looking at it. We sipped our coffees, as silence descended on the table. I began to think of a nice afternoon nap, when Novello's voice kicked me out of bed.

"I have a comment for both of you, but I don't want either of you to respond. Okay?"

"Okay," Abby and I responded simultaneously.

Novello moved his cup to the side and folded his hands on the table. "Connor, when you and I took our walk to One Ashburton Street, a few weeks back, I noticed an odd looking fellow across the street watching us. I filed it away. Then, when we met at Boston Common, I saw him again. I have not seen him since. I looked for him today because I think he is following you, not me. I also think that odd fellow is the person you call Freddy." Novello spoke slowly and quietly every word coming out as if it were being pulled by an invisible wire. "I don't want you to respond. Because if I am correct, and you admit it, I will be required to take action. I don't want to take action. You were very helpful on the Governor Hands matter. Far as I'm concerned you and that Freddy character solved it. I asked for help on I.RISE, and I have received it. So consider my comments as just the musings of a homicide detective."

Novello patted his lips with a napkin and smiled. "I say this as a friend. I believe this Freddy, or whatever his real name, is dangerous and unpredictable. I figure he has contacted Connor by now and knows more about this case than he should." The waiter returned with a bill on a small tray. Novello signed it and handed it back with a smile. "Please tell David everything was great," he said.

Novello turned back to us. "One last thing, then we can depart as friends. If you happen to be contacted again by Freddy, please do not tell him anything more than he might already know. I still want you both to meet with this Monsignor Roche, and I'll get back to you on the time and place. But you are not, I repeat not, to tell Freddy or anyone anything about this meeting, what we learn from it, or anything about I.RISE, or what's in this envelope."

Novello stood and smiled. "I have had a wonderful afternoon. Thank you for joining me." He took the envelope and left using the stairs to the upper deck and inside dining.

"Fucking Freddy," Abby muttered. You haven't told him anything, have you?"

"Not since the bus ride," I said. "By the way, did you catch Novello asking the waiter to thank David? He knows the owner."

Less than ten minutes later, I pulled into our driveway. Something rolled in the pit of my stomach as I glanced to the side entrance to our house. A yellow card was taped to the door. I touched Abby and pointed to the card.

We exited the car and walked to the door. The card read:

> I WAS NOT THE ONLY ONE WATCHING YOU.
> BE CAREFUL – TRUST NO ONE
> F.

Chapter 23

Carmela Bartoni strode into the Jefferson Street Gymnasium with a copy of her husband's death certificate and a demand for the contents of his locker. To her left, about twenty men and women walked on tread mills, rode stationery bikes, and a few lifted weights. Carmela saw all of them as sweaty and repulsive.

She walked to a blond veneer counter where a perplexed, young attendant with acne and bad breath told her the locker was in the men's shower area, and he lacked authority to allow her to open it.

"Well, I have the authority," Carmela declared. "I was his wife. He's dead. He's not coming back here to collect his stuff." She leaned across the counter bringing her pointed nose within inches of his face. "I am legally obligated to gather his belongings. My husband was an important judge, a good friend of the Governor and a member of clubs more prestigious than this dump. Not one of them has given me any trouble." She stared at him. "You think, I'm going to jump through hoops at this sweat hole?"

Carmela backed away and pulled out her phone. She stared at the young man. "If you value your job, you'll get me the contents of that locker in the next five minutes. Don't make me use this phone, or you'll be looking for a new job before I finish the call."

"You know the combination?" He asked.

Carmela smiled, and put the phone away. "What kind of lock is it? Combination wheel like a high school locker, or a digital number code, like a hotel safe?"

"Like the hotel safe. You punch in four to six numbers."

Carmela's smile grew and her face softened. She handed the man a piece of paper. "Here are three sets of numbers. One of them will open the locker."

———

Anthony Novello sat in a soft leather chair in the immaculate living room of his two-bedroom condominium on Richmond Street in Boston's North End. A brandy snifter of St. Remy VSOP, with a single ice cube, sat on a table positioned to his left. The window on Novello's right provided a partially obstructed view of a dog park. Novello considered the creation of the park conclusive evidence the gentrification of the North End was complete.

Earlier, Novello returned the state vehicle he had driven to Falmouth, and spent an hour in his office reviewing the murder book he and McGonagle created on Bartoni. Reading everything a third and fourth time had not triggered new thoughts or removed lingering doubts. What it had done was infuriate Novello. Bartoni was murdered two weeks ago today. He had captured and secured confessions from killers in far less time, usually within hours or days of the killing. Novello's anger did not weaken his confidence in himself or McGonagle. They would first find the killer, and then focus on those who had lied, misled or deliberately distracted them. Those people would pay a heavy price.

At five o'clock, he walked home, stopping at Mike's Pastry. A regular customer, Novello avoided the long line by pre-ordering and flashing a smile and his badge to all onlookers. He picked up a box with an Expresso Cannoli and six pistachio macaroons, and left two twenty dollar bills. On the last Monday of each month, which would be the day after tomorrow, Novello visited the shop to settle his bill for the past month. It generally ended up with the establishment owing Novello money, which he left as a tip.

Novello leaned back in the chair and closed his eyes. His mind drifted to D'Alessandro and their breakfast meeting. His body tightened with anger at the Chief Justice's affair with Win Allen and their cavalier and illegal conspiracy to deny justice to the plaintiffs in the *Sheehan* case. He would bring justice to the doors of both.

His mind shifted to Carmela Bartoni. His earlier call reached only a machine. His message asking her to call and providing his cell and office numbers had not been returned. Why would a woman whose husband was murdered two weeks ago go away for the weekend? Visit family? Novello remembered Carmela's cynical reference to her family when she bragged of her own investments following the sale of Rothwell Industries. Novello reached for a small leather notebook he kept in the drawer of the table where his glass of brandy rested, the ice cube now just a sliver of cold floating on the amber liquid. He retrieved the notebook and a small pen attached to it with a piece of leather twine. He jotted a note: *Rothwell Industries?*

Novello's eyes focused on another table across the room. The envelope Connor McNeill gave him at lunch, lay next to an old wooden box Novello used to dump mail and his keys. He got up from the chair and went to the envelope. Instead of returning to the chair, Novello walked to a rustic walnut farm table he used as his office, and occasionally as a dining table for entertaining. He opened the envelope and separated the papers into three piles: McNeill, I.RISE, and EZ DUZ IT Realty Trust. He put Connor's overview of his research and written comments on the contents of the envelope into the McNeill pile. Novello wrote "McNeill" on a piece of plain paper and placed it on the top of the pile. He used a large elastic to keep the pages together, and moved them to the end of the table. He would read these later, perhaps in bed. He had a good grasp of what they contained from his discussion with Connor and Abby at lunch. He picked up the I.RISE pile and brought it over to his chair and sat down. This would require a careful review. Novello reached for the snifter.

———

While Anthony Novello sat in his comfortable chair reviewing the papers on I.RISE, Carmela Bartoni, about twenty-one miles away, paced the oriental carpet in her living room with a cold glass of Kendall-Jackson Vintner's Reserve Chardonnay. She wore an expensive dark business suit from Ralph Lauren. She stole a glance of herself in the mirror over the fireplace. *My thinness works for me,* she thought. It provides an air of the aristocratic. Carmela believed she was a woman who looked better – more comfortable – in formal clothing than casual attire. She could not remember ever wearing jeans or a mini skirt, not even in high school.

Although model thin, Carmela also believed her age and pride precluded the fashions currently being designed for anemic millennials and others who had never grown up or purchased mirrors. She believed Jimmy Choo shoes belonged on hookers or comedic transvestites. In preparation for her husband's burial, Carmela used the Internet to search for female designers her age or older. She spent hours looking for clothing with the labels of Muccio Pravda, Diane von Furstenberg or Carolina Herrera. In the end, she settled for a basic black outfit off the rack at Nordstrom's.

She took another look at the mirror, and this time stopped and stepped closer to it. She turned sideways and then a full 360 making a careful assessment on everything she saw. Carmela deliberately carried herself with an air of intelligence that would attract only serious men – not the scammers or Romeos. So why the marriage to Robert Bartoni, she wondered. Carmela shrugged and smiled. *Who cares? Yesterday's news.*

She paced and soon found herself in Robert's study. Carmela glanced over to the desk and the dark blue canvas duffel bag with the tacky white NIKE swoosh. Earlier, she had opened it and reviewed its contents. She was horrified repulsed to see articles that had touched her husband's skin. The note book, Carmela concluded, was worthless. She had been told it had information on her husband's secret investigation of her foundation. But, it appeared to be notes for a memoire and some coded gibberish. *Who the hell is he to investigate my foundation?* She stared at the bag, as if willing it out of existence. *Be happy to get rid of it, as well as the pissant who asked me to take it.* She shuddered at the memory of sweaty bodies at the Jefferson Street Gym, and took a sip of wine.

She stood in the doorway considering her husband's desk and his soft leather chair. Her marriage to Robert had been a quiet ordeal. Neither was prone to yelling or other antics. They simply co-existed and, for the most part, ignored each other. She remembered a time Robert sat at the desk, calling out to her with questions about her Foundation.

"Come out here and sit with me. I'll answer any questions you have," she called back. That ended the questioning. The study was Robert's turf, the rest of the house was hers.

Another time she had come home and found him sitting at the kitchen table rummaging through papers. "Can I help you with anything?" She asked.

"I'm trying to come up with something to do with my life when I give up the robes," Robert said. "The Governor wants to put me in charge of a special study commission, but he wants me to come up with the subject."

"Any ideas?" She asked, surprised he was conversing with her.

"Maybe I'll expose the charlatans running OUI programs across the state," Robert said. And the foundations that support them."

That had ended that conversation and began her concern about what he knew about her foundation.

Carmela strolled into the kitchen and glanced at her land line. She heard Novello's message when he called over an hour ago. She had no intention of calling him or answering the phone if it rang again. "I told people I was going away for a few days, and, by God, I am staying away at least until Sunday afternoon," she announced to her empty house. She smiled, toasted her glass to the air and took a long sip.

There was no way Carmela could know she would never see another Sunday afternoon.

———

By six-thirty Novello was about half way through the I.RISE pile of papers. He studied the list of its board of directors, principal officers, and the original incorporators. On Monday, he would ask McGonagle to run each of the names through the system for arrest records, convictions or prior involvement with the courts. He jotted a reminder note in the leather note book to ask Connor if he could find the original board of directors. Thinking of Connor reminded Novello he would have to schedule a meeting with Monsignor Roche and notify Connor and Abby of its time and place. These thoughts resulted in yet another note. Novello cursed his addiction to notes and resolved to ask McGonagle to teach him how to use the voice memo function on his phone. Of course, this thought required him to jot another note in his leather throw-back to the nineties. "You are history," Novello muttered to the book as he wrote the reminder note.

He next grabbed I.RISE's most recent annual report and began reading. It contained much of the information Connor and Abby had conveyed at lunch, but Novello wanted to see it in the words I.RISE chose, rather than those chosen by Connor or Abby. There was the obligatory section on success stories with a smattering of quotes attributed to unnamed parents, clients and former clients by first names only and some fully named individuals, identified simply as a community leader or advocate. Novello underlined those identified by full name, and wrote "systems check" in the margin of the page.

There were sections describing I.RISE's successful programs for the treatment of alcohol and substance use disorders. A boxed paragraph announced I.RISE was a certified and approved treatment program for those convicted of, on probation for, or facing operating while under the influence of alcohol or drugs charges in any court of the Commonwealth.

A color coded pie chart, which depicted I.RISES's major sources of revenue, appeared to have been designed to look attractive while conveying as little information as possible. The largest piece of pie – grants, donations and contracts – was a bright red 62%; a second piece – court ordered programs or referrals – a Kelly green 30%; and the remaining wedge – Other – a deep blue.

The next page was captioned: Supporters and Benefactors. Novello shifted to a more upright position. A quick glance captured a three column listing of individual names, organizations and foundations, with no information as to the amount of any donation. Nothing to separate supporters from benefactors or even a monetary limit or distinction between them. To make matters worse, the list was not alphabetized. Novello got up from his chair and walked over to the farmer's table. He opened a small box, took out an index card and returned to his chair. He slid the card under the top name and slowly moved down the column to the bottom and then to the top of the next. About midway down the third column he hit a name that meant something: Rothwell Foundation.

Novello grabbed his phone and called Connor McNeill. He connected with a voice after the third ring. "Connor, it's me." Novello paused a few seconds. "The guy who paid for lunch today." He paused again. "That's okay. Listen, I need you to do some research and get me as much information as you can, as fast as you can, on The Rothwell Foundation. And, hey Connor, thanks for doing this, and thanks for not asking any questions." Novello ended the call and swallowed the last of the amber liquid.

Chapter 24

When Novello called, we were in our upstairs den. Abby was at her desk in a small alcove facing a back window. She was wearing a Boston Celtics T-Shirt and cut-off dungarees, no shoes or socks. Her auburn hair was up, and it seemed obvious we were not going out. Still, she looked great. I was wearing an old faded blue golf shirt with a red polo player, tan Bermuda shorts, no socks and low cut white canvass sneakers. Dressed and ready to go or stay.

I sat in a recliner watching the highlights of a Red Sox win over the Cleveland Indians. Every time I moved, the recliner made noises like an animal groaning. It interfered with the TV's volume. Whenever I complain about the noises, Abby says I'm passing along the blame for a loud fart.

Since she was generating billable hours, and I was loafing, I answered the phone. Novello pronounced my marching orders in a few words, but this time thanked me twice. Must have been embarrassed by his display of gratitude, he hung up before I could say you're welcome.

"Another assignment?" Abby said when I hung up the phone. "You working for him or for Vinnie? Let me check to see who signs your paycheck."

"I think we can do this tonight in less than an hour," I said. "And, he actually said thanks. Twice."

"Maybe the next time you'll get a please and thank you. Before you know it, the two of you will be hugging and singing 'Kumbaya.'"

"That's not going to be an easy image to get out of my head," I said.

"A perfect T&T might help."

"We should get the work done before we party," I said. "Can you go on your computer and print out whatever you can find on The Rothwell Foundation? Board of directors, an annual report, list of supporters. The kind of crap I got on I.RISE. I'll go on mine and take a look at its latest 990 tax form."

Abby stared at me. "Let me see if I have this right."

Whenever she says that, I know she has it exactly right, and I am about to receive some constructive criticism. "Go ahead,' I said.

"You want me to stop making money for us, so I can go online and dig up some information on the Rothwell Foundation because Novello needs it, but doesn't want to do it himself, or pay someone to do it. Do I have this right?"

"You have it exactly right," I said.

"And I should do this because?"

"Because while you think Novello can be an authoritarian asshole, you also think he's hot. And, because I'm adorable, and I do the dishes."

"You have it exactly right," Abby said. She glanced at her watch. "We'll meet at the recliners at eight o'clock. See what we've got."

———

It didn't take long, and Abby & I were comparing notes less than an hour later. Abby scooted over in her swivel chair to the cluttered round oak table I use as a desk. She spread out several sheets of paper printed from her computer. "Let me go first," she said.

"Go ahead."

"The Rothwell Foundation was established in 1985 by Zachery and Eleanor Rothwell with a three million dollar gift." Abby read from a sheet of paper. "It provides funding for the treatment, education and support of people with alcohol or substance use disorders." She dropped the sheet on my table. "It also runs a hotline and helps people find treatment or other services."

"You print out a listing of its officers and board of directors?" I asked.

"Hold on Sherlock," Abby said. "Let me do this my way."

"You sound like Novello," I said. "No questions."

"Well then," Abby said. She deepened her voice. "I'll answer your question, not because you asked it, but because I decided I wanted you to have the information. You don't seem to understand your role in this investigation. The answer is yes, and there are surprises, maybe clues."

"You have my attention."

Abby grinned. "That's better. "The Foundation is a volunteer organization. It has a Treasurer and a CEO. Both positions are unpaid and both are occupied by the same person. Care to guess who that is?"

"No idea,' I said. "Wait. That reminds me of an old joke. What do you call a deer with no eyes?"

"No idea," Abby said. "Very clever. Can we get back to The Rothwell Foundation?"

"Wait," I said. "There's more. What do you call a deer with no eyes and no legs?"

Abby shook her head. "Okay, tell me."

"Still no idea," I said. I stared at her. "I know you're laughing inside. I can hear it. Right?"

"Wrong. You lose ten points and any chance to get lucky tonight. Now, do you want to know who it is?"

"Yes."

According to the website, it's Carmela Rothwell," Abby said.

"And, I'm supposed to know her because?"

Abby smiled harder. "Wait for it, Sherlock. I followed your advice and went to the Secretary of State's website. The name listed as Treasurer and CEO is Carmela Rothwell Bartoni."

"No shit."

"Has to be the Judge's wife," Abby said.

I pulled out my copy of I.RISE's Annual Report, turned to the page listing its supporters and benefactors and showed it to Abby. "We should check to see if Rothwell Foundation is listed as a supporter or benefactor."

It took a few minutes since the list was not alphabetized, but there in the third column was *The Rothwell Foundation.* "Bingo," I said.

"I have another surprise," Abby said. She reached for her research notes.

"Elvis is alive?"

"Elvis is alive, and he's a member of the Rothwell Foundation's Board of Directors, along with Carmela Bartoni, Susan Landry, our friend at I.RISE, and Nelson Decker, the odd looking guy who's the clinical director of I.RISE."

"Huh. I.RISE and the Rothwell Foundation are joined at the hip," I said.

"Or somewhere."

"Speaking of which," I said. How can I get those 10 points back and improve my chances of getting lucky?"

"Make the T&Ts when we're done."

"Deal."

"We should compare the board of directors of Rothwell with I.RISE to see if there are other surprises." Abby said. She glanced over to the notes I had written on my part of the research. "So did you learn anything?"

I confessed to Abby she had discovered the important information. The 990 Tax I reviewed offered nothing. It made no mention of I.RISE, which as not surprising since I.RISE was a for-profit corporation and it would be unusual for a tax exempt foundation to donate to a for-profit. I told Abby I suspected the Foundation was listed as a supporter of I.RISE because it purchased its services. Since the Foundation ran a hot line and made referrals, I thought the referrals might go to I. RISE. My theory was the Rothwell Foundation would purchase the initial treatment plan for any referral until Mass Health or another insurance plan took over.

Abby reaction was succinct and on target. "Did you learn anything from the 990, other than it's useless?"

"Nothing," I said.

"I can feel the wind going out of my sails." Abby said. "I wanted these crooks to be crooks."

I shrugged. "I know what you mean. But, we know I.RISE and Rothwell are connected. I.RISE bought its building in 1987, two years after The Rothwell Foundation was established. We know the land is mortgage free, and is owned by the EZ DUZ IT Realty Trust. Who knows? Maybe Carmela Rothwell is the EZ DUZ IT Realty Trust, or at least one of its beneficiaries."

"Why would she do it that way?' Abby said.

"To hide ownership. Maybe Carmela Rothwell Bartoni didn't want her husband to know she owned the I.RISE property. Maybe she and the judge owned the building and put it in trust to avoid people knowing about any conflict of interest."

"Christ, my teeth hurt," Abby said. "We're talking maybes and running in circles."

Silence claimed the room, as the two of us fiddled with papers.

"Let's take a break," I said. "T&T?"

"Yes! Use big glasses."

————

An hour later, refreshed and still sober, we rested on our recliners. We looked at the TV, each waiting for the other to turn it on. "I thing you have the remote," I said.

"You had it last," Abby said. "You were watching the Red Sox when Novello called."

I groaned. "When you're right, you're right." I got up from the recliner and began fishing through its crevices.

"Found it," Abby said. "It was under the I.RISE annual report you left on the table."

I picked up the report I had printed from the I.RISE website. "According to this," I said to Abby, "I.RISE has annual revenues of nine million and annual expenses of six million, including occupancy. I remember wondering how much of the nine million came from the Sunday collection boxes."

"I don't want to do anymore work," Abby said. "Let's find a movie and relax."

"Fair enough. Thanks for the help tonight." I picked up the remote and placed the Report on the table. What'd you feel like watching?"

"Wait a minute!" Abby said. She sat up and shifted her body towards me. "Nine million annually?" The place was emptier than a broken bottle when we were there Friday."

"Yeah, and six million in expenses seems too high, as well."

"Something doesn't make sense," Abby said. "Or, maybe I'm trying too hard to make all of them crooks."

"Need more information. Tax returns would help," I said. "Novello might be able to get those."

"Why would I.RISE inflate revenue and expenses?" Abby said.

"What if it's a money laundering operation? I said. "Maybe there're taking care of more than drunks and pedophile priests."

"Ooh, I just felt the wind filling my sails," Abby said.

"And, I'm feeling lucky," I said.

"You promised me a movie."

Chapter 25

Carmela Rothwell Bartoni was an early riser. On the last Sunday of her life, she completed her forty-five minute exercise routine, showered and dressed before six o'clock. She entered her kitchen wearing a dark blue running outfit with fuchsia piping. Her hair was up, and she wore no visible makeup. Carmela sat at the large kitchen table and took small bites of her unbuttered toast. She glanced at the telephone with its winking red light from two messages left by Novello. She shook off her annoyance. Suddenly, the loud thump of the Sunday *Globe* hitting the back door came into the room. Carmela stood, walked through the mud room and opened the door.

———

Less than a mile away, Archie hid behind a large oak tree. The cloth hand-made cover-ups on both shoes obscured the small marker he was standing on. It read: The Echo Tree.

Archie preferred the paper shoe covers worn in the operating room. But this would be an outdoor killing, and that required cloth. He watched the seconds tick away on his watch. It was easy for him to remain still, it always had been. He glanced towards the meeting place, a concrete slab bench, perhaps sixty feet away, but the topography of the land and trees obstructed his view.

Archie thought about what had to be done, how he would do it, and the consequences. He felt neither anger nor remorse. The killing was simply a consequence of changing and unforeseen circumstances. Something that had to be done, like tying your shoes or carrying an umbrella on a rainy day. Any discomfort or unpleasantness about this killing was something he needed to bear in order to avoid a greater displeasure. He peeled back his surgical gloves to take another look at his watch. 6:26.

Robes

————

Carmela scanned the Sunday *Globe*, starting as she always did, with the obituary pages, and then moving to the Business Section. At six-thirty, she dumped the remainder of her coffee in the sink, rinsed the cup and placed it in the dish washer. She walked over to the desk in the living room, took her burner phone from the drawer and slid it into the zippered packet of her dark blue top. She collected the blue duffel bag with the Nike swoosh and walked out the front door. A steady – neither brisk nor leisurely – walk would bring her to her destination about five minutes early. Carmela arrived early for all her meetings or appointments. She believed it gave her control, placed her in charge, and put the other person in a defensive posture. Oh, Mrs. Bartoni, you're a bit early. Carmela's smile would be her only reply. She enjoyed watching others quicken their pace to catch up with her.

She walked along Bedford Street and came to the Wood Gate entrance. The cemetery opened at seven, but the closed gate prevented only vehicles from entering. Carmela stepped over a small stone wall and entered Sleepy Hollow Cemetery at six forty-seven.

The grass, freshly cut and heavy with the morning mist, carried the smell of spring. Carmela walked along the paved road. *Should I visit Robert while I'm here?* Carmela quickly dismissed the idea. *He's still decomposing.* She shuddered. *I might even smell him.* Tall pine and oak trees on a ridge to the left hovered over her as she continued walking. The cemetery was quiet and still. No birds chirping, breezes whistling, or squirrels scurrying across the grass, circling up trees or digging up food supplies. In an hour or two, Sleepy Hollow would be filled with tourists and mourners, many walking the same route as Carmela towards Authors' Ridge and the burial sites of Henry David Thoreau, Louisa May Alcott, Ralph Waldo Emerson, and Nathaniel Hawthorne.

Carmela walked past stone steps leading up the hill to large, moss stained gravestones dotting the high ridge. She approached an empty parking area that could accommodate three, perhaps four, vehicles. She smiled at the thought of being a few minutes early.

She turned left and started up the steep incline to Authors' Ridge. Carmela knew at the top of the hill, at The Echo Tree, the paved walkway turned to the right towards Thoreau's grave, about thirty steps away. There, the path curved left and about ten steps more to a low concrete slab bench – the meeting place – in front of a small stone marking the grave of Louise May Alcott. Carmela could not see the bench from her position near the top of the incline, but she knew of its presence. As she began the right turn at the top of the incline, she glanced at her watch 6:54.

––––––

Archie stepped out from behind the Echo Tree and walked two quick steps to come up behind Carmela, whose was walking erect about twenty steps from Thoreau's grave. Before she could turn, he pushed the suppressor on his gun to the base of her head and fired upward. The bullet sped through the brain stem, ricocheted through the hypothalamus, the cerebrum and exited her skull just above her left ear. She was dead in a tenth of a second, she'd felt nothing but a sudden apprehension. The killer caught her before she could hit the pavement. He dragged the body behind the echo tree. He took her burner, following a quick pat down search. He went back to the walkway for the duffel bag, and placed her phone in it. Archie carried the body over to the top of a steep sloping hill leading down to a reedy marsh. This would be risky. He needed to get away from the popular site, but knew the advantage of time if he hid the body in the tall weeds and grasses at the bottom of the hill.

He edged down the hill sideways carrying Carmela in his arms. About half way down, his arms aching, he dropped her. The dead weight that was once Carmela Bartoni lay flat on the side of the hill. Archie dropped to his knees and slid his arms under her body.

He lifted the mass and tried to roll it closer to the reeds. It was like moving a five foot slab of cement. Heavy with absolutely no roll. He tried dragging her by the legs, but that required him to go down the hill backwards. Too risky. He dropped to his knees and resumed using his arms to lift and push the body. Each lift moved the body another foot towards the reeds. He repeated the process, grunting and dripping in sweat, until the body entered the reeds. Archie collapsed on the side of the hill and closed his eyes. He took a series of deep breaths into his nostrils and expelled them out his mouth, trying to control his breathing. He regained his breath and composure, scampered back up the hill and grabbed the duffel bag. He stripped off the surgical gloves, removed the shoe coverings and placed them in the duffel bag. Archie walked past the cement bench and began a leisurely stroll among the trees, shrubs and gravestones of Sleepy Hollow Cemetery. He looked at his watch, 7:13.

Chapter 26

Archie sat in his wing back chair back in his safe place admiring the small fire in the wood stove positioned in the southwest corner of the living room. The outside temperature did not warrant a fire, and the small room would soon become uncomfortably warm. He knew this, of course, but he wanted the fire for purposes other than heat. The duffel bag taken from Carmela sat at his feet. He had crushed her burner phone against one of the boulders in Sleepy Hollow and deposited the remains in a trash barrel outside a shopping mall.

Archie unzipped the bag and hoisted it onto his lap. He removed a small towel and a pair of shower tongs and placed them on the floor beside his chair. Next came a large three ring binder, which he placed on the floor on the other side of his chair. He ran his hand along the inside of the bag. Empty. He shook it and heard only the ambient noise of the room. He looked for outside compartments and found none. He got up from his chair and retrieved a large black trash bag from under a small sink. He brought the trash bag back to his chair and put the tongs, towel and duffel bag into it. He moved the bag over to the rear door and went back to his chair and opened the large binder.

The binder contained two sections, separated by a standard manila divider with a brightly colored plastic tab. The first section appeared to be the outline of a memoir, along with notations as to potential chapters, incidents or cases to be included. Archie carefully read each page, running his finger down and across the center of each line. He searched for his name or any reference to an investigation. About halfway through the forty-seven pages, he concluded Bartoni was devoid of literary skills. He continued his slog through the pages and saw nothing of consequence. His opinion of Bartoni's writing skills remained unchanged. He removed the pages from the binder and placed them, one at a time, in the wood burning stove. Archie watched as the edges of each page curled up, turned brown and erupted into bright orange flames. Once satisfied all the pages were now ashes, he went back to his chair and turned his attention to the second section.

———

Novello sat in his state vehicle outside Carmela Bartoni's house. An attractive, thirty something African-American woman opened the passenger side front door and flashed a Concord Police Detective Identification Card. She climbed into the passenger seat and extended her hand. "Kenisha Williams. How can I help?" She wore dark blue sneakers, jeans, a cotton green turtle neck and a blue windbreaker.

Novello liked Kenisha Williams immediately. No what's going on? What are you doing here? Whadyawant? Instead, an immediate offer of assistance with no bullshit. He grabbed her hand. "Anthony Novello, AG's Office, Homicide Bureau."

"Cool," Kenisha replied. Whadyaneed?"

"I'm investigating the murder of Judge Bartoni. This past Friday, we learned the Judge had a locker at the Jefferson Street Gym in Boston. We think he may have hidden some important notes. The Gym told us we needed either a search warrant, or Mrs. Bartoni to get it opened. Mrs. Bartoni told one of my officers she was going out of town and she'd meet me at the Gym Monday morning."

"Wait a sec," Kenisha said. "Her husband's been murdered, and her trip out of town was more important to her than finding out what was in the locker?" Williams shifted in the seat to face Novello. "Have you checked to see if the locker's been opened?'

Novello nodded. His initial instinct about her was correct. She gets it, good cop. Instinctively, he checked for a wedding ring. None. "I called this morning. The voice at the desk said you can't tell if a locker's been opened. It was locked when he tested it."

"Did she know the location of the club?" Kenisha said.

"Until my officer called, she didn't know her husband was a member of the club or that he had a locker. She learned everything on Friday when the officer called."

"He still with the Bureau?" Kenisha said. "Or she." She shook her head. "Don't answer, that's none of my business, sorry."

"Don't be sorry, wish it had been you and not that idiot," Novello said.

She smiled. "So, why you here? You think she might be in danger?"

"My gut tells me she never went out of town, or if she did, she's back. Both cars are in the driveway, a neighbor said he saw her walking out of her house in some kind of exercise clothes about six thirty this morning, and she had a duffel bag. She hasn't answered her land line since, and no one has reported seeing her."

"You think she took the duffel bag from that locker?"

"The thought occurred to me," Novello said.

"She didn't know the locker existed until Friday, maybe she doesn't know the combination," Kenisha said. "Something to hope for."

"Most people tend to use the same series of numbers for combinations, pin numbers or passwords; wedding anniversary, birthdates," Novello said. "She might have been able to figure it out, if she went there. But you're right, we have some reason to hope, but I keep thinking about that duffel bag she was carrying."

Kenisha nodded. "But, you really just want to be sure she's not hurt or unconscious on the floor in her house, right?"

Novello knew the signal when he heard it. "Right."

"Let's go," Kenisha said, as she opened the car door.

She rushed up the walkway and knocked loudly on the front door to Carmela Bartoni's house. She pushed the mail slot in and shouted. "Mrs. Bartoni! Concord Police, please come to the door." Novello stood behind her, wondering if he could recruit her for his team. There was no response to the knocking or shout. "Let's try the back door, they're usually less secure," Kenisha said.

"Your turf, your call," Novello said. He followed her around the house and to a small back porch with an unlocked screen door.

Kenisha knocked on the window pane to the back door. No answer. She pulled out a small black case, unzipped it and removed two picks. "This shouldn't take long," she said more to herself than to Novello.

"Street skills are good," Novello said.

"Well, as you may have guessed, I didn't grow up in Concord," Kenisha said.

"How'd you end up here?" Novello said.

Kenisha spoke, but kept her focus on the lock and her picks. "Bussed from Boston. Concord-Carlisle High School wanted a little diversity, and the fact I could run the two, four and one hundred meters in record times helped. After graduation, I did a stint at a teaching college, and decided I wanted to be a cop. When I graduated from the academy, a guy I met at the high school called. He was Chief of Detectives and asked me to join the force." She maneuvered the two picks and a soft click broke the silence. "We're in," Kenisha said. The door opened and the two stepped inside.

"Mrs. Bartoni," Kenisha shouted. "Concord Police, are you okay?"

"I'll take the upstairs," Novello said as he rushed past her.

"I'm checking the basement," Kenisha said. "Meet me in the living room."

———

The second section of Bartoni's binder consisted of five pages of cryptic hand written notes and questions. It seemed to be a series of disjointed thoughts, a To Do List, amid a few paragraphs of what appeared to be coded messages. Persons and organizations were referred to by random letters of the alphabet: X, K, W, M, O, and Organizations R, B and Q.

Archie concluded a separate code page existed since no one could remember the letters that corresponded to each name. He did not find one. "Shit," he shouted to the empty room. He took a deep breath and expelled it slowly. It doesn't matter, he thought. No one would ever see these pages, and even if a code page were found, what would it mean to anyone? What would it prove? Nothing.

Archie tore the pages from the binder and threw them into the fire. He watched them burn and become ashes drifting to the bottom of the stove. He stood before the fire and examined the now empty binder, looking for any markings that could identify it as Bartoni's. He found none and placed it on the bottom shelf of a bookcase. A souvenir.

Archie returned to his chair and closed his eyes. What impact would the killing of Carmela Bartoni have on the investigation of her husband's death? Misdirection or would it push Novello and Flaherty in a different, more threatening direction? How will the others react to the second killing? Who cares? No point in second guessing. It was done. It had to be done. Someone had to take charge.

Archie opened the drawer and removed his gun. He placed it on his lap and gently caressed it with his hands. *Are there other loose ends?*

———

"Beds are made and the rooms are immaculate," Novello said. "Didn't see any luggage or signs of packing or unpacking."

"Saw some luggage on a shelf in the basement. There was dust on it," Kenisha said. "Just a cup and small plate in the dishwasher. Refrigerator is well stocked, for a single lady. Didn't see a duffel bag."

"Neighbor saw her with one this morning," Novello said.

"Her purse and cell phone were in the living room," Kenisha said. "Probably wouldn't take the purse if she went running or for a walk, but surprised she left the phone behind."

"What's your gut say?"

Kenisha laughed. "I've been a cop five years. No one's ever asked for my gut reaction. Other parts of my anatomy, but not gut."

"So?" Novello said.

"She went to the gym and took the bag from her husband's locker. She could have her own bag, and maybe that's the one the neighbor saw. But, I don't like coincidences. Besides there's no gym nearby. If that's where she was going she'd drive. I think she was either walking some place to get rid of the bag, or to meet with someone to hand it over. The fact she's not home and the cars are here tells me she either went somewhere with that person she was meeting, or she's dead." Kenisha waved her hands. "I know I'm jumping to conclusions, but you asked for my gut, not what I know, suspect or can prove."

"My gut's telling me the same thing," Novello said. "And, I've learned to trust it. We both know she could show up here in ten minutes and tell us she went off with a friend for a day's ride to nowhere. She could tell us she never got into her husband's locker at the club and the duffle bag the neighbor saw was her own. We both know that could happen." Novello stared at Kenisha. "Do either of us believe it will? Do either of us think it makes sense to go home and wait for Carmela to call, or show up here? Do either of us believe she's going to show up at her husband's gym on Monday morning?" Novello said. "I'm afraid she got herself into something and it got her killed. Our gut reactions never solve or close cases, but they tell us the next steps."

"So, what's next?" Kenisha said.

"There a place nearby where people exercise or walk? Someplace a woman in her late sixties would feel comfortable."

"Half or three quarters of a mile from here is the Sleepy Hollow Cemetery," Kenisha said. "It's scenic, hilly, some think breathtakingly beautiful. If she was going for a walk, that's where she'd go."

"She mentioned Sleepy Hollow when I interviewed her," Novello said. "Said her husband wanted to be buried there, among the famous writers."

"Well there's no room on Author's Ridge," Kenisha said. "But there are sections where folks can still purchase lots. And, it's a great place to walk or jog."

"Sleepy Hollow's what's next," Novello said.

Chapter 27

Kenisha Williams rode with Novello in his state vehicle along the paths and hills of Sleepy Hollow Cemetery. Two Concord police offices in separate vehicles traveled different routes in the sprawling cemetery. "If she's here, she's dead," Novello said. "No pun intended. If she was going for a walk, she'd have been home long ago. And why take a duffel bag on a walk? If she was going to a gym, she'd have taken her car, and she'd be home. Why are there two cars in her garage?"

"She came here to meet somebody," Williams said.

"Yeah, but for an eight hour meeting?" Novello said. "If it was just a meeting, to hand off the duffel bag, she'd be home. If she was going to go off with someone, why not get picked up at her house? Why meet in a cemetery?" He looked around, peering through the windows of the car. "Security cameras here?"

"Anything not here during the Revolutionary War, won't be here now," Kenisha said. "Just like you won't find a Jiffy Lube or a Burger King in this part of town. Want to keep looking? There's a pond at the top of the hill."

"If she walked here to meet someone, why go all the way to the top of the cemetery? Unless she was meeting a fitness nut," Novello said.

"What if there was no planned meeting?" Kenisha said. "What if walking here was part of her exercise regimen and something happened – she got mugged, or." She stopped. "No. Nobody gets mugged in a fuckin' cemetery at seven or eight on a Sunday morning."

"And it doesn't explain the duffel bag," Novello said. "Where's that Authors' Ridge you mentioned?"

Kenisha pointed. "Over there. "There's a large reedy area and water at the bottom of the ridge, near that small parking area."

"Let's look there," Novello said.

Robes

——

I sat at my computer in the upstairs den putting together a written report for Novello on everything Abby and I learned about the Rothwell Foundation. Novello didn't text or use email. He gave me an email address for Ed McGonagle and asked me to send everything to him. I wanted my report to be concise, easy to read, and contain all we knew or suspected about Rothwell and its connections to I.RISE.

It took about nine minutes.

Whenever Abby and I think aloud with each other, we tend to convince ourselves that we know or have discovered more than we have. A couple of Tanqueray and Tonics exponentially increases our enthusiasm. Also makes everything more fun, or at least less boring. The task of reducing our discoveries, thoughts, and energy to paper, sharpens the focus, and I quickly realize how little we know. Yet the clear connections among the Rothwell Foundation, Mrs. Bartoni, and I. RISE were, at least to us, new and important information. Perhaps not as important as we thought and hoped, but still important.

I looked at my single page report and decided to include a visual to show the connections. Lawyers draft documents as if being paid by the word or page. I'm as guilty of this as any barrister even when I'm not getting paid. I thought a simple chart with lines connected to squares, rectangles and circles – like an organization chart – could show the connections and what Abby and I discovered. It added some bulk to the report and might even impress Novello.

I started by listing the names: Eleanor Rothwell and Zachery Rothwell in a square and drawing a line from that square to another square with the words Rothwell Foundation. I created a line from the right side of the Rothwell Foundation square to a circle with the name Carmela Rothwell Bartoni, CEO & Treasurer. A second line under that went to a rectangle, which listed in bright red coloring the names Susan Landry and Nelson Decker. I made Carmela Rothwell Bartoni's name a bright green.

Next, I inserted a line running from the bottom of the Rothwell Foundation square down to a third square, which I labeled I. RISE. A line on the right side of that square connected to a circle with the words Susan Landry, Exec. Dir. Nelson Decker, Clinical Dir. I put their names in red. I had searched for additional common names between the two listed boards of directors, but found none.

I paused to look at my work. I needed to illustrate the Rothwell Foundation was a supporter of I. RISE, so I inserted a dollar sign on the line running from the Foundation's square to I. RISE. There was still something missing. I thumbed through the papers in my file and saw the notes I had taken on my title search. I went back to my chart and drew a line from the bottom of the I.RISE square to another square, which I labeled EZ DUZ IT Realty Trust. I inserted the words ten-year lease across the line. I decided on a final line running down from the bottom of the EZ DUZ IT square to a circle with the word Beneficiaries and a question mark.

I stood and looked at my chart. Because they were in red, my eyes were drawn immediately to the names Susan Landry and Nelson Decker. I wished there were more connections and searched for them. Nothing.

Whenever I work on something, particularly when drafting a document, Abby urges me to walk away from it every hour or so for 10 minutes to let my mind clear. She says I'll have a fresh perspective when I return to it. I decided to follow her advice, and I used that time to make a perfect T&T.

———

Novello and Kenisha stood in the small parking area at the bottom of Authors' Ridge. They watched the patrol cars with the other two officers, their hands waving out the window, circle and exit the cemetery through the Wood Gate.

"You don't live in Concord." Novello said.

"God no," Kenisha responded. "It's a nice town and a great place to visit, but I couldn't afford to live here."

"You don't commute here from Boston, do you?"

"I'm in Waltham. It has a nice city vibe and I can take back roads and get here in fifteen, twenty minutes." Kenisha smiled. "You a Boston guy?"

Novello nodded. "North End," he said. "Most of my life."

"Nice," Kenisha said. "I remember going to Paul Revere's House as part of a high school field trip. There's a stone marker in a park not too far from here where the British captured him. Eight or nine of us met there, and our civics teacher drove us in this huge van to Paul Revere's House and the Old North Church. I remember we had lunch at some famous pizza joint."

"Probably Regina's or the European," Novello said.

Kenisha shook her head and smiled. "Don't remember. "It was a nice day ruined when the van dropped me off at the three decker in Roxbury where I lived. Teacher said it didn't makes sense for me to go to Concord just so I could get on a bus back to Boston. Prick said it loud enough to make sure everyone knew I came to school on a bus from Boston." Kenisha shrugged. "Of course everyone knew I came on a bus, but they never saw where I lived." She tried for a smile, but it wasn't there. "I remember how sad I felt and how quiet everyone was when they got out of the van so I could get off." She shook away the memory. "Sorry, didn't mean to get into my life story."

"That sucks," Novello said. "If it's any consolation, today that three decker is probably worth over a million dollars."

"We rented," Kenisha said. "The real consolation is the teacher still lives in Concord, and I know his car. I give it special attention and a fair amount of tickets." Kenisha laughed. "Hey, enough about me, let's get back to Mrs. Bartoni."

Novello pointed to the pond. "How deep is this?" Novello said.

"I'd guess ten, maybe twenty feet," Kenisha said. She pointed to the high reeds. "If we try to get over to the reeds walking along the water's edge, I'm afraid we'll end up at least knee deep in muck." She pointed to her right and the pathway to Authors' Ridge. "If we go up to the ridge, we might be able to crab walk down the hill to the reeds."

"Let's go," Novello said.

———

Abby joined me in the upstairs den and immediately went to my computer. I rested in my recliner with a Tanqueray and Tonic and waited for her reaction to the report I drafted for Novello.

"I like it," Abby said. "Particularly, the chart. Makes the connections clearer. I did notice something, and I made two changes."

"You made changes to the flow chart?" I got up from my chair.

"Sure did," she said.

I went to the computer and peered over her shoulder. My eyes immediately went to the new additions of red. The E in Eleanor Rothwell and the Z in Zachery Rothwell in the top box were now red, as were the letters EZ in EZ DUZ IT in the bottom box, signifying the Realty Trust that owned the property in New Bedford that housed I. RISE.

"Sonofabitch," I said. "You've always said if I walk away from something I'm working on, I'd get a new perspective when I came back to it." We exchanged fist bumps.

Chapter 28

Novello and Kenisha Williams walked up the steep path to Authors' Ridge. They stayed on the narrow path, Kenisha in front, past the Echo Tree, the Thoreau Family site to a cement slab bench. "Let's go back here," Novello said. He stepped over the cement bench and across the flat ground to where the steep ridge dropped some forty feet to the pond and its reedy shoreline.

Kenisha followed him over and they looked down. "Steeper than I thought," she said. "Glad I have sneakers."

Novello looked at his tasseled loafers and grunted. "Hill's not as steep over there," he said, pointing to his left and to the area at the top of the pathway they'd climbed minutes earlier. "Let's start over there. Once we get to the bottom, we can move along the shoreline towards this area."

"Your shoes, your call," Kenisha teased.

They retreated their steps, past the famous grave sites and to a large tree at the top of the walkway. Novello pointed to a small plaque at the bottom of the tree. "The Echo Tree? Know what that's all about?"

"Actually, I do," Kenisha said. "Part of the ceremonies on Memorial Day, and, I think, Veterans Day, was a playing of Taps and Echo by members of the High School Band. The Taps player would be in the valley in front of the audience, and the echo player would be behind this tree playing towards the swamp. No one seems to know when the tradition of using this tree started, but when I was at the school every trumpeter wanted to play echo. I think the band's alumni group put up the marker."

"You in the band?" Novello said.

"No, I was strictly track."

They moved away from the tree to the edge of the ridge, and

looked down the steep hill. Scrub pines and larger maples dotted the hillside. Several bushes had been trampled on. Novello crouched like a baseball catcher, turned his body to the right and placed both hands on the ground. He started moving down the hill. "Can you turn towards the left and follow me down the same way?

"Got it," Kenisha said.

"No snakes here, right?' Novello said. "Hate snakes."

She laughed. "You and Indiana Jones. Don't think there's anything here that can hurt you. Might see a garter snake near the water, maybe a frog. You okay with frogs?'

Novello didn't answer. The two slowly made their way down the hill. About two thirds down, Novello stood and used a tree for support. Williams joined him and they scanned the hillsides to their left and right. Nothing.

"Probably can make it the rest of the way standing up if we're careful," Novello said. "You see a snake shoot it." They proceeded another fifteen feet when Novello stretched out his arm to stop Williams."

"Snake?"

"Body," Novello said. He pointed to his right.

There in the swampy reeds the body of a woman in a dark track suit, her face streaked with black mud and her right arm rigid with two fingers pointing to the sky.

———

Abby and I looked at the flow chart. "Could be a coincidence," I said. "But I'd bet the name EZ DUZ IT was partly a tribute to Eleanor and Zachery Rothwell."

"I agree," Abby said. She tucked some loose strands of hair behind her left ear. "Given the other connections and the roles Carmela Bartoni has with the foundation, we need to point this out to Novello."

"Agreed," I said. Although the 990 for Rothwell doesn't mention any interest in EZ DUZ IT, or any realty trust,"

"Maybe the $425,000 came directly from Eleanor and Zachery Rothwell," Abby said.

"Could have happened that way. Rothwells give it to Carmela, who buys the building, and puts title in a realty trust," I said. "That works."

"Carmela names the realty trust EZ DUZ IT to pay homage to her folks," Abby said. "And it has a subtle irony because EZ DUZ IT is a slogan for the recovery community, and Carmela knows it was Eleanor and Zachery who made the purchase possible."

"EZ made it possible, EZ did it, or EZ DUZ IT," I said. "Definitely works."

"Even without proof," Abby said.

"Not gonna ruin a good theory looking for facts," I said. "I'm sending this to McGonagle."

———

By five o'clock, uniformed officers of the Massachusetts State Police, some still wearing their black wrap around fuck-you sun glasses, swarmed Sleepy Hollow Cemetery. A team from the Medical Examiner's Office, working with the Concord Fire Department, removed the body and placed it in a black body bag for transport to an autopsy team in Boston. Almost half of her head had been blown apart, and forensic teams scoured the reedy marsh area and the hillside for skin, bone fragments and other evidence.

Novello identified the body as Carmela Bartoni, relying on his memory of her height, weight, and the description a neighbor had provided the Concord Police that morning. The task of securing a more formal identification through family members, DNA, finger prints, dental records or other methods fell to others. But there was no doubt in Novello's mind who the body was. He leaned against his car with Williams, watching the organized frenzy the discovery of a murder victim brought to any scene.

"Kenisha, let's get something to eat. My treat," he said. "They don't need us here, and we'll be writing reports until late."

"Thanks," Kenisha said. She smiled. "You make it sound so romantic." She lowered her voice and put her hands on her hips. "Let's get food before the grueling work of reports. Anthony Novello, you make it hard for a girl to refuse."

Novello smiled. "Let me rephrase that. "Kenisha, may I have the pleasure of taking you to dinner?"

"Thank you, that would be very nice," Kenisha said. She walked towards the passenger door and looked back to Novello. "Not every day a girl gets invited to dinner at a murder scene."

Chapter 29

I arrived at work at seven thirty on Monday, the last day of April. A light rain drizzled on the porch steps as I unlocked the door. I was surprised to find the office empty. Vinnie left a note on my desk advising he'd be in by noon. He left a shorter than usual "TO DO" list.

I scanned the list. I had completed many of the assignments the previous week. Vinnie must have been distracted. I prepared a morning pot of coffee to ease into the work week. While the coffee was brewing, I glanced into Vinnie's office. The shiny brass telescope pointing out the window and across Falmouth Harbor brought an uneasiness to my stomach. I walked over and peered through it. I adjusted a knob near the eyepiece and the Falmouth Band Stand came into focus. It was close to the Flying Bridge, but far enough way to help me relax. But it didn't. The office seemed to close in on me. A loud thump at the front door startled me. "Jesus," I shouted into the empty room. I rushed from Vinnie's office to the reception area. The noise was *The Boston Globe* hitting the front door. I retrieved the paper and brought it to my desk. A soft beeping tone signaled the coffee was ready. Back in the small kitchen, I poured a cup and walked to my desk. The office seemed unusually quiet and the air stale. Outside, a car hissed by on the wet street. I sat and unfolded the paper, trying to shake away the hollowness in my stomach. My eyes drifted to a headline in the lower right corner of the front page: WIFE OF MURDERED JUDGE FOUND DEAD.

———

Novello and McGonagle met at the Jefferson Street Gym. One attendant shouted as McGonagle used a large orange pry bar to open Judge Bartoni's locker. It was empty. Another attendant with horrible breath acknowledged he had opened the locker for a woman identifying herself as Carmela Bartoni. He gave her a dark blue duffel bag. "I hope I was helpful," he said to McGonagle. "Yeah," McGonagle responded. "You're a prince. Keep up the good work."

The trip to the gym confirmed what Novello had concluded, but it needed to be done.

Novello's next task involved a call to State Trooper Douglas Tanner, the officer who told Carmela Bartoni about the locker. It was also Tanner who mislabeled the contents of Judge Bartoni's briefcase. "Should have gotten rid of him then," Novello said to McGonagle, as he waited for a connection. The call went to voice mail. Novello told Tanner he was no longer assigned to the Homicide Bureau. "Learn from your mistakes," Novello spoke slowly to the machine. "Or, you'll be writing citations on the Pike your whole career."

At eight-thirty, Novello and Ed McGonagle sat across from each other at the square table in the bullpen adjacent to Novello's office. Each had a large cup of coffee. A box of plain donuts centered the space between them. The news of Carmela Bartoni's murder spread quickly. Both *The Boston Globe,* and *Boston Herald* had front page stories. Novello briefed Attorney General Flaherty Sunday evening, and the two agreed to meet today at ten. A team of officers searched Bartoni's house shortly after her body was discovered. Other officers removed electronic equipment, including a computer, laptop, and an iPad. Her cell phone had not been located.

"So tell me about this Kenisha Williams," McGonagle said. "She the reason you didn't call me? Even after the body was found?"

"Good cop, good looking," Novello said. "Cooperative from the get go. No jurisdictional bullshit, no who's in charge bullshit. No I'll have to check with my chief bullshit. She's like us – let's get it done. We might still be looking for Carmela Bartoni if it weren't for Kenisha."

McGonagle nodded, his mouth full of donut.

Novello said, "Did I mention she's hot?"

———

I worked on the assignments listed on my "TO DO" list. It was a slog as my mind kept returning to *The Globe* story on Carmela Bartoni. Abby called after seeing the news on television. We agreed to do nothing. The last thing Novello needed was to hear from us. We assumed the meeting with Monsignor Roche would be cancelled. We were both unnerved by the murder. Neither of us knew or had ever met Mrs. Bartoni, but we had learned things about her, and she had become a part of our lives.

It was a few minutes after ten when I heard the door open.

"Top of the morning to you, Connor McNeill," Vinnie's voice boomed.

"And the rest of the day to yourself, Vincent Preskin." I started to get up from my chair, but Vinnie came into my office. I sat down. "You heard about Mrs. Bartoni?" I said.

"I did. Judge Fisher called me early this morning. Wanted to know if I could drive him up to Concord later this week or whenever the wake is." Vinnie shrugged. "I told him the police will have the body for a few days. Suggested he give me a call when he finds out about the wake, and I'd see what I could do." Vinnie slumped into one of the chairs facing my desk. He looked tired. "I think Fisher wanted me – or us – actually you – to get the details from Novello. He never asked, and I sure as hell didn't offer." He started to get up, but slumped back. "Fisher's not a bad guy, and I know he's old, but I don't want to become the son he never had, or the manservant he's too cheap to hire." He smiled. "How was your long weekend? Go anywhere special?"

I had to think a moment. The Friday Abby and I went to New Bedford seemed a month ago. "Not really," I said. "Abby's grandmother was raised in New Bedford, and her mother was born there. Both have passed on, but Abby had never seen the old homestead. So we took a day trip, had a nice lunch at a place called the Black Whale."

"Find the old homestead?' Vinnie said.

Vinnie didn't seem suspicious, just making conversation. "Yeah, a two decker on Acushnet Ave. near the St. Anthony of Padua Church. Got home by five and golfed Saturday." I knew Acushnet Ave was one of the main drags in New Bedford. I had noticed the church as we were driving in. It stuck in my memory because as a kid I prayed to St. Anthony whenever I lost something.

"Golf, that reminds me," Vinnie said, his mind had drifted away from New Bedford and my long weekend. "You and Abby interested in playing in a foursome with me and a golfer to be named later a couple of weeks from this Saturday? It's a charitable event, the course is in Plymouth. Office will pay. I sponsor a hole every year."

"Sounds great," I said. "Let me call Abby to make sure we're free. Not sure we're up to your caliber of golf."

"Not a problem," Vinnie said. "Nobody at this tournament takes golf seriously. Well, on this one day they don't. There's a dinner, and they usually have a comedian. It'll be fun, lot of laughs. Best of all there're not a lot of lawyers fucking up the night with shop talk."

"You've played this a lot of years?" I said.

"Nine or ten," Vinnie said. "My foursome won one year." He nodded towards his office, where the picture of Vinnie and three other guys grinning over a brass trophy hung over his golf clubs.

"Nice, what's the charity?" I said.

"An alcohol and substance abuse program called I.RISE."

———

"The duffel bag changes everything," Novello said to McGonagle. "Think about it. There was no reason for Carmela to take the duffel bag from the locker, or to bring it with her to Sleepy Hollow. Unless, she thought or was told something inside that bag incriminated her." Novello rose from his seat and paced the room.

McGonagle knew not to interrupt with a question or comment. He sat sipping his coffee and waited.

"When that asshole Tanner told her we had located the locker, she must have called someone. They developed a plan for her to take the duffel bag and bring it to a prearranged meeting spot." He looked at McGonagle and raised his eyebrows.

"We got telephone records on both her cell and the land line," McGonagle said. He took out his notebook and flipped a few pages. "Tanner called her on Friday. Records show the only calls Carmela made on Friday and Saturday were to a grave stone company, her foundation, and two calls to her church. There were no calls on Sunday."

Novello came back and stood behind his chair. He leaned in towards McGonagle, resting his forearms on the back of the chair. "She used a burner. I know she called someone. Have someone check who she spoke to at the foundation."

He walked over to the window and suddenly turned to McGonagle, snapping to attention as if slapped by a hand he didn't see coming. "The duffel bag also means Fisher lied to us," Novello came back to the table and sat down. "If Judge Bartoni was really investigating D'Alessandro and Win Allen, the duffel bag would have been in his locker when we were there this morning. Carmela Bartoni wouldn't give a shit about a scandal involving those two. Why would she retrieve something involving either D'Alessandro or Allen? She wouldn't. She got it because it involved her. Nothing makes sense about Carmela taking the duffel bag, unless she was afraid something in it implicated her and the person she was meeting at Sleepy Hollow. And that person took the bag and killed her."

Novello stared at McGonagle. "Ed, we need to start over and look at this case from a different perspective. Bartoni wasn't investigating the Chief Justice and Win Allen. It was never about them." He held up his hand like a crossing guard. "We're not forgetting them. We're gonna jack up those two assholes, but this murder investigation is not about them. This case is about Carmela Bartoni and whatever she and the person who killed her were up to. Bitch was cuter than a shit house rat," Novello said. "I sat in her living room and she spent the first ten minutes trying to establish control. Even taped our conversation. She confirmed what Fisher told us. Said her husband was investigating something involving the church." Novello paused. "Funny, as I say those words now, they have the same rehearsed quality as our interviews with D'Alessandro and Win Allen."

"Rehearsed it with whom?" McGonagle said. "Fisher mentioned D'Alessandro and Win Allen. Mrs. Bartoni didn't. Right?"

"I should've pushed her harder." Novello ran the fingers of his left hand into his hair, pushing his palm into his forehead. He waived his hand, the signal McGonagle needed to respond.

"Okay," McGonagle started. "Let's go over what we know or are fairly certain is true. Let's see if it supports calling Fisher a liar. Let's see if it supports our original theory, or the new direction you want to go. Sound like a plan?"

Novello looked up and sat erect in his chair. "Sounds like something I've asked you to do on more than one occasion."

McGonagle smiled. "I thought you'd recognize the approach." He took a bite of his donut and a sip of coffee. "First, Fisher told us Judge Bartoni and he were friends, and that they met every couple of months or so for lunch. Judge Bartoni's appointment book and Mrs. Bartoni confirm that. Second, Fisher told us Judge Bartoni said he was investigating a scandal involving the Catholic Church. Mrs. Bartoni said he was investigating something involving the church. Third, Bartoni's clerk, Joe Colby, said the Judge was up to something, and he had taken a serious interest in the church abuse scandal. Fourth, Fisher said Bartoni told him he had seen Win Allen and Chief Justice D'Alessandro travelling in a car together late at night. Our own investigation tells us D'Alessandro and Win Allen are more than friends. D'Alessandro admitted to you they were lovers, and Win Allen admitted to me at the Fill-A-Buster that he was getting his ashes hauled by the Chief Justice." McGonagle picked up his coffee, but then set it down. "Two other things. When you asked Mrs. Bartoni if she thought her husband would have confided in anyone about whatever he was investigating, she said Judge Fisher. The other thing is a point in your favor. Mrs. Bartoni told you the name Win Allen didn't mean anything to her. But she knew or assumed he was a lawyer." McGonagle took a deep breath and smiled. "Now, we need to ask ourselves whether what we know helps or hurts your new theory." He nodded at Novello for a response.

"Win Allen said he was getting his ashes hauled?" Novello said.

———

At the same time and just over fifty miles away, Bobby Morelli balanced his 240 pounds on a pale brown wooden stool at The Rogues Club, a bucket of blood with a bar, 2 pool tables, a broken pinball machine and 4 tables of varying design and sturdiness. Each table was surrounded by four metal folding chairs. Its entrance a dark green door under a small sign in an alley, a block from Purchase Street in Fall River.

Bobby was wearing baggy gray sweat pants and a matching sweatshirt two sizes smaller than a circus tent. In front of him stood a tall thin glass of vodka and grapefruit juice, beads of water rolling down the sides and staining the bar. The room smelled of empty beer bottles and wet cardboard.

Bobby ran a Fall River neighborhood for Anthony Bonfiglio. He was one of twelve neighborhood bosses, but the only one with a single area of the city. This made Bobby a big man in his neighborhood, but not in the organization.

To fulfill his responsibilities and avoid the wrath of Bonfiglio, Bobby used three teenage dropouts as runners. He paid each runner from his own share of the weekly earnings of his neighborhood. The runners collected from those who owed money to Bobby or Bonfiglio. Any loans made in his neighborhood became Bobby's task to collect. "Don't matter if he's in prison or a dirt farmer in fuckin' Kansas. Your problem," Bonfiglio once told Bobby. "You collect it or you pay it. Don't matter to me."

Bobby's runners collected from those who owed. They also collected the names of those who were delinquent. But, they never threatened or hurt delinquents, even those who failed to make the weekly vig. That task fell to Bobby or Simon, a red-headed Ukrainian-born seven-foot behemoth on Bonfiglio's payroll. Simon the Redhead was known and feared in the shadows and corners across Fall River and New Bedford. Part of his legend said he once crushed a delinquent man's testicle between his fingers after receiving an amount nine dollars short of the balance due. The Redhead was to be avoided at all costs.

Bobby knew neighborhood bosses who went to Bonfiglio for help too often didn't remain neighborhood bosses. Sometimes they found the Redhead waiting at their front door, or in their garage. Bobby kept a wooden Louisville slugger for those clients who needed a hurtin'. Bobby liked to tell people that he once gave a home run swing of the bat up between a delinquent's legs. "Effective, and I didn't have to wash my hands," Bobby told his runners.

The runners also distributed small amounts of drugs, pills, crack, heroin and whatever to four street merchants spread across Bobby's neighborhood. Unlike the runners, these pushers took their agreed share of the profits before turning the cash over to the runners. Neither Bobby nor Bonfiglio relied on an honor system or the integrity of the merchants. Each had been assigned a quota, and deviations resulted in a summons to visit Bonfiglio, or worse, a visit from Simon the Redhead.

Occasionally, Bobby and one or more of his runners would show initiative and steal a truck loaded with goods, or break into a warehouse or a pharmacy. These activities generated additional income for Bobby and his runners, which were shared equally. But only after the payment of a 25% tribute to Anthony Bonfiglio.

Bobby lifted a canvas bag filled with cash onto the bar. A pale green sheet of paper filled with numbers and letters told him the week's take and its sources. An average week for Bobby brought in just over forty-one hundred. From this he would pay each of his runners three percent. Not much, but easier than bagging groceries. And, someday they might run a neighborhood. Another forty percent went to Bonfiglio. This left Bobby, on average, about twenty-one hundred, or a yearly cash haul just shy of one hundred ten thousand. Last year, the occasional initiatives pushed Bobby's yearly income to a little over one hundred forty thousand.

Bobby considered himself a financial wizard. He once hid all his cash in old paint cans stored in a wooden cabinet in the basement, an idea given to him by someone he no longer remembered. Now the cans were used only for "walking around" money. The rest he laundered through a legitimate business, and he paid taxes on what came back to him. Bobby hated paying taxes, but that was how they got Al Capone, and Bobby would be smarter than Capone. One hundred forty thousand, and this year he was on track to maybe crack two hundred grand. Not bad, for a slug who rarely left the bar stool.

Not enough for a man with Bobby's dreams.

He wanted more neighborhoods.

Bobby sat at the bar with the canvass bag, the pale green sheet and a small calculator. He had done the math earlier, but Bobby did everything at least twice, particularly when it came to money. A voice cut into his concentration.

"Bobby Shits, as I live and breathe. A beautiful day in your neighborhood?"

Bobby turned. The man Connor O'Neill knew as Freddy stood just inside the door, casually holding a pool cue.

"No need to call me that," Bobby said. "Unless you want that stick up your ass." He slid off the stool. "Whadyawant?"

"You know who I am," Freddy said. "And who I work for?"

"Yeah, I know who you work for." Bobby took a step and was about five feet from Freddy. "You know who I work for?"

Freddy smiled. "I do." He extended a hand. "Sorry about using your old nickname, won't do it again."

Bobby grabbed the hand, but kept his eyes on the pool stick. "A drink?"

"Cold beer would be nice," Freddy said. "From the bottle is fine."

Bobby went behind the bar to an old-fashioned red top-opening cooler with beer bottles bathed in six inches of icy water. He lifted the top and took out a long neck bottle of Rolling Rock. He shook off the drippings and handed it across the bar to Freddy.

"Thanks, you do remember."

"Don't forget much," Bobby said. "Unless the right people tell me to."

"Smart," Freddy said.

Bobby nodded. He came around the bar and sat on his stool, next to Freddy. "So, now that we're best friends, the fuck you want?"

Freddy took a long swallow of his beer. He grabbed a small napkin from a pile on the bar and centered the bottle on it. He turned towards Bobby to his right. "What were you doing at The Flying Bridge this past Saturday?"

"Eating. The fuck you think I was doing?" Bobby said. His eyes stayed focused on the glass of vodka and grapefruit juice in front of him.

"I think you were watching someone. I'd like to know why."

Bobby looked over to Freddy. "And I should tell you, why? The fuck you've ever done for me?"

"Because you know who I work for," Freddy said.

Bobby shifted on his stool to face Freddy, their knees almost touching. "I was asked to keep an eye out. That's all I'm saying. And, you know who I work for. You have a problem, have the person you work for talk to the person I work for. Now do me a favor. Finish your beer. Get the fuck out of here. I got work to do."

"Not an unreasonable response to my question," Freddy said.

"And, thank you for admitting you were at The Bridge and that you were watching someone. I hate wasting time with lies and bullshit. Thank you for the courtesy of telling me the truth, at least up to a point." Freddy took a pull on his beer. "Now listen carefully to what I say, because I don't want there to be any misunderstanding. Are you listening, Bobby?"

"Yeah, I'm fuckin' listening." His eyes drifted downward.

"Look at me, Bobby. "This is important. I want you to see my words."

Bobby stared at Freddy. "I'm looking and listening. Get this the fuck over with."

"There is a person I care about, whom I consider a friend. His name is Connor McNeill, and he's working with your cousin Vinnie." Freddy smiled. "Like the movie."

"Fuckin' hilarious," Bobby said. "Haven't heard that one in probably 2 days."

"Still listening? Good. So my friend Connor isn't in the game, and I think he's gotten himself entangled with something that may involve your cousin Vinnie, a Judge Fisher and perhaps some other people you know."

"Don't know any Judge Fisher. I got nothing to do with Vinnie."

"Shut up!" Freddy screamed, his voice echoing across the room. "I told you to listen, not talk. Told you I don't have time for lies and bullshit."

Freddy took a deep breath and smiled. "Sorry about shouting, Bobby. I have temper issues. Working on them. The reason I am here is to tell you two things." Freddy held up a finger. "First, I don't care what game, scam or hustle you, Fisher, Vinnie or anyone else is up to. I don't give a shit, I really don't." A second finger popped up. "But the second thing," Freddy said, "I really do care about. Are you still listening, Bobby?" The second finger closed and the first pointed towards and nearly touched Bobby's large nose. "If anything bad happens to Connor McNeill or to his wife, I will come back here, or to your house, to wherever you are, and I will kill you. I don't give a shit about the Redhead, or who you work for. I will hunt you down and kill you. Is that clear?"

"Fuck you," Bobby snarled. He tried to swat away Freddy's finger with the back of his right hand. "I ain't afraid…"

Freddy pulled back his finger and avoided Bobby's passing hand. He then pushed it deep into Bobby's left eye. Bobby screamed, bringing both hands to his face. At the same time, Freddy slid off his stool, grabbed the back of Bobby's head and brought it down so his nose met Freddy's rising right knee. Blood spluttered over Bobby's hands and face. Freddy pushed him off the bar stool and to the floor.

"Motherfucker, I'll kill you," Bobby screeched. His body rolling with pain, blood running into his mouth and down his chin and neck.

"Thanks for the beer," Freddy said. "Remember what I said."

Chapter 30

Vinnie hustled out of the office at eleven o'clock, his briefcase bulging with documents, notes and papers for a commercial sales transaction.

Tension wrapped itself around me. Mrs. Bartoni's connection to I. RISE and her murder made everything sinister. My research on I.RISE, and Novello's investigation on Judge Bartoni's murder had now merged.

Had our trip to I. RISE been reckless? Were we in danger? I looked at the flow chart I emailed to McGonagle. The box with the name Carmela Rothwell Bartoni in bright green stared back at me. I realized she was dead when I prepared the chart. I added a line off the I.RISE box to a circle with Vinnie's name and a dollar sign. I went to Vinnie's office and walked over to his golf clubs. I studied the picture of Vinnie's foursome behind the trophy. Something in my mind clicked. Next to Vinnie, second from the right, was the guy I saw in the picture at I.RISE of the group standing behind the opening day ribbon. The picture was on Abby's phone, but I was certain it was the same guy. I took a picture of Vinnie's foursome with my phone and sent it to Abby. "Anyone look familiar?" I texted.

I picked up the I.RISE Annual Report and looked for Vinnie's name under the list of supporters. It wasn't there.

So what? Maybe he didn't want to be hounded by other non-profits or charities.

But, why not? If he sponsored a hole at their annual golf tournament, why wouldn't he be listed as a sponsor in the annual report?

What the fuck was going on?

The phone rang, shattering the silence. "That's the guy in the picture we saw at I. RISE," Abby said. "He was cutting the ribbon on opening day."

"Bingo," I said. I told Abby about Vinnie's invitation for us to play in the I.RISE golf tournament.

"You made up an excuse why we can't go," Abby said.

"I thought we'd go," I said. "Might learn something."

"Connor, don't you think Susan Landry will be there? Were you planning on asking Vinnie to register us as Pete and Amy Coumounduros?'

―――

"I might have added some local flavor to his statement," McGonagle said. "Getting your ashes hauled is probably not part of Winfield's lexicon. He used the term 'lovers.' In any case, does what we know support or detract from your new theory?"

"Almost everything we know came from Judge Fisher and Carmela Bartoni," Novello said. "If they were involved in something, they'd corroborate each other." Novello took a sip of coffee and carefully placed the cup on a small napkin. "Tell me, do you think it strange Fisher felt it was important that he tell me the information he had?"

McGonagle shrugged. "Fisher's a judge. He wanted to talk with the top dog."

"So, call me,' Novello said. "Make an appointment. Why does the Judge get Vinnie Preskin to drag Connor to a meeting? Why does Fisher need Connor to set up the meeting? Fisher must have friends on the job in Falmouth. He could have asked them to contact me, or given them a written statement to get to me. It all seems forced."

"Maybe he figured if he called he'd get shuffled off to someone. Remember how pissed he was that he had to deal with me?" McGonagle said. "Preskin said the Judge knew you'd see his name in Bartoni's appointment book and want to talk to him. Fisher decided he'd save you the trouble, and come directly to you."

"If we had seen his name in Bartoni's book, we'd have asked a Falmouth detective to interview him," Novello said. "Fisher would know that, but he wanted a face to face. Why?"

McGonagle shook his head. "If Fisher's dirty, the last thing he'd want is a face to face. He'd want to deal with his friends in Falmouth, where he has clout. And, why in hell would he say Bartoni's investigating something? He could have said they had lunch and talked about the Red Sox, the weather or other judges, the usual bullshit."

"Because he didn't know what we knew or if Bartoni had already mentioned his investigation to anyone else. So he uses our meeting – your meeting – to distract us. To get us to focus on the Chief Justice and Win Allen," Novello said.

"But what you now call a distraction turned out to be accurate," McGonagle said.

"Don't forget the duffel bag. You think Carmela was meeting D'Alessandro or Win Allen? You think she was part of that scandal? Maybe a threesome?"

"No," McGonagle said. "And, thanks for putting a picture in my head that'll keep me up all night" He put out an exaggerated shudder. "Tell me this. You think Fisher made up the story and by coincidence it happened to be true?"

"You know I don't. Maybe Judge Bartoni did see them in a car together and mentioned it in passing to Fisher. Fisher adds the part about Bartoni saying he had other sources and that he was investigating them," Novello said. "Then he tells us, and we're off and running."

"So what was Bartoni talking to Fisher about? The Red Sox, the weather?"

Novello shrugged. "We don't know. But Fisher's no dope. We both know the best lies are those close to the truth." Novello picked up his cup of coffee. He put it down with taking a sip. "Maybe, Bartoni did say he was investigating a scandal involving the church. He mentions it to Fisher, not realizing Fisher is somehow involved. Maybe Bartoni figured out his wife was somehow involved. He says enough to Fisher. Fisher kills him."

"Lot of maybes," McGonagle said. Doubt raced across his face. "Hard to see a ninety plus old man killing anybody."

"Fuckin' guns make it easy to kill," Novello said. "Just pull the trigger."

———

I was nine pages into the financing agreement and loan application Vinnie negotiated for a Hyannis Medical Practice hoping to establish a satellite office in Falmouth. Although dry as dust, the document interested me because the medical group could become a source of business for Abby. The draft agreement mentioned a business plan and projected revenue charts. Vinnie told me the client would prepare these for our review later this week. The financing agreement said the business plan would outline the community need for the services, and the client's marketing strategy to secure enough medical referrals to generate income to repay the loan. I wondered if I. RISE had a business plan when it was created. How did it market itself?

Susan Landry, the Executive Director of I.RISE, told us most of the referrals came from New Bedford, Falmouth and the Upper Cape. I wondered if Judge Tobias Fisher was part of I. RISES's marketing strategy.

I knew how to find out. I grabbed my phone and called the Probation Office at the Falmouth District Court.

———

How you want to handle I. RISE?' McGonagle said. "You look at the stuff McNeill emailed me?"

"Yeah," Novello said. "We got lucky on that. When Flaherty asked me to have someone look into I. RISE, I farmed it out to Connor, never thinking it would amount to anything. He's found connections between I. RISE and Mrs. Bartoni. Gives us a place to start. I have people combing her files at home and her bank records. IT's going over her computer and electronic toys. Not sure we'd have found the connection between Carmela Bartoni and I. RISE if Flaherty hadn't asked about the company."

"What's next?" McGonagle said.

"Connor and Abby are meeting with Monsignor Roche tomorrow at 2. He's the Archdiocese's point person with I. RISE. Abby has some expertise in reimbursement and how insurer's pay for services. She thinks the church is paying I. RISE for services it isn't receiving, and someone's getting a kick back."

"I saw her report," McGonagle said. "Nothing would surprise me about the church, but she and Connor are making some big leaps."

"You said the same thing about me less than two minutes ago," Novello said. "Maybe, maybe not. Let's see what they learn at the meeting with Roche, and go from there. I need to text Abby with the details on the meeting."

"You text?"

"You're going to teach me that and how to use the voice memo function on my phone."

"Before or after we solve the Bartoni murders?" McGonagle said. "You want me at that meeting with the Monsignor?"

"Got that covered," Novello said. "Right now, you and I are going to Falmouth. Judge Fisher wanted a face to face? Well, in about ninety minutes he's getting one."

Chapter 31

I was with Francis (don't call me Frank) McNulty the day he learned he would be appointed Chief Probation Officer for the Falmouth District Court. Francis was Senate Chair of the Joint Committee on Insurance. I was lobbying him as part of a coalition to support more funding for the Nantucket Land Trust. It was an easy sell and took about twelve seconds. We were a half hour into a serious discussion on why the Red Sox were doomed when one of McNulty's aides interrupted to say the Governor was on the phone. McNulty signaled I should stay. As he sat listening to a voice I couldn't hear, the smile spread over his face. McNulty didn't smile with just his mouth, he used his whole head. The creases in his face ran up to his glistening eyes. On this occasion, I think even his hair danced. "Connor," he said to me. "I have held my last fundraiser, kissed my last ugly baby and laughed at the last shitty joke. In about a month, my daily commute will go from eighty miles to less than five. My wife will be ecstatic. I might even get lucky tonight."

That was almost twelve years ago.

Today, a few minutes before noon, I sat in The Quarterdeck, a popular restaurant in downtown Falmouth waiting for McNulty to arrive for the lunch I promised him in my phone call from Vinnie's office. I asked Francis to see what the probation officers thought of I.RISE, and if they knew whether Judge Fisher or anyone else had promoted the organization when it was established. He said it wouldn't take long and he'd meet me for lunch today at "The Deck."

The Quarterdeck's sloping ceiling, fashioned from thick old ship timbers, gave diners a cramped feeling, as if on the below deck of a sailing vessel, which, of course, was the point of the name and ambience. Several stained glass windows commandeered from a church provided some light during lunch hours. Evening diners often used cell phones to read the menu. I had no such problem as the light rain that started the day had succumbed to brilliant sunshine and a breeze carrying a hint of humidity. I sat at a small table near the bar sipping a tonic water with a lime, but no Tanqueray. If I have as much as a swallow of alcohol in the middle of a work-day, I spend the rest of it looking for a place to nap.

McNulty walked in at noon. Like the opening notes to a popular song, his personality filled the room. He flashed me a quick smile of recognition and turned his attention to those seated at the bar. "Hey Jimmy, howareya?" he barked to a man on the third stool, their eyes connecting in the mirror behind the bartender. McNulty walked over and patted Jimmy's shoulder, while his attention focused on the woman beside him. "Hey Darlin'," he said, offering his cheek for an air kiss. I stood as he drifted over to the table. McNulty was somewhere in his sixties, about six-one and, a few more pounds over two hundred. He had a round friendly face, dark brown mischievous eyes and his thick hair was the color of wet sand. We exchanged a hug. "Connor, great to see you. Been too long. The hell you up to these days?"

"Life's good, Senator," I said. "I work part-time for a lawyer and still do some lobbying for the Clean Environment Campaign," I said. "Gets me into The Building, one or two days a week." Anyone who has ever held office, lobbied or worked in the State House always calls it The Building.

McNulty nodded approval and sat down. He immediately turned and signaled to the bartender. "Coffee, Billy. The usual." He turned back and winked. "Strong, black and with a shot of Jameson." His eyes glanced a menu and returned to mine. "How's that pretty wife of yours? Still in health care? The hell she see in you?"

"Told her I was rich," I said. "Abby's great and still in health care. How's your family? Everyone good?"

"Just me and Maureen, now. The kids and four grandchildren are all off Cape. My oldest grandson is captain of the Bentley Baseball Team. I've got one who graduated from URI, one in high school and one in the seventh grade. They're all in Massachusetts, which is nice, but nobody seems interested in living on the Cape. So, we have to go off Cape for dance recitals and birthday parties. Not that I'm complaining, but, of course, I am." He laughed.

"We were both smart enough to marry up," I said.

A waitress came to the table with a steaming mug of coffee and placed it before McNulty.

He took the careful sip people do when confronting a cup of hot liquid. The mug disappeared in his large hands. "Perfect Billy," he shouted without turning. "Connor, let's order so we can get down to business." He looked up to the waitress and handed her his menu. "I'll have the scallop salad, house dressing."

I ordered a corned beef Reuben without fries and asked that the sandwich not be cut. We sat in silence as the waitress walked back to the bar. McNulty took over. "So, what's up?"

"As I said on the phone, this is off the record. Your name or the probation department will not be used. I'm doing research on OUI Programs. I came across one called I.RISE. Heard they get a lot of cases from Falmouth. What'd you know about them?"

"You didn't get nabbed on an OUI?" McNulty said. "I know I asked earlier, but c'mon who the hell researches drunk driving programs?"

"This isn't about me or anyone getting arrested for OUI," I said. "Just want to know about I.RISE."

"That's easy," McNulty said. "It's a good organization. Easy to work with, they return our calls and file reports on time. For the most part, the folks we send them haven't complained about the program, or the fees." He took a larger sip of his coffee. "Of course, drunks are chronic complainers, but they seem to like I.RISE, more or less. Used to get all of our cases, until a program, opened up in Mashpee a couple years ago. Connor, I'm not sure what you're really asking. What's up?"

"Did you find out if Judge Fisher was involved with I.RISE or promoted it?" The front door opened and the screech of chair legs scraping along floors and the movement of bodies filling empty spaces surrounded us.

"Fisher," McNulty said with a shake of his head. "Christ, he's over ninety and still hanging around the courthouse every day. Even has an office. I talked to Gus Ferraro, he's older than dirt. Gus was around when I.RISE first started. Know him?"

"Only the name," I said.

"Gus says Fisher pushed hard for OUI referrals to go to I.RISE. Fisher was presiding justice in those days, so his words mattered. Of course, back then the only choice for somebody bagged for drunk driving was a program in Hyannis or I.RISE. So it wasn't a hard sell. When it first started, I.RISE even held classes in Falmouth at a storefront it rented in the old theater block. That helped its business." McNulty picked up his cup. "Particularly with the folks who picked convenience over the risk a neighbor might see them at a drunk driving school." He took a deep sip and returned the cup to a stained napkin. "Later, I.RISE ran a free shuttle from the courthouse to New Bedford. That helped business."

"Fisher do anything else?" I said.

"Gus says Fisher would arrange tours of the facility in New Bedford for the POs. A dog and pony show, but there's nothing untoward about that." McNulty shrugged. "I.RISE puts a lot of effort in getting business. Like I said, they're easy to deal with. One of their folks comes around the court every month or so to leave information, shoot the shit with the POs. "Like the salesmen who visit customers to catch up, stay in touch. That kind of thing."

The waitress came over with our lunches. My sandwich was cut diagonally and surrounded by fries. I accepted the plate with a smile and asked for another tonic water. She placed a plate before

McNulty and backed away. McNulty looked at me and smiled. "If you tell a waitress to substitute, like a salad instead of fries or squash instead of peas, they write it down and remember. If you tell them not to do something like no fries and don't cut the sandwich, they don't write it down and they forget."

"I'll try to remember that next time," I said.

"Write it down, or you'll forget," McNulty said around a grin.

"Know if Fisher had any help with promoting I.RISE?"

McNulty nodded and reached over to stab a few of my fries with his fork. "He had some members of the local bar pushing. Guys like Paul Cunningham, Dick Jendrysik, maybe a few others. But most of the work was done by either Fisher or I.RISE itself."

"Know if Vinnie Preskin got involved?" I asked as casually as I could.

"Preskin?" McNulty said with more than a hint of derision. "Smoother than shit on the sole of your shoe." He stabbed two more fries. "His brother, Bobby Shits, is mob connected."

"Not his brother," I said with some vehemence. "It's his cousin, Bobby Morelli." I picked up half of my sandwich. "We don't pick our cousins, and Vinnie has nothing to do with him." I bit into the sandwich. Delicious.

McNulty shrugged a concession. "Don't pick our brothers or parents either. In any case, I haven't heard Preskin's name in connection with I.RISE. I don't think he does criminal work. Not sure what he does, besides golf and make money. He might have had an ownership interest in the old theater block, where I.RISE once ran classes, but fuck, Preskin owns property all over Falmouth." He smiled. "He'd buy the ocean if he could find somebody to sign the deed." McNulty shoved the fries into his mouth and chewed. "Connor, the fries are good. Should try some."

"Maybe I'll just stab one of your scallops instead," I said.

"Good way to lose a finger,' McNulty said. "I ordered these scallops, you didn't order the fries. They're fair game."

I grinned. "When you're right you're right. Anything else you can tell me?"

McNulty stared at me. "Connor, what the fuck is going on?"

———

Twenty minutes later, I drove Francis McNulty back to the Falmouth District Court. I never told him what the fuck was going on or anything more than I had been asked to learn what I could about I.RISE. McNulty knew there was more to the story, but he was not the type to keep pushing. He also knew "off the record" ran both ways, and he would let the matter drop unless I raised it again. The rest of our lunch was spent trading stories about experiences in The Building and political and sports predictions neither of us would remember. I pulled in front of the courthouse, and we exchanged the obligatory promises to get together soon. I watched him through the windshield of my car. He walked towards the front door and my attention was drawn to the two men approaching the same door. McNulty smiled as he held the door for them to enter.

Anthony Novello and Ed McGonagle.

Chapter 32

Judge Tobias Fisher, impeccable in a dark blue suit, crisp white shirt and a yellow power tie with small dark blue dots, stood behind his desk when Novello and McGonagle entered his office at the Falmouth Courthouse.

Novello scanned the desk. No loose papers, folders or books. The computer on the credenza was off. A *Boston Globe* and the depression in an old leather chair told him the Judge had been sitting and reading the paper when his secretary announced their arrival. He then moved to the desk to greet them. In the time it took Novello to make this assessment, he, McGonagle and Fisher met at a spot three feet in front of the desk to exchange handshake

Novello wore a dark brown double-breasted suit, pale yellow shirt, and olive tie. McGonagle arrived in tan slacks, blue blazer, white shirt and no tie.

"Well, this is a surprise," Fisher said. "You should have called. Almost took today off." He extended a thin, oily hand to Novello.

"Anthony Novello, Judge, thanks for seeing us." He gestured to McGonagle. "You remember Detective McGonagle."

Fisher smiled and extended his hand to McGonagle. "I do, nice to see you again." Fisher extended an arm towards the sitting area, an old leather sofa and two chairs. "We'll be more comfortable over there. May I get you anything? Coffee? Tea? Ice water?"

"We're fine," Novello said. He went over to one of the chairs and sat down. McGonagle steered Fisher to the sofa and took the other leather chair.

"Think I'll have an ice water, if you don't mind," Fisher said. He walked over to his desk and pushed a button on the black desk phone. "Muriel, I'd like some water when you get a chance." He covered the mouth piece with his hand. "Sure I can't get you something?"

"We're good," McGonagle said.

Fisher smiled and hung up the phone. He walked over to the sofa and sat on the cushion closest to Novello's chair. "So, Detective Novello, what brings you to Falmouth?"

"You," Novello said. "We have additional questions we need to ask."

"Fine," Fisher answered with a smile. "Can you tell me what progress, if any, you've made on Judge Bartoni's murder?" He paused a moment then waved his hands, as if to erase his words. "No, of course you can't. Forget I asked. Sorry, I know better than that. It's just," Fisher shivered as though struck by a bolt of ice. "Now his wife is murdered. Horrible turn of events. I hope I can be of some help. I believe I told Detective McGonagle everything I know." Fisher gave out a self-evident shrug. "But go ahead, I'm at your disposal."

"Well, first could you tell us about the last time you saw Judge Bartoni," Novello said.

"You're referring to the lunch at the restaurant in Plymouth I told Detective McGonagle about?" Fisher said.

"I'm referring to the last time you saw Bartoni," Novello said.

"That was the last time," Fisher said. He glanced at his watch.

"Tell me. I wasn't there when you met with Detective McGonagle."

Fisher shrugged and for the next five minutes repeated what he told McGonagle. Novello remained silent throughout. McGonagle kept his eyes focused on his small notebook, occasionally jotting a few words. When he finished, Fisher crossed his arms and waited.

"How well did you know Mrs. Bartoni?" Novello said.

"Hardly at all," Fisher answered, confusion creeping across his face. "I think I met her at his swearing in, but, frankly I have no real memory of even that."

"Know her maiden name?' McGonagle said.

"No. Should I?"

"Ever been in her home?" McGonagle said.

"Just said I didn't know her. Why would I be in her home?" Fisher unbuttoned his suitcoat and crossed his legs.

"Her husband's home, as well," Novello said. "Two of you were friends. Weren't you?"

"I was never in the house." Fisher said. He glanced at his watch.

"Know where the Judge lived? What city or town?" McGonagle said.

"No," Fisher said. "Well, I don't think so. He might have mentioned it off hand, but I don't remember. What the hell does this have to do with anything?"

"Bartoni was murdered in his home," McGonagle said. "Pretty sure the news coverage of the crime mentioned it was in Concord. Just a little surprised you didn't remember. He being a friend and all."

"Are you being cute with me, Detective?" Fisher said. "I lost a good friend when Robert was murdered. I didn't read every fuckin' word of every article. If you don't have more important questions to ask or comments to make, you can get the hell out of here." Fisher pointed a finger at McGonagle. "You're a smartass, Detective. I knew it when we first met, and everything you've said today confirms it. You and I are done, Detective." To emphasize the point, Fisher shifted his body towards Novello.

"You drive, Judge?" Novello said.

"I'm almost ninety-one, Detective."

"You drive?"

"No," Fisher said.

"But, you have a driver's license," Novello said.

"I do," Fisher said. "It expires in September, next year. Want to see it?"

"You have a car?" Novello said.

"Yes," Fisher said. "Probably wouldn't start, it's been so long since it was used. I think it's boorish to ask people to drive me somewhere, without at least offering to provide the car. Most people decline the offer. They prefer driving their own car."

"The Rothwell Foundation mean anything to you?" McGonagle said.

"I said I'm done with you," Fisher said.

"Okay," Novello said, rising from his chair. "We'll finish this in Boston, some other day."

Fisher sighed. "I don't believe I have ever heard of The Rothwell Foundation."

Novello sat down. "What about I. RISE?"

"It's an alcohol and substance abuse program in New Bedford. A very good one, I'm told."

"When was the last time you saw or spoke with Carmela Bartoni?" McGonagle said.

Fisher stroked his chin in thought. "I don't know if I ever spoke with her," Fisher said. "I told you I may have met her at Robert's swearing in ceremony, but I can't even be certain of that."

"Did you see her at Judge Bartoni's funeral?" Novello said.

The door opened and the woman who had let Novello and McGonagle into the office came in with a bottle of water and a glass full of ice. She placed it on the coffee table in front of Fisher.

"Thought you had forgotten," Fisher muttered. He gave her a dismissive wave. She turned and walked out of the room. Fisher unscrewed the cap and took a long drink from the bottle. When he finished, he emptied the remainder into the glass. He looked towards Novello. "Where were we?"

"I asked if you had seen Mrs. Bartoni at her husband's funeral."

"I didn't go to the funeral," Fisher said. "Couldn't get a ride."

"When's the last time you spoke with anyone at I.RISE," McGonagle said.

Fisher shrugged and ran the fingers of his right hand through his hair. "I don't know, Detective. Jesus, you think I keep a diary? Certainly not since my retirement. Maybe as long as fifteen years, more or less." Fisher turned towards Novello. "What the hell do any of these questions have to do with Chief Justice D'Alessandro or the matters I told Detective McGonagle a few weeks ago?'

Novello smiled. "We appreciate your patience, Judge. We have our own way of doing things, and I know it may seem a bit scatter shot to you, but everything we've asked is important, and it's helpful to the investigation to get your answers. We're almost done."

"Thank you for that, I guess," Fisher said. "I want to help."

"Ever own a gun, Judge?" Novello said.

"What?"

Novello heard the response as the transparent "what" of a person who is afraid he's made a mistake. "Simple enough question, Judge, ever own a gun?"

"No. Well, maybe a BB gun as a youth. Does that count? How about a slingshot?"

"Ever shoot a gun?" Novello said.

"Do carnivals count?" Fisher said. "Think I may have shot one at one of those booths they have. That'd be more than fifty years ago."

Novello remained expressionless. "When's the last time you shot a gun?"

"I don't know if I have ever shot a gun," Fisher said.

"Ever talk with Judge Bartoni by telephone? Or, were all your meetings face to face?" McGonagle said.

"I may have," Fisher said. "I don't remember."

"Did Judge Bartoni ever talk to you about his wife? Her interests? Background? What she did?"

Fisher took a sip of water. "Not that I can recall. I know I don't know or remember much about her, her interests or what she did."

"You own or have any interest in any real estate?" Novello said. "Other than your home on Linden Road."

"No. I am a man of relatively modest means," Fisher said. "I never saw the need to acquire properties."

"Ever been to Sleepy Hollow Cemetery?" Novello said. "It's in Concord."

"No," Fisher said. He took a long swallow of water from the glass, emptying it.

"Anything you want to add to your previous statements that we haven't covered today? Novello said.

"Far as I can tell, you haven't covered any of the matters we previously discussed," Fisher said.

"Anything you want to add?" Novello said.

"No."

"Have you seen or had any contact with either Chief Justice D'Alessandro or Win Allen, since you gave Detective McGonagle your statement?"

"No," Fisher said. "Don't you think I would have mentioned that?" Fisher said, trying for incredulity and succeeding only in sounding afraid.

"Anything else?" Novello said to McGonagle.

"I think we're done," McGonagle said. He rose from his chair. "Thanks, Judge. Good to see you again. Always a pleasure."

Novello saw the faint surprise at the abrupt ending of the interview sprint across Fisher's face. He stood and extended his hand. "Thank you, Judge. You've been generous with your time and answers. We can see our way out."

———

The door closed behind Novello and McGonagle. Fisher stood in front of his desk, his arms crossed, and stared at the closed door. "Assholes," he muttered to the empty room. He walked over to the chair Novello had occupied and sat down.

———

Twenty-three minutes later, McGonagle drove over the Bourne Bridge on the way back to Boston. The two had not exchanged a word since leaving the courthouse. McGonagle knew Novello needed quiet and some time to absorb all that had been said. He sensed Novello stirring in the seat and looked over. "Ready?"

Novello nodded. "Ready."

"You think he's lying?" McGonagle said.

"He knows more than he's telling us." Novello said.

"I saw some tells," McGonagle said. "But I'm not sure about anything. You're positive?"

Novello tapped his fingers on his knees. "You know, when you think you remember a past event, you're really remembering the last time you remembered it. So details from the actual event tend to fade with each repeating. Unless, instead of remember something you saw or experienced, you're simply reciting the lines of a script. Memorize your lines and deliver them. Comes out almost the same each time."

"The nose knows," McGonagle said.

Novello laughed. "That's a story that got pushed when I made the mistake of telling a newsman that lies can make people stink. Some folks do sweat and stink when they lie, but there are a lot of other tells to look for. Fisher showed almost all of them."

"But."

"Can't prove a fucking thing," Novello said. The silent beat of his fingers continued. "But we will. Take that to the bank."

Chapter 33

McGonagle flashed his badge to the attendant at the Bowdoin Street entrance to the state parking garage. The yellow mechanical arm rose, and he pulled the two year old black Ford Explorer with the pale blue Commonwealth of Massachusetts plates into one of the spaces reserved for the Homicide Bureau. Apart from his declaration that Fisher knew more than he was saying, Novello had been quiet the entire ride from Falmouth. McGonagle was neither surprised nor disturbed by his friend's silence. He knew Novello would not start a conversation until he chewed and digested all he learned from Judge Fisher.

"Walk with me," Novello said when the two met at the rear of the car. They walked passed the attendant and through the garage opening they had entered. Novello paused a moment and stretched, flexing his shoulders and back muscles. They turned left and walked up Bowdoin towards the State House. Novello stopped and used his arm to stop McGonagle. "Ed, tell me what you think." He started walking. "Nice job getting under Fisher's skin."

"That was easy," McGonagle said. "He pisses me off. Officious little prick."

They turned into the private parking area behind the front building of the State House, showing their badges to the Capitol Police Officer, who smiled and waved them on. "You think Fisher was lying or telling the truth as he knows it?" Novello said.

"Well, he sure as hell didn't waste any time emptying the bottle of water," McGonagle said. "But two cops showing up unexpectedly would make the Pope nervous. Not sure we should put too much stock in that." They walked under the arch connecting the front State House Building to the back. "He answered questions with questions. 'Do you own a gun?' 'Do BB guns count?' 'Ever shoot a

189

gun?' 'Do carnivals count? Preskin said the Judge rarely drove – his words – especially long distances. Today, Fisher said he doesn't drive and people sometimes drive him in his car. Small inconsistency and so what? He put away the notebook. We got a few may haves and don't remembers. There was some grooming and he gave too much detail on some things. I'd have to check my notebook."

"But," Novello said.

They stepped out of the shadows of the arch. McGonagle stopped and turned to Novello. "I saw the signs of deception, but frankly I'm having a hard time getting my head around the idea he murdered either Bartoni, let alone both of them."

"Because he's ninety-one and a retired judge?" Novello said.

"No, because he came to us and gave us information that proved to be accurate," McGonagle said.

"Remember the duffel bag," Novello said. "Why would Carmela take the duffle bag?"

"I know, I know. We've talked about this, but it's still hard to see that little prick as a cold blooded murderer."

A large shiny black Cadillac Escalade came up Dern Street and turned towards the arch. It stopped in front of them. The uniformed state police officer at the wheel gestured with his fingers for them to approach. "It's the Governor," Novello muttered to McGonagle.

———

Ten minutes later, Novello and McGonagle sat on opposite sides of the mahogany conference table in the Governor's third floor State House office. Governor Paul Francis Concanon, a wiry, solemn man in his mid-sixties, with thinning hair and blotchy Irish skin, sat at the head of the table, flipping through a pile of pink "While you were out" messages. Novello's eyes scanned the office. Six or seven years ago it had undergone a substantial renovation, which included refurbishing with late seventeen hundred period appropriate artifacts, furniture and wallpaper. Novello thought the office looked like the waiting room at a Parisian brothel.

Concanon looked up from the messages. "What can you tell me about the Bartoni investigation?" Concanon stared at Novello. "Bartoni was a friend, and you and I have worked together on some pretty sensitive matters. You know I can keep my mouth shut."

"We have, and I do," Novello said. "And, we've been wanting to speak with you since Flaherty told us of your friendship with Bartoni."

"You mean when Flaherty complained about my frequent calls for information," Concanon said.

"He might have mentioned that" Novello said. "There's not much to report. The investigation started in one direction as a result of information we received that Bartoni was looking into a serious scandal, the details of which you don't want to know." Novello paused to let Concanon react.

"Go on," Concanon said.

"While we're not done looking at the scandal, Mrs. Bartoni's murder has caused us to look in other directions."

"You think both were killed by the same person?' Concanon said.

The drone of ringing phones, a cranky copier and scurrying footsteps infiltrated the office.

"We're not sure," Novello said. "But we're certain the killings were connected, and we believe they may involve something Judge Bartoni was investigating. In broad strokes, Mrs. Bartoni might have been caught up in something. The Judge discovered it, perhaps not even realizing his wife was somehow connected. It got both of them killed."

"Jesus. This is not what I expected. You have any suspects?" Concanon said.

"Rather not throw names around until we do some more work, but our eyes are on someone. Want the name?"

"No." Concanon expelled a loud gust of air. "This is incredible. How can I help? You need resources? More people?"

"Tell us what you know about Judge Bartoni, and his wife," McGonagle said. He fished a small notebook from the inside pocket of his blazer.

"Everyone knows the Judge was a media hound and more than a little self-centered," Concanon said. "But he was also very smart, and he was passionate about the criminal justice system." Concanon glanced at his watch. "I've got time," he said more to himself than to Novello or McGonagle. "When I was district attorney, we'd occasionally meet to discuss the ADAs that appeared in his courtroom. Who was good, who needed help, who was too fast or too slow, prepared or not prepared. He told me he wasn't looking to get anyone fired, but to let me know who needed help with courtroom presence or strategy."

"He was a prosecutor's judge," Novello said.

"Everyone says that," Concanon said. "And, I guess it's true because of his tough sentences. But I discovered he also met with the head of the Public Defenders' Office to discuss his people. Bartoni believed the system only worked if both sides were smart and strong."

"You have more recent contacts with Bartoni?" McGonagle said. "Been a long time since you were DA."

Concanon nodded. "We'd run into each other every once in a while – usually on the street. We'd give each other a hug, swap a few stories and promise to get together soon, but we rarely did. We'd see each other at bar association dinners or events. That changed when I became governor.

"Tell us," Novello said.

"He sent a congratulatory note and said he wanted to meet or speak with me. He asked me to send him the name and phone number of the person he should call to set up a time and date for either a face to face or a call. He added his private number in the event my staff person would rather call him directly." Concanon smiled at the memory. "So, of course, I did what Bartoni hoped I would do, and I called him."

"When was this, if you remember," Novello said.

"Early January, two years ago. We set up a meeting for here," Concanon gestured to indicate his office. "Pretty sure the meeting was in January. I'll have someone check the appointment book and telephone log and send you the dates. I know sometimes the dates becomes important."

"You were a good prosecutor," Novello said.

"Anything of interest discussed at this meeting?" McGonagle asked.

"There was," Concanon said. "The Judge was anxious about retirement. I think he was sixty-six at the time, so he had four years before he hit the mandatory age. But he was nervous or worried, and he wanted to know what he'd be doing once he turned in his robes. It bothered him."

There was a soft knock on the door, and a young woman entered. Her face twisted into apology mode for the interruption. "I'm so sorry, Governor, the Speaker would like a word with you."

"Maura, no need to apologize for doing your job. Tell the Speaker, I'll come to his office in twenty minutes. If he's on the phone, tell him I'll call him in twenty minutes."

Maura backed out of the room, her apologetic face replaced by a veil of uncertainty."

Concanon smiled. "Maura's my niece. The oldest daughter of a brother who rarely spoke to me until I became governor."

"Funny how that happens," Novello said.

"Yeah, hilarious," Concanon said. "She's a nice kid. Not her fault her father's an asshole." He gave a dismissive wave. "Besides, what's the point of public service if you can't help family?" Concanon shook his head, as if to clear it of extraneous thoughts. "Let's get back to Bartoni."

"You said he was concerned about hitting retirement," Novello said.

"Well, the long and short of it is I suggested I could appoint him to lead a special commission to study some issue of public importance. It would carry a small stipend and be set up to last a few years. It would keep his name in the news and allow him to feel busy and important. Of course, I didn't say it that way, but I wanted to be helpful. I felt bad for him. I reminded him we had plenty of time, and he should put some ideas on paper. You know, the subject matter, the membership of the commission, maybe even funding requirements. That sort of stuff."

"Was he interested?' McGonagle said. Did he ever follow up with a subject?"

"Very much so. Wait a minute!" Concanon said, his body shifting upright in the leather chair. "You said earlier Bartoni was investigating something? What?"

"We're not sure," Novello said. "At first, we believed it had something to do with judges, lawyers and the *Sheehan* case. Now, we're not so sure, but we do believe he was investigating something and keeping notes or a journal on whatever it was."

"The *Sheehan* case?" Concanon said. "This is bizarre. How does the *Sheehan* case fit into this?"

"Sure you want to know?' Novello said.

"You're right, forget I asked. Bartoni never mentioned the *Sheehan* case to me, but for several weeks after our meeting in January, he would send notes suggesting topics for the special commission. But they were always too grand. A reorganization of the trial court, or the juvenile court system. If I were to propose something that big, all hell would break loose and everybody and their brother would be scrambling to get their interests protected by getting a seat on the commission. It would die of its own weight. I told him he should consider a limited and concrete subject."

"The Judge ever come up with anything?" Novello said.

Concanon nodded. "He did and frankly I was surprised by what he suggested." He pushed a button on the telephone console at the head of the conference table. "Sam, call the Speaker and tell him I'm caught up in something. Ask if I can call or meet with him at five today. Thanks." Concanon hung up and looked at Novello and McGonagle. "You guys want something? Water? Coffee?"

The question reminded Novello of his meeting with Fisher earlier. "Water would be nice. Thanks."

Concanon pushed the button again. "Sam, bring in some water when you get a chance." He hung up. "Should have thought of this earlier."

"No problem. As long as it's cold," McGonagle said.

Concanon laughed. "I was talking about Bartoni's topic for the commission not the water."

"Well, we want both," Novello said.

———

Just under sixty miles away, in the back room of an auto body shop on South Main Street in Fall River, Anthony Bonfiglio sat in a tufted leather tub chair across a table from Bobby Morelli. The room smelled of spray paint, diesel, and coconut. Morelli's nose was heavily bandaged in white and protruded from between a blackened right eye and a large cone shaped patch covering the left eye. The bandage on his nose appeared to be part of the elaborate eye patch. Morelli was dressed in his usual garb: sweat pants and a hooded sweatshirt. He sat on a matching tub chair fidgeting his fingers and moving his tongue in a losing effort to moisten his mouth.

"You let some wiseass jerk give you a beating in your own club? 'Smatter with you," Bonfiglio barked at Morelli.

"He suckered punched me, Mr. Bonfiglio," Morelli said. It sounded like: thucker funched me.

Bonfiglio wore tan slacks, running down to brown tasseled loafers and no socks. He wore a large, untucked tan and yellow shirt with glossy buttons down the front. He looked like what he was: a mob boss. But, he was a smart, hard kind of hoodlum. One who worked his way up; who had shot and been shot. His muscles had gone soft and he now weighed close to two-fifty. Still full of the piss, but not much vinegar. His thick, scarred neck supported a large round face creased like a walnut. It rested on wide sloping shoulders. At six-one, he was square with a large nose and heavy lids over dark eyes. Thick, oily black hair was combed straight back and stained the back collar of his shirt. His fingers resembled the short stubby cigars he smoked.

"I asked you to keep an eye on Anthony Novello. I wanted to know why he was in Falmouth. Instead, you let some asshole beat you up. Because of Connor McNeill? Who the fuck is Connor McNeill? Why's he working with your cousin? Why's he important to Salamanca? Why's he breaking bread with Novello?" Bonfiglio leaned forward. "Bobby, talk to me. The fuck is going on?"

"Don't know if McNeill is important to Mr. Salamanca. Guy only said he was important to him. This guy works for Mr. Salamanca. Said he'd kill me if any harm came to McNeill or his wife. That's when he sucker punched me. I'm gonna kill the prick," Morelli said. "I promise you that Mr. Bonfiglio."

"Ya don't even know his name," Bonfiglio said. "You let me talk with Sally. We're not gonna kill anyone who works for Sally without an okay. Not gonna start a fuckin' war because you let someone smack you around."

"He sucker punched me," Morelli said.

Chapter 34

Three bottled waters arrived less than a minute after the Governor's request. Sam placed them in front of Concanon, and whispered, "Speaker says five is fine, and he'll come here."

Sam retreated from the room. Concanon started talking before the door closed.

"Bartoni called one day. Maybe a year, year and a half ago. I'll get you the specific date. He wanted to use the commission to examine the criminal justice system's treatment of drug offenders. Bartoni thought the jails and prisons were overcrowded with people who didn't belong there. I told Bartoni I liked his idea and suggested the idea of drug courts and other programs to deal with non-violent drug offenders. I reminded him his reputation of being tough would provide credibility to the idea of pushing treatment." Concanon paused as if seeking a reaction to his sage political advice.

"Makes sense," Novello said. "What'd Bartoni think?"

"He agreed and seemed to be excited about the fact we were making progress on the idea of the commission." Concanon laughed. "By this time, Bartoni was referring to it as our idea."

"What happened next?" Novello said. He glanced over to McGonagle, scribbling in his notebook.

"I made the mistake of mentioning I thought his wife's connections to the alcohol and substance abuse communities could help put him in touch with the right people." Concanon frowned as though remembering an unpleasant experience.

"Judge didn't care for that?" Novello said.

"I remember a long silence," Concanon said. "Bartoni told me Carmela was mostly involved with alcohol treatment and the charlatans – his word – who ran drunk driving schools."

Novello locked eyes with McGonagle. Neither spoke.

"Needless to say, the conversation got awkward,' Concanon said. "I asked Bartoni to send me a written outline of his ideas. I said I would have an aide flush them out for us to review, perhaps over lunch. I wanted to end the call on a friendly positive note, but I could feel tension creeping through the telephone line."

"Interesting reaction," McGonagle said.

"Well, it gets more interesting," Concanon said. "A month or so later, Bartoni sent me the outline I requested. And it was very different from what we had discussed."

"How so," Novello said.

"Bartoni wanted a special commission to review the effectiveness and cost efficiency of all the operating under the influence programs in the Commonwealth. He wanted the commission to have subpoena powers, the authority to hold hearings and to take testimony under oath. He also wanted to review probation office referrals, as well as any judicial influences over the referrals. It was surreal. He went from trying to help people with substance use disorders charged with non-violent crimes to some sort of Star Chamber to kick the shit out of OUI Programs."

"You still have a copy of the outline, or whatever he sent you?' Novello said.

"You kidding? We don't throw away gum wrappers in this place. I'll get someone to track it down and run a copy over to you tomorrow."

"Ever talk to Bartoni about this?" McGonagle said.

"Yeah. I called him the day or day after I received it. I was afraid he might leak the idea to some reporter, and I'd be chasing my ass trying to put this shit back in the tube. I politely told the Judge this was too controversial. I reminded him these programs were popular, had been around for a hundred years and I wasn't aware of anything that justified this type of investigation. And that's the word I used investigation."

"How did he react?' Novello said.

"Eventually, he seemed to agree with me. He admitted he might have gone too far. He said these programs were something the criminal defense bar came up with to let drunks keep their licenses." Concanon shrugged. "The conversation ended peacefully. He admitted he let his bias against these programs get the best of him." Concanon laughed. "He said he'd go back to his – and he called it his – idea on drug courts." He shook his head in bewilderment. "It's been over a year, and I never received anything from him. Not a call, an outline or a note. Nothing. I have to admit until today, I haven't thought about the idea of a commission or Bartoni's aversion to OUI programs."

"This is helpful, Governor," Novello said. "We don't want to impose on your time, but what can you tell us about Mrs. Bartoni? Earlier, you referred to her as Carmela. Did you know her well?"

"I knew she was a Rothwell, and had more money than God," Concanon said.

"Remember how you met?' McGonagle said.

"I do," Concanon said. "Stephanie Nelson, my Chief of the Division of Public Charities, organized a meeting with the financial officers of the public charities that register with us. The point was to provide them with some guidance on the kinds of records they should be keeping, and the laws or regulations that govern public charities. I was there just to give some welcoming remarks."

Concanon took a gulp of water. "I met Carmela at that meeting." Concanon put his hands up. "The reason I remember is the meeting began with one of those painful exercises where everybody says a few words about his or her organization. Must have been a half hour before that was finished. It's never one sentence. These people believe they're doing God's work, so they're always selling their organization as the most important, most critical group of folks that ever existed. The population they serve is the most vulnerable God ever put on this earth. Christ, I thought the meeting would be over before it began." Concanon shrugged.

"Sorry, I digress. Anyway, when it was her turn, Carmela introduced herself as Carmela Rothwell Bartoni, and described her foundation in about twenty seconds. Then, and this was classic, she said something like I came here to learn how the AG wants us to report, not to learn what every public charity in Massachusetts does." Concanon shook his head. "You can image how that was received. But, it made an impression and I still remember it." He took another sip of water. "I stayed for the entire meeting, and when it finished I asked her if she was related to Judge Bartoni. I learned she was his wife, and we had a nice, but short, conversation about her foundation's interest in alcohol and substance abuse treatment programs. She thanked me for having the meeting, told me she thought it was important. I think she may have mentioned her husband had high regard for me, but she did it in a way that made clear – at least to me – she didn't care what her husband's opinion of me was; that she would form her own."

"A no-nonsense, no-bullshit woman," Novello said.

"Exactly. You've met her?"

"Just once, a few days after her husband' murder." Novello said.

"Have any other interactions with her?" McGonagle said.

Concanon nodded. "I saw her a few times at other meetings Stephanie organized, but only to say hello. I checked out her foundation on the Internet, and read some of the reports they filed with us."

"Foundation funded many OUI Programs?" McGonagle asked.

"Don't remember," Concanon said. "I was more interested in the finances. The amount of its revenue. I knew the Rothwell family had a lot of dough, but my recollection is that the Foundation was pretty modest. Something like two or three million. If it's important, I can reach out to Flaherty and ask him to have Stephanie prepare a more detailed report for you. I don't want to go around Flaherty, unless you want me to."

"I'll ask Flaherty," Novello said. "We have a good working

relationship. Much better than I thought it would be."

"Glad to hear that," Concanon said. "Never can be sure what you'll get with Gypo. I figure the sonofabitch will be running against me as soon as he loses interest in being a bureaucratic crime fighter."

———

Anthony Bonfiglio spooned some linguine onto his fork, dipped it into a small bowl of tomato sauce, parmesan cheese; and a drizzle of olive oil and pushed the folk into his mouth. He brought a corner of the large white cloth napkin tied around his neck up to his mouth and patted his lips. "Sorry you can't enjoy some, Bobby. Maybe next time."

Across the table from Bonfiglio, Bobby Morelli sat sipping a chocolate milk shake through a straw. "Hurts to eat," he said. It sounded like furts to heap.

A thin mechanic in greased stained blue coveralls came into the room with a cell phone on a silver tray. He placed the tray in front of Bonfiglio, and backed out of the room. The mob boss picked up the phone and tapped a number. "It's me. He available?" While he waited, Bonfiglio waved off Bobby's offer to leave the table. "Mr. Salamanca, thanks for taking my call." Bonfiglio laughed and said. "Sally, it is. You know I begin our conversations with a note of respect. And, out of respect is why I am calling. A day or so ago, a fellow who once did some work for you, skinny guy with glasses and a fucked up eye, came into Bobby Morelli's club and put a beating on him."

"He sucker punched me," Morelli whispered from across the table.

"Bonfiglio gave Morelli a dismissive wave while he listened to Salamanca. "Well I'm calling to ask if this guy stills works for you and to find out if Bobby somehow disrespected you or earned this beating. Because if you don't care about this guy, and if Bobby didn't disrespect you, then I want to tell Bobby it's okay to hurt him – maybe kill him."

Bonfiglio listened for a few seconds and said, "Okay, that's fine.

I have one more question, if you have time. Does Connor McNeill mean anything to you?" As he listened, Bonfiglio's tongue briefly scanned the inside of his mouth searching for morsels of pasta. "Okay, enjoy your evening, Mr. Salamanca."

"Wish you'd stop saying this guy beat me up. He sucker punched me," Morelli said. "Nuthin' I could do."

Bonfiglio spooned some linguini. "Well now you can do something. Sally doesn't give a shit about the guy who sucker punched you, and he doesn't know McNeill. Far as he's concerned, you can hurt or kill both of them. And, Bobby, you can use the Redhead if you want." The fork full of pasta went into his mouth.

"Gotta find the prick first," Bobby said.

Bonfiglio dropped his fork on the table. "Bobby, if you put a hurt on McNeill, the guy will come and find you. So fuck up McNeill, and be sure to have the Redhead with you when this guy comes looking for you."

———

At four-thirty, Novello and McGonagle sat in the Bullpen at One Ashburton Place. Novello called Attorney General Kevin Flaherty's Chief of Staff to ask for copies of every financial report filed with the Division of Public Charities by the Rothwell Foundation.

"I have a friend at Revenue," McGonagle said. "I'll get off-book copies of the Bartoni's tax returns for the last ten years."

"If they filed separately, just get hers," Novello said. "See if he'll get you whatever her foundation and I.RISE have filed over the years."

"Done," McGonagle said as he jotted a note.

"Good," Novello said. "I've got someone putting a microscope to her bank statements, investment accounts, whatever she had. We need to send another team to the house to look for safes, or places to hide documents, thumb drives, or whatever the fuck you call them. Those two kept secrets from each other. We need to find out where they're hidden and what they are."

"The computers we found are clean. Forensics got zilch," McGonagle said.

"Tell them to start looking outside the home. The Judge had a locker, maybe Carmella had her own special place."

"Got it," McGonagle said, his nose buried in the small notebook. "By the way, on I.RISE, we set for that meeting with the Monsignor guy?"

"It's covered,' Novello said. "You and I are going to be balls deep in paper work and financial records tomorrow. Connor and Abby will meet with us about four. They'll fill us in on the Roche meeting." Novello stood and stretched both arms over his head. He sat down.

"Want to talk about Fisher and what we heard from the Governor?' McGonagle said.

"Not yet, Novello said. "I want you to take time tonight to go over everything we heard. Develop some scenarios on paper or in your head, as to what you think happened. Then we meet here tomorrow at eight, and we solve this case."

"Sounds like a plan," McGonagle said. "I'll shine up my cuffs. Maybe bring an extra pair to work."

Novello smiled. "We've learned a lot. Tomorrow's a long day, and the next one even longer. I think we're beginning to turn a corner. This case is taking shape. I can feel it coming together. I can fucking feel it."

—————

Bonfiglio's stubby fingers did not fit in a traditional cappuccino cup. So, he was sipping his favorite drink from a large white coffee mug emblazoned with a cardinal bird perched on a tree branch. Under the bird in bright red script were the words: "Good Morning Asshole."

"Tell me something Bobby," Bonfiglio said. "Besides getting sucker punched, did you ever find out why Novello and this McNeill guy were having lunch?"

"I wasn't close enough to hear anything, Mr. Bonfiglio. But Novello got there first. The McNeills came together. Dressed like golfers. The McNeill broad gives Novello a hug, so I figure it's just a social call. But, after they sat down, McNeill gives Novello one of those large yellow envelops. Looked like it had a bunch of papers in it. Novello never opened it. They're there a long time, eating and talking. They get up exchange hugs and leave about two, two fifteen." Morelli shrugged to indicate his information flow had ended.

Bonfiglio gave a satisfied nod and took a swallow of cappuccino. The red stained white napkin was still tied around his neck. He brought a piece of it to his lips. "Bobby, things are fucked up. Don't like it when things are fucked up. Who is Connor McNeill? Why is Novello meeting with him in Falmouth? Why is he working with your cousin? Why does the freak that sucker punched you care about McNeill?" He took another careful sip of his cappuccino. "I don't like not knowing the answers to these questions. Maybe you need to speak with your cousin. Understand?" Bonfiglio moved his cup of cappuccino to the side and folded his hands on the table. "Bobby, do you know the answers to any of these questions?"

Bobby shook his head. "I don't, Mr. Bonfiglio. But I'll get them for ya. Just wait and see. I'll get them."

Bonfiglio smiled. "Bobby, maybe you should use the Redhead for this. He has tools and devises that are very effective in getting information. Let him help you with this."

Morelli gave a non-committal grunt. "Thanks, Mr. Bonfiglio."

Bonfiglio nodded, his tongue resuming the jaunt inside his mouth and along his teeth. "And Bobby, I sure as fuck don't like not knowing why Bartoni and his wife were killed and who ordered it. It has fucked things up and I don't 'preciate it when things get fucked up." He took a sip of cappuccino. "Bobby, I want you to find out who killed Judge Bartoni and his wife. And I want you to have Red kill him."

"No shit, Mr. Bonfiglio," Morelli said. "Somebody killed a judge?"

Chapter 35

The next day started early for Novello and McGonagle. At six-thirty, over a cup of coffee in the Beacon Hill Coffee Shop across from Ashburton Place, McGonagle pleaded, cajoled and eventually promised a pair of box seat tickets for ten Red Sox games to his friend at the Massachusetts Department of Revenue. In return, copies of Carmela's tax returns for every year following creation of the Rothwell Foundation would be delivered to his office by nine-thirty. Ed was also promised copies of tax returns filed by I.RISE, and the EZ DUZ IT Realty Trust.

While McGonagle worked his miracles, Novello called in favors and secured the services of three forensic auditors on loan from the Boston Office of the FBI. They would review each return, and copies of all financial statements and records I.RISE or the Rothwell Foundation filed with the Secretary of State. Interns from Attorney General Flaherty's Office were assigned the task of collecting and copying these records.

At eleven o'clock, McGonagle and Novello sat across from each other at the small table in the Bullpen, a twelve inch pile of pale blue forms centered between them. These were the filings of the Rothwell Foundation with the Public Charities Division of the Attorney General's Office. Next door, the hum of copiers, printers and the muted conversations of the three forensic auditors wafted into the room.

"I feel I should have an eye shade and a pocket protector," McGonagle said.

———

Malcolm Butts was a nervous, narrow-shouldered man in a gray suit, white shirt and a pale blue tie that ended a full two inches above his silver belt buckle. He had a blond comb-over and looked to be somewhere between twenty-five and forty, Novello thought. One of those men who would never look his age. Novello had been told that if he wanted a great – not good – forensic accountant, Malcolm Butts was his man. And so, at two o'clock in the afternoon, Novello and Butts sat with McGonagle at the square table in the bullpen with a stack of tax returns, credit reports, and three tall bottles of water.

Butts looked around the small room with the hanging lamp. He picked up the leather sap Novello had placed on one of the piles as a paperweight and cradled it in his small hands. "You've squeezed out some information in this room," he said around a nervous laugh.

"Mostly atmospheric," Novello said. "But we've found a few surprises when we use the bullpen instead of one of the larger conference rooms. What can you tell us?"

"Well, I've squeezed out some information, myself," Butts said with a smile. "And I didn't need to sweat it out of anyone. Just a sharp eye, experience and this." He tapped the side of his head with his right forefinger. "I'm very good at detecting criminal activity."

"That's wonderful," McGonagle said. "And, you're going to share that information with us. Right?"

"Of course." Butts smiled his head shifting from McGonagle to Novello, like a center court spectator.

"When?" McGonagle said.

Butts seemed surprised. "Oh, I assumed you'd be asking me questions, and I'd be answering them. Isn't that how you usually work these things?"

"You can go ahead and tell us what you've learned. If we have any questions, we'll ask them as you go along," Novello said. "That okay?"

"That's fine," Butts said. Energy seemed to descend upon him. "Let's start with Mrs. Bartoni. That fuckin' bitch may be the most interesting of the lot." Then, he stood up, pulled off the clip-on tie and removed the theatrical comb-over headpiece, revealing a shaved gleaming head. "Gotcha," Butts said through a wide smile.

"Jesus Christ," Novello said around a shocked laugh. "Sure as hell did."
McGonagle doubled over in laughter.

———

After exchanging personal information, two cop stories for every
financial audit exposure of a white-collar asshole, the dog sniffing
ended. Butts picked up a tax return and began. "I reviewed Mrs.
Bartoni's tax return, and I ran, as we say in the Bureau, 'her
financials,' which is FBI speak for a sophisticated credit report."
Butts nodded, and a satisfied smile spread across his face. "She and
Judge Bartoni filed separate returns. Not unusual given the fact she
had considerably more income. I suspect she wasn't interested in
having her finances subjected to the scrutiny and exposure a state
judge might be required to allow."

"I notice you're now calling her Mrs. Bartoni, instead of 'that
fuckin' bitch'," McGonagle said.

"Well, don't wish to speak ill of the dead." Butts said.

"Kind of you," McGonagle said.

"Mrs. Bartoni paid taxes on monthly income she received from
an investment fund. She started taking withdrawals from the fund
when she hit sixty. Her father set it up the year she was born. Every
year until he died in 1986, Zachery Rothwell gifted the maximum
allowable amount in his daughter's name to the fund. Today,
principal and accumulated income total a little more than two
million dollars, all legal and all taxes have been paid. Questions?"

"So, she's rich and pays her taxes?" Novello said.

Butts squinted. "She's not Bill Gates rich, but who is? She is very
comfortable. No mortgages on her property or any outstanding
loans, but her financials do get a little hinky. I wanted to give you
the whole picture."

"Go ahead," Novello said.

"She is also a beneficiary of the Easy Does It Realty Trust. The
actual name is spelled phonetically."

"We're familiar with it," McGonagle said. "Any other beneficiaries?"

"She's the only one getting disbursements," Butts said. "Of course, she could share them with others, but she's the one declaring and paying taxes." Butts took a swallow of water. "She pays taxes on the interest income she receives from the trust. Before she died she was doing very well with Easy Does It. Distributions were in excess of a hundred grand. I'd guess the trust has holdings in excess of five million. Again, outwardly, it appears legal and taxes are being paid on the distributions."

"So when does it get hinky?" McGonagle said. "Understand, of course, I am enthralled with nuances of high finance, taxes and trusts. I mean. I could listen to this all day." He glanced at his watch. "Unfortunately, we have people coming at four o'clock."

Butts looked towards Novello. "Every team has at least one ball busting wiseass. He's yours?"

Novello smiled. "But he brings donuts."

Butts nodded. "Okay, let's get hinky." He took a swallow of water. "Mrs. Bartoni had only one credit card, and based on our review she used it infrequently, and only for those purchases where a credit card is required. Like airline tickets. I'm told her closet was full of high end clothes, yet she had no clothing store cards. Only a VISA Card that was rarely used."

"She used cash for everything," Novello said.

"Yeah, she didn't charge groceries, gasoline purchases, clothing, nothing. Christ, it's more convenient and quicker to pay for gas at the pump with a credit card. Bing bang, you're done. With cash, you've got to run to the window or into the store, wait ten minutes in line with two rednecks buying dozen scratch tickets each, and an adolescent broad with spiked hair and tattoos. The only time I use cash is for the collection plate at church."

"So, she had cash flowing into her life from somewhere, which she used for everything and didn't pay taxes on?" Novello said.

Butts nodded. "A good size cash flow, and it's been running for a good number of years."

"How long? Any idea how much?' McGonagle said.

"Based on the review of her credit activity, I'd guess it started around 1989-90, and increased about fifteen years ago. That's when almost all credit card activity ceased." Butts rested the elbow of his right hand on the table's edge and drummed his fingers on the side of his shaved head. "Hard to say how much, but given her lifestyle, and considering the Judge's income must have contributed to the household and living expenses, I'd guess ten or fifteen thousand a month."

"As much as two hundred thousand a year?" Novello said.

"Could be," Butts said. "And, we've got some questions on the Rothwell Foundation."

"Go ahead," Novello said.

"We checked all the 990s. The foundation gave some small grants to organizations that we don't think exist. Probably shells. Not enough to cause suspicion, but enough to tell us the Foundation wasn't everything it purported to be."

"If you're right we got tax fraud. She could have been siphoning or cleaning her outside cash flow through her foundation. Doesn't feel like the kind of thing that would get her killed," McGonagle said.

"We need to find the source of the cash flow. That will get us the answers," Novello said.

"And, that brings us to I.RISE," Butts said in a triumphant note.

Chapter 36

"So you've got twenty thousand in dirty money, and you want to clean it quick and easy," Butts began. "You send four guys into a casino, each with five thousand in cash. They each get five thousand in chips and go have lunch, or catch a show. They go back to the cashier and turn in their chips. Now you have twenty thousand in cash, which is clean; provided you claim it as gambling winnings." Butts extended his arms like a magician in a Ta-Dah moment. "I like to use that example because it's simple and easy to understand. It also illustrates two points. One, you have to pay taxes on the money once it's clean, or you defeat the whole point of laundering. Second, one or more of the four guys could abscond with his five thousand. So you have to set up some kind of commission for the folks who are essential to the scheme."

"We know this," Novello said in a polite tone. He figured Butts started this way for a reason.

Butts nodded. "I know you do, but I like to start with the simple and then move to the more sophisticated scheme I think may be in operation at I.RISE. Sorry."

"No need to apologize," Novello sad. "We all have our idiosyncrasies."

"Ya think?" McGonagle said, glancing at Novello.

"Okay, thanks to someone's good efforts, I've looked at tax returns filed by I.RISE, as well as their financials," Butts said. "They opened up in 1987 and almost from the beginning did very well. Too well."

"Hold on a sec.," Novello said. He stood and retrieved his phone from the inside pocket of his charcoal suit jacket. "Novello." He stood silently for close to a minute. "Thanks, good work. I'll tell Ed and the others." He slid the phone back to the inside pocket. And sat down. "Staties are searching Bartoni's house. They found ninety thousand in cash stuffed in three one-gallon paint cans in the back of an old wooden cupboard in the basement."

Butts smiled. "Did I mention I was very good at detecting criminal activity?"

———

The three kicked around theories on how best to discover the sources of Carmela's cash influx. The conversation drifted back to I.RISE and its financial success.

"I.RISE opened its doors in 1987," Butts repeated as a way of restarting. "That first year it reported revenues in excess of two million. Anything's possible, but a program targeted at a narrow population – folks arrested for drunk driving – is not going to have two million the first year."

"We can check other companies doing the same thing," Novello said.

"Don't bother," Butts said. "I'm telling you, they are getting a cash influx that makes Carmela's paint cans look like she's been running a lemonade stand. By 1990, it doubled to a little over four mil, and now it's close to ten."

"Let's say you're right," McGonagle said. "How's it work?"

"Let's say," Butts paused and looked to Novello, "give me a name."

"Salvatore 'Sally' Salamanca," Novello said.

Butts smiled. "Providence Mob boss, good choice. So let's say Sally has a few million he wants to clean. He drops seventy-five thousand in cash to I.RISE every other week. I.RISE makes up phony case files and invoices, and cooks its books to show the cash as insurance reimbursements, grants, and client payments, whatever. It keeps a percentage, say eight percent, and sends the rest back to one or more shell companies controlled by Salamanca. Maybe he or his goons are on the shell's board of directors. Maybe I.RISE is one of Salamanca's shells. There are for-profits that pay each member of its board more than thirty grand a month." He took a long pull of water, emptying the bottle. "Another way to get money back to Salamanca, would be for I.RISE to pay for fake services provided by shell corporations. Could be anything from cleaning and laundry – no pun intended – therapy services, data processing, office supplies, etcetera."

"Wait a sec," Novello said. "Somebody suggested to me I.RISE was getting paid for treatment services it never delivered, and part of the payment was being kicked back to the Archdiocese. Could that be part of the laundry operation?"

Doubt raced across Butts' face. "That's the reverse of what I described in the Salamanca hypo. I suppose it could be part of a laundry, but do you really think the Archdiocese of Boston is using I.RISE to launder money?"

"No, but could Sally be using a priest in the Archdiocese as part of a scheme to launder money."

Butts sat a bit straighter in his chair. Talk to me."

"Let's say Monsignor X is in a position to refer priests to I.RISE for treatment. Let's say he is also in charge of handling payment for those services. Father Y is referred to I.RISE for treatment of pedophilia. I.RISE sends a monthly bill to Monsignor X for these services, let's say it's six thousand a month. Monsignor X pays the bill, but does it with a check for three thousand from Archdiocesan funds and three thousand in cash from Salamanca. How would that show on the books or financials?"

"I.RISE would set up a file for Father Y. It would show a six thousand dollar monthly invoice going out to the church and coming back paid. Its books would just show the full six thousand being received, going into its general treasury, bank accounts, whatever. Or, it could send out an invoice to the church for three thousand. Then when Monsignor X delivers the check for three and cash for the second three, a new invoice of six thousand is created, never sent to anyone, but marked paid. If, as your people suggest, no services are being rendered, then the full six thousand is profit."

"You're sure I.RISE is a laundry?" McGonagle said.

"One hundred percent sure," Butts said. "Best proof, of course, is to get some weak link to talk. You could try to get a seizure warrant, but I.RISE will raise all kinds of confidentiality issues even for its fictitious clients. The court will appoint a Master or someone to go over the files you seize to help safeguard confidentiality."

"Won't be easy to convince a judge to give us even a seizure warrant," McGonagle said. "All we have is your opinion. No offense."

"None taken," Butts said.

"We could find the weak link," Novello said.

"There is another option," Butts said. "I.RISE has to create phony patient files by the barrel load to support all the money coming in and out the door. That takes time, discipline and work. The phony files are probably created by one of the dummy corporations controlled by Salamanca." Butts shrugged. "We'll keep using Salamanca as the hypothetical mastermind."

"Good as any," Novello said.

"So we look for a corporation that gets regular payments from I. RISE. I've already identified two or three candidates. My top two are Secure Data Technologies in New Bedford and Cape Business Systems in Bourne. An analyst can check out both companies, their owners, boards of directors, who owns the building and property at the addresses provided on invoices. All sorts of good stuff."

"How quickly can you do this?" Novello said.

"It's being done as we speak," Butts said. He smiled at Novello. "I'm checking all of the companies that regularly receive payments from I.RISE."

"Okay, what else is being done?" Novello said.

"If Secure Data Technologies, or one of the other companies I'm looking at is creating the fake files, they'll be sending them to I.RISE electronically. My analyst will discreetly hack into their systems and verify whether or not my suspicions are accurate."

"And if they are?" Novello said.

"They are," Butts said. "I'm very good at detecting criminal activity. And when I'm proven right, you'll have found the weak link to pull," Butts said.

"Discreetly hack? Not exactly kosher," McGonagle said.

"Says the man who got me tax returns to examine," Butts said.

Chapter 37

I drove down Beacon Street with Abby, both of us searching for the elusive parking spot. I hate driving in Boston. The streets often have no signs and the grid makes little sense. One-way streets intersect with more one-ways and, in certain areas, with trolley tracks designed to destroy tires.

Boston drivers have their own idiosyncrasies. Using blinkers is optional; a yellow light means speed up; and a red is interpreted as proceed with caution. Boston has the worst drivers because we have the worst pedestrians. Jaywalking is as common as breathing. The few who do use crosswalks, consider Walk / Don't Walk signals as suggestions. To make the driving experience worse, once you've reach your destination, parking spaces are as rare as antiquities.

A dark maroon sedan pulled out five feet ahead of us. I slammed on my brakes, put on the blinker and claimed ownership of the eight by twenty piece of asphalt in front of 489 Beacon Street. Our destination – the Catholic Chancery Office – was less than a hundred yards away. A significant victory. Close counts in horseshoes, grenades and parking spaces. We were twenty-five minutes early for our two o'clock meeting with Monsignor Roche. Abby hates being early for anything. Almost as much as I hate driving in Boston.

"Let's walk up to Mass Ave.," I said. "That'll kill some time."

"When I was in college, I used to go to a club called Crossroads," Abby said. "Just on the other side of Mass Ave. Wonder if it's still there."

"Let's find out," I said. "Good to have a goal."

We were 40 feet from Massachusetts Avenue when a black Plymouth sedan drove past us and swung into a convenient space in front of a no parking sign, a few steps ahead of us. A hand placed a POLICE OFFICIAL BUSINESS sign on the dashboard.

"We need one those," I said.

An attractive African-American woman got out wearing a dark blue blazer and tan slacks. She saw us watching and smiled. Her eyes gave us a quick scan.

"Abby and Connor McNeill?" She said.

Her smile grew larger when we answered yes.

"I'm Kenisha Williams with the Concord Police. Captain Novello asked me to join you for the meeting with Monsignor Roche."

———

At two o'clock I sat between Kenisha and Abby on one side of a large glass-top oval conference table in a front, first floor room. Tall windows provided us a view of Beacon Street and helped distract from the drab flowered wallpaper surrounding us. A sixty-something receptionist with brownish-orange hair informed us Monsignor Roche was running a bit late, but she promised he would be with us "shortly."

"We'll wait. Some coffee or water would be nice." When the woman left, Kenisha leaned in to Abby. "If they're going to make you wait, make them work."

"How much do you know about this meeting?" I asked.

"I got a full briefing, and I read what you prepared for Novello. He said to let you and Abby take the lead. I'll make the introductions, then you guys take over."

"You're being polite including me in that," I said. "Pretty sure Novello told you to let Abby take the lead."

"You're as perceptive as you look," Kenisha said.

"You *are* polite," Abby said.

We laughed. The door opened and the receptionist entered balancing a plastic tray with three bottles of water.

"Couldn't find any coffee," she said. She placed the tray in front of Kenisha and left. It was now five after two.

I took a bottle. "It's room temperature.

"She really makes you feel welcomed, Kenisha said."

"How did you know us?" Abby said. "Outside, when you got out of your car."

"Sounds like you're fishing to learn how Novello described you."

"I am," Abby said.

"He told me to look for a couple your age. Said you were attractive, exuded confidence, and you would appear as if you put some time and thought in picking out your wardrobe." Kenisha turned towards me. "Want to know how he described you?"

"No offense," I said. "I don't give a shit."

"Amazing, that's exactly what Novello said."

"Not sure I believe that," I said. "I give a shit about a lot of things, and Novello knows that. I just don't give a shit about how he would describe me."

Kenisha touched my arm. "Connor, Novello likes and respects both of you. He made that clear. I was only describing how he said you'd be dressed. Like you didn't give a shit."

I smiled. "Since you're a detective, I assume you've noticed we're both wearing blue blazers and tan slacks. Your shoes are cleaner, and probably more expensive." I was wearing brown Rockports with thick soles. They hadn't been shined since I bought them two or three years ago.

"I did notice that," Kenisha said. "You see Connor, I don't give a shit either."

We were all laughing when the door suddenly opened and a swirl of black entered the room I glanced at the rotating numbers on the small clock on a low two-shelf bookcase in the corner. 2:09.

——

His back to us, Monsignor Roche shrugged out of his long black raincoat. He turned and removed the black fedora covering his longish grey-brown hair. Carefully draping the coat over a chair he looked at us. "Hello, I'm so sorry to have kept you waiting. The

Cardinal has me running around like a Shriner's Parade." He gave a short bow. "I'm Monsignor Paul Roche, like the house pest. Hopefully more charming."

There was polite laugher, and Abby squeezed my hand. *It's him.*

I squeezed back. We simultaneously realized we were looking at the man in the picture we saw at I. RISE. He was also in the picture over the golf bags in Vinnie Preskin's office. Monsignor Roche was one of the men standing behind the trophy with Vinnie Preskin and two others at the I.RISE annual golf tournament fundraiser.

Chapter 38

Monsignor Roche sat at the head of the table, an expectant look on his face. Kenisha stood up and introduced herself. "I'm on temporary assignment to Attorney General Flaherty's Office. The Attorney General appreciates your strong commitment to treatment and to doing what is necessary to prevent a reoccurrence of the incidents all of us regret, and want to avoid."

Inwardly, I smiled at her careful words.

"With me today, Monsignor, are Connor and Abby McNeill who are helping us with the task of developing what you might call a best practices manual to help other organizations, whether religious or not, to learn from the good work you have done to correct the mistakes of the past and, as I said before, to help avoid any reoccurrence." Kenisha turned to Abby. "Abby, would you like to start?'

Abby stood, and Roche immediately signaled she should sit. "No need to stand. We can be informal and comfortable. And, Abby please tell me a little about your background, education and experience, or whatever else you might want me to know about you."

"Thank you Monsignor," Abby began. "I'm a registered nurse with degrees in Biology and Public Administration. I've worked on all sides of health care: direct care nursing, management and financing."

"That's impressive," Roche said, a smile filling his face. "Tell me about each of the positions. What you took from them, and how they made you the person you are today."

A bullshit request and question. Roche wanted to suck the time out of the meeting. The less he said the less chance for a mistake. I wasn't worried. I knew Abby would recognize the ploy. She made her living negotiating contracts with highly paid and smart health care bureaucrats, clinicians, lawyers and accountants. She wouldn't be intimated or fooled by a roman collar with a small patch of red to signify monsignor.

"With respect, Monsignor, I don't want this meeting to be about me, but about the good work the Archdiocese is doing with treatment and prevention programs. I've prepared a comprehensive bio on myself, which I'm happy to leave. Right now, I want to give Connor a chance to introduce himself. Then, we can get down to work."

I jumped in before Roche could say anything. "Afternoon Monsignor, I'm Connor McNeill. I'm a lawyer by training, and have held legal positions in the areas of public health and health care financing. I have some expertise in public policy development." I didn't offer a copy of my resume since it would reveal much of what I said was bullshit. Always safer to lie verbally. "Two things we want you to know," I said. "First, this meeting is not about looking back or assigning blame. It's about learning the treatment programs you use, what works and what you think can be improved. Second, we don't want any names. We want data, not names. Data will help us to measure or evaluate the great work you and the Archdiocese are doing." Another definition of bullshit is saying you want to evaluate something you've already called great.

Abby shuffled some papers. Roche's eyes shifted to her. A shadow of annoyance crossed his face. I suspect he thought all of this was going too fast.

"Monsignor," Abby said. "I know you use four treatment providers for most of your referrals. Do they all use the same basic approach, or is there one you think we should pay particular attention to?"

Roche shifted in his chair and cleared his throat. "Before I begin, would anyone like more water or something else?'

"We're fine," Kenisha said.

"Okay," Roche sighed. "Well, the three affiliated with the church are all fine programs, and each was providing services before I arrived. When His Eminence gave me this assignment, I searched to find what other options might be available. The Institute for Recovery, Independence and Self-Empowerment came to my attention. We've been very happy with the services they offer."

"Is the approach – I'm sorry I've forgotten the full name of that service provider," Abby said.

"You can call them I. RISE," Roche said.

"Is their approach to treatment different from the three other providers?"

Roche cleared his voice again. "I.RISE uses a holistic approach. They'll do a full assessment and then sit down with the client and develop a treatment plan aimed at his particular needs. And," Roche paused for emphasis. "The client is free to reject any part of the plan. That approach, I'm told, helps secure the client's buy-in to his own treatment."

It was the same spiel Susan Landry, the Executive Director of I.RISE, gave Abby and me when we were Pete and Amy Coumounduros looking to help our son, Brandon.

"Do you get copies of these individualized treatment plans?' Abby said.

Roche seemed startled. "What? I'm not sure what you mean. Why would I get a treatment plan?"

"Perhaps as part of a periodic report, or a monthly progress report or whenever I. RISE provides a cost statement for a particular plan," I suggested.

"Well, of course, I'm kept abreast of everything, but I think you'd have to speak with the people of I.RISE to get a better idea of the treatment options and costs."

"Perhaps you could contact them with our names and encourage their cooperation to get the information we need," I said. "Again, we don't want to see any names, just an idea as to what these treatment plans include."

"Of course," Roche said. "I'm confident I.RISE will provide whatever you need." He looked at his watch.

"Can you tell us how many referrals you've made to I.RISE?" Abby said.

Roche gave a dry little cough. "Not off the top of my head."

"Could you send it to us?" I said.

"I'll ask that something be prepared and sent to you. Don't know how long it will take. I didn't realize you'd be asking for this level of detail."

"That's okay, Monsignor," Abby said. "We can get the numbers from I.RISE. We'll also want some idea as to average length of stay if it's residential treatment."

"Again, Monsignor, if you could contact them and request their cooperation with us it would help." I said. The model of reasonableness. "By the way," I said. "Do you have a special contact at I.RISE?"

"What'd you mean special contact?" Roche said.

"The person you call to get information or if there's a problem," I said.

"No, whoever answers the telephone, is the person I deal with."

"Let's talk in more general terms," Abby said. "I've been assuming, there is no insurance coverage or any kind of third party-payment – other than the Archdiocese – for this treatment."

"That's correct" Roche said.

"So take me through the payment process," Abby said. "Do the bills come directly to you? How often? Do you make the payment or send it to someone else?"

"I approve for payment each bill that arrives. Payment is made out of a special health account I manage." Roche took a sip of water. "I send Chancery copies of all invoices, a monthly record of all disbursement, and the amount I expect to need for the next month. May I ask how this is relevant to developing a best practices journal?"

I heard more than a hint of annoyance in Roche's voice.

Abby was unfazed. "It's a part of quality assurance and monitoring, but not critical to today's discussion."

"Today's discussion?" Roche said. "I'm not sure what you mean by today's discussion. I agreed to a meeting not a continuous dialogue. We're trying to put all this behind us, not spend the rest of our lives talking or answering questions about it."

If the good Monsignor was expecting Abby to apologize or stop, he'd be disappointed.

"Well, if you're the person who approves an invoice for payment, and you write out the check, how do you go about determining if the bill should be paid? Abby said

"We, the Archdiocese that is, have a good working relationship with I.RISE. We agree to a cost and we pay our bills."

"Okay," Abby said. "Since you indicated earlier, you didn't get progress reports, how do you know Father X is still in treatment when you get a bill with his name on it?"

"I didn't say I didn't get progress reports," Roche stammered. "I told you I was fully apprised of everything. I don't carry the damn things around with me."

Abby smiled, which I'm sure infuriated Monsignor Roche, although he simply stared back. Kenisha knee tapped against mine. She was enjoying the show.

"Okay, let's move to another topic," Abby said. "Do you or I.RISE have any data on readmission rates or – and I apologize for using this word – recidivism rates?"

"I'll try to get that to you," Roche said.

"Perhaps you can add that to the cooperation letter, you send to I.RISE," I said. "I can prepare a draft for you if you'd like." Connor McNeill, available and eager to help.

"What happens once you learn a client has completed his treatment?" Abby asked.

Roche sat a bit more straight, as if uplifted by a question he knew how to answer. "We have a series of meetings before, during and after treatment. Often the individual is placed on what we call a 'restrictive ministry.'" He flashed the universal quotation sign.

"It all depends what the treatment team recommends."

"Does I.RISE have follow up or after-care program? Abby said.

"Yes, it's a very thorough, professional and competent organization," Roche said, a tone of finality creeping into his voice.

"How do its rates compare to the other organizations? Do you know the average monthly rate for a residential program at I.RISE?" Abby said.

Roche smiled as if he had been waiting for this question. "The rates compare very favorably. I.RISE is almost half of what the others charge. It's just under three thousand a month."

"Good," Abby said as if pleased by the answer. "And the rate for the follow-up or after-care programs?"

Roche shrugged. "I think it ranges from one to two thousand a month. I.RISE can tell you. But it's considerably less than what the others charge."

Just to bug him, I chirped in again. "And if you could write…"

"I know. I know, I'll send them a letter." He glanced at his watch. "Are we about done?"

I got another knee tap from Kenisha.

"Do you work with other dioceses in making referrals to I.RISE?" Abby said.

Roche shifted in his chair. "Well, sometimes I'm asked by another diocese both in and outside Massachusetts about recommended programs."

"That makes sense," Abby said. "I know priests coming out of programs in one state or diocese are often reassigned to another state or diocese."

"Nothing nefarious about that," Roche said, hurriedly. "There are a limited number of good programs. We're not trying to hide priests, as *The Globe* would want you to believe." He took another look at his watch.

"When it's a patient from another diocese or state, do you make the referral?

"I sometimes help with the logistics of getting the people together," Roche said. "I don't get a finder's fee if that's what you're implying."

"It wasn't," Abby said. "I'm just trying to get a clear picture as to how everything works."

"Do you remember how you came to learn about I.RISE?" Kenisha said.

"Probably through the Internet," Roche said. "I was doing research on a number of programs." Roche gave an exasperated look. "It was over fifteen years ago."

"So you don't remember if it was a particular person or group that brought I.RISE to your attention?" Kenisha pressed.

Roche shook his head. "No." He stared at her for probably five or six seconds. It felt like a full minute. "Do you mind if I ask you a question?"

Keisha smiled. "Sure."

"Why in the name of all that's holy is it important how I learned about I.RISE? How is that even closely relevant to writing a best practices journal, or whatever you call it?"

"It isn't," Kenisha said. "I'm just curious. I.RISE apparently does good work. You said it came to your attention. I think most people as a follow up would ask how." Kenisha lifted her pocket book onto the table, as if preparing to leave. "Must admit I'm a bit surprised you prefer not to answer, but that's certainly your prerogative."

"Just a moment young lady," Roche stammered, his face turning red. "I said I didn't remember. It was more than fifteen years ago. Don't you dare suggest I am refusing to answer." Roche turned to face Kenisha head on. "I'm not some two-bit thug, whose words you can twist to suit your own needs." Roche stood. "This meeting is over. And, don't think Attorney General Flaherty won't hear about this." He draped his black raincoat over his arm and walked out of the room.

"That went well," I said. "Don't suppose he wants me to draft his letter to I.RISE."

"What happened to keeping it friendly, non-confrontational?" Abby said.

"Relax. The meeting went exactly as I expected," Kenisha said. "He was evasive and lying from the get go. C'mon, let's get out of here. When we meet Captain Novello, you'll learn more."

"Only if we don't ask questions," Abby said.

Kenisha laughed and gave Abby a high five.

Chapter 39

When I was a state representative, I shared a small office and took home a small salary. But I had a great space in a parking garage at the top of Bowdoin Street. Abby and I followed Kenisha's maroon Toyota into that garage. We drove to the lower level and waited in the car while she removed small orange cones at the top of two spaces. The damp cool air infiltrated our car. She popped her trunk, threw the cones inside and parked her car. I drove into the space beside her. The garage echoed with slamming car doors.

"You can have the police official business sign," Abby whispered to me. "I want one of those cones."

We rode the elevator to the lobby of One Ashburton Place and avoided security by following Kenisha and her badge through a special entrance. Another elevator ride took us to the eighteenth floor and a conference room. Inside were Anthony Novello, Ed McGonagle and Attorney General Kevin Flaherty. Novello and McGonagle were side by side and Flaherty sat at the head of the table. Water bottles had been placed in front of each of them, as well as in front of an empty chair on Novello's right and the two across from him. Kenisha took the chair next to Novello. Abby and I took the remaining two seats at the table. An old school clock on the wall showed the time at quarter to four.

———

Monsignor Roche took a quick sip from a bottle of water as he listened to the voice on the other end of his phone. "Yeah, well I've had the kind of day that would depress St. Francis of Assisi," Roche said. "And it's not over yet." He listened and nodded affirmatively. "The meeting was a waste of time. I told them nothing, and, frankly, I doubt they'll be back. You'll have to take care of things at your end."

227

Roche doodled on a white note pad with the legend: From the Desk of Philip Cardinal Mulcahy. "Three of them," Roche said. "Some smartass named Connor McNeill, his wife, Abby, and an asshole cop Kenisha or Kenosha Williams. Thought she could push me around, but got her head handed to her." Roche felt his face flush and tighten at the response. He stood up from his desk. "No, no, don't worry. It didn't get out of hand. The meeting was almost over, and she made a flip remark that didn't sit well with me. I told her so, and she apologized. It's all good. Nothing to worry about. But, you have to take care of things at your end."

Roche sat back down. "Look," he said. "They can't catch me in a lie, because I didn't tell them anything."

———

"He lied his ass off," Kenisha said. She extended her arm across the table to Abby and me and said to Novello. "Connor and Abby have a picture of the Monsignor at I.RISE's opening day ceremony. And, he can't remember how he learned of its existence? Gimme a break."

"That the picture you showed me at the Flying Bridge last Saturday?" Novello said to us.

Abby said, "It is, and he's also in a picture with Vinnie Preskin at the annual I.RISE golf tournament fundraiser."

"Vinnie didn't hide his connection with I.RISE," I said. He even invited us to play in the golf tournament this year. The picture's hanging right over his golf clubs, there for all to see."

"Yeah, but Roche was lying his ass off," Kenisha said. "No way, he couldn't remember when I.RISE came to his attention. Claimed it was fifteen years ago. Bullshit. May have been fifteen years since he started sending pedophiles to them, but he was there when it opened its doors in 1987. He was connected to that organization from its beginning."

"Another thing, which may be important," Abby said. "Monsignor

Roche told us I.RISE charges less than three thousand a month for its services. Said that was about half of what the others charged. When we were at I.RISE, we saw a residential rate charge of forty-eight hundred per month. Archdiocese is getting a discount."

Novello looked towards McGonagle. "Or, the Archdiocese may not be paying the total bill, as Butts predicted." He turned towards us. "We'll get into that later. Tell me what you thought of Roche."

"Kenisha's right," I said. "He's lying about not remembering how he heard about I.RISE. He was defensive and got angry when she pushed him on his connection with I.RISE."

"And we now know he's somehow connected to Vinnie Preskin," Novello said. "At least enough to play in his foursome at an I.RISE fundraiser. And, we know Vinnie is connected to I. RISE, as a financial supporter. And, he's connected to Judge Fisher."

"And Vinnie's connected to Bobby Shits Morelli, who works for Anthony Bonfiglio, who runs the Fall River and New Bedford mob," McGonagle said.

"Hold on," I said. "Morelli is Vinnie's cousin. You're the second person in as many days to bad-mouth Vinnie to me because of his cousin. Christ, I'm connected to Vinnie. You indicting me?"

Novello stared at me. "No one's indicting anyone. We are just stating what we know to be facts. A fact that offends you is still a fact. Is any connection that's been mentioned inaccurate?"

"Morelli is a cousin not a connection," I said. "Connection implies something more than a genealogical fact. Morelli is connected to the mob. He's not connected to Vinnie." The side of Abby's knee hit mine. A signal to shut up.

"And, you know this to be a fact?" Novello said.

"No I don't," I said.

Novello smiled. I saw it as an effort to ease the tension. "Connor, you sent me a report on the possibility of money laundering at I.RISE. You added a flow chart that showed a number of connections between I.RISE, the Rothwell Foundation, EZ DUZ IT and others.

Remember those communications?"

"I do." I knew where this was going, and realized my defense of Vinnie was doomed.

"Well if we were to draw a flow chart on what we're discussing now, wouldn't you draw a line from the Vinnie Preskin box to a Bobby Morelli box?"

"I guess I would," I said. "And there may be another Vinnie connection to I.RISE. Someone told me Vinnie rented property in Falmouth to I.RISE as kind of a satellite clinic, when they first started doing OUI programs. I haven't had time to check it out."

"Good. Nice work," Novello said. "Let's move on."

Abby reached down and squeezed my hand.

Chapter 40

That afternoon, while Novello, McGonagle, Flaherty, Williams and the McNeills were discussing Monsignor Roche and I.RISE, Attorney Mitchell Isaac Garofalo sat at his oak roll top desk opening the day's mail.

Garofalo, a wiry shark in a brown suit with shiny pants, spent most days cruising the halls of the Suffolk Superior Court in Boston, swinging a battered briefcase. Fifty-six, bald with a monk's ring of tight curly brown hair, Garofalo graduated fourth from the bottom of his class at New England School of Law. He practiced law from a three-room suite above a barber shop on North Street in Boston's North End. One of the rooms was his bedroom.

Garofalo muttered to himself, a habit he picked up in law school. It helped him remember things, prepare for confrontations, and relax. Behind his back, some court personnel and courtroom spectators scoffed and underestimated Garofalo. Insurance companies and their attorneys did not. In the last eighteen months, Garofalo recovered over four million dollars, representing plaintiffs injured in automobile accidents, and a dozen or so who alleged abuse by Catholic priests in the Archdiocese of Boston.

Garofalo dropped the daily assortment of circulars and advertising materials in the wire basket in the knee hole of his desk. He separated the invoices into two piles. Those charged to his law practice he placed in a red shoe box to be paid on Friday. His personal bills went into a blue shoe box for payment each Sunday. Garofalo paid his bills by check and all of them on time. He carried zero balances on his personal and business credit cards, and he maintained scrupulous records on every financial transaction. The Internal Revenue Service audited Garofalo three times over the past fifteen years. Each audit ended with the government sending him a check.

Garofalo turned his attention to a large manila envelope with a handwritten address. It had been pushed through the mail slot of his office door. There was no postage and no return address. He opened the envelope and tipped it, spilling its contents onto his desk. A number of photographs slid from the envelope. Garofalo counted eight color pictures of Chief Justice D'Alessandro along with four pictures of Win Allen and D'Alessandro walking together and a picture of D'Alessandro exiting a vehicle with a large scarf covering her head. Garofalo peered into the envelope and removed Anthony Novello's business card. On the back was a short note: "A petition for a rehearing of the *Sheehan* case is in order. Call me for details."

"Nice," Garofalo muttered. "I smell money, impeachment and disbarment. Cool beans."

————

I kept my mouth shut and tried not to sulk. I wasn't sure why I had reacted so strongly. Vinnie had been good to me, and it felt shitty to sit around a table with folks ready to include him in a murder plot. It didn't help that a guy often compared to Gypo Nolan sat at the head.

"What's the status on the Chief Justice and Win Allen? Are we done with them or are they still in the mix?" Attorney General Flaherty said to the group. His eyes locked on Novello.

"They're still in the mix, and are being dealt with," Novell said. "Haven't ruled them out, but I want to keep the focus on I.RISE and our curious cast of characters."

"How are they being dealt with?' Flaherty said.

"Sure you want to know?' Novello said.

Flaherty answered with an I-understand shrug and silence.

I kept my eyes on Novello. Any new information or surprises would come from him. The pile of papers in front of him included the reports and flow chart Abby and I prepared. I took that as the justification for our being at the table. The other documents appeared to be a compilation of financial and corporate reports. In the middle of the pile were pale blue sheets, which were the forms tax exempt non-profits file with the Attorney General.

"Before we get started, my thanks to the Attorney General for getting us much of the information we will be discussing," Novello said.

"I can hear the word 'but' coming next," Flaherty said good-naturedly.

"Nothing wrong with your hearing," Novello said around a smile. "I'll provide a detailed briefing on where this investigation is going. The Bureau is part of the Office of the Attorney General, and you're the Attorney General. Obviously, you're free to stay. But – there's that word – you probably don't want to know all the details of what happened or what's coming next."

I assumed all this was rehearsed earlier, as Flaherty was up from his chair before Novello had finished asking him to leave the meeting.

Flaherty thanked us all and walked towards the door. He stopped behind my chair and patted my shoulder. "Connor, good to see you again. Maybe next time we'll have a chance to catch up."

I couldn't remember ever having a conversation with Flaherty. We were not friends. Former state representatives always talk to other former reps. as if family members. Part of being a member of the club. "I'd like that, General," I said. My use of Flaherty's formal title did not surprise him. He probably expected it. Not because I was a former rep., but because I lobbied. Sucking up is an important part of that club.

When the door closed, Novello spoke. "Anybody have someplace they have to be in the next two hours?"

Silence claimed the room.

"Good. Let's get started."

Chapter 41

"Let me state the obvious," Novello began. "Nothing said or shown here is shared with anyone." He looked around the room. "We know police and politicians leak like colanders, but that's not the case here. I won't tell Flaherty anything unless I'm prepared to see it on the front page of *The Globe* or *Herald.* The officers to my left and right are the exceptions that prove the rule." Novello looked at me. "Connor, if I didn't trust you and Abby, neither of you would be here."

"Thanks," I said. "Okay to take notes?"

"Sure," Novello said. He slid a green spiral notebook across the table to each of us. Yellow number 2 pencils followed.

Old school.

"The Attorney General convened a special grand jury earlier this afternoon. Subpoenas will be going out in the next day or so. Things are going to happen fast," Novello said. "We have also placed surveillance teams on certain people of interest. He looked to McGonagle. "Ed, tell them what we know. And Abby," Novello smiled, "it's okay to ask questions."

I squeezed Abby's hand.

McGonagle reached down to the floor near his chair and brought up another green spiral notebook. He opened and placed it in front of himself. "We got an off the record peek at tax returns filed by Carmela Bartoni, her parents, the Rothwell Foundation, the EZ DUZ IT Realty Trust, and I.RISE. We've arranged to have forensic accountants review these returns. We have their preliminary reactions. We'll get more information tonight or sometime tomorrow, but we don't expect them to change."

McGonagle flipped a page and glanced around. "We looked at some public records old enough to have beards. We've learned things. A lot of it is interesting and moves the investigation. We're not ready to indict, but we're confident in what we believe and that the proof is out there. We'll get it."

Because of the seating arrangements, McGonagle's eyes looked towards Abby and me. I realized that's why we were on this side of the table. When we left the meeting with Monsignor Roche, Kenisha said Abby and I would learn what she already knew. This presentation was all for our benefit. My eyes caught Novello watching me. He flashed the briefest smile and an almost imperceptible nod. I think he knew I had just figured it out. I returned a quick grin and settled in my chair. I felt bad I had pushed back on Novello about Vinnie, but the surge of adrenalin at being in the room pushed the guilt away as if it never existed.

McGonagle cleared his throat. "Remember, this investigation is fluid and I can only tell you where we think it's heading, and go from there. Mrs. Bartoni was receiving large amounts of cash. We know this. We don't know the source of these funds, but we will find out. We also know her foundation made at least some questionable donations or grants to organizations that may be shells or non-existent. We don't know how this is connected to her death, or if Judge Bartoni was aware of it."

McGonagle reached under the table and pulled up a bottle of water. He unscrewed the cap, but did not take a sip. "We're certain I.RISE is at the center of at least two separate criminal schemes, including kickbacks, fraud and whatever else a hot-to-trot prosecutor might come up with. We suspect the first one started shortly after it opened and is still going on. The second involves the priests accused of pedophilia, who were referred to I.RISE for treatment. We think Judge Bartoni was killed because he discovered, or was close to discovering, one or both of these schemes. Another theory is that he was killed by mistake. Mrs. Bartoni was the target."

McGonagle took a breath and picked up the bottle. He took a short sip. "We are certain I.RISE is a money laundry either for

Anthony Bonfiglio, who runs Fall River and New Bedford or Sal Salamanca, who runs Providence, or both. We think the mob controlled I.RISE the day its doors opened, and they are still running things. We don't know if Judge Bartoni discovered the laundry operation. But, we can't rule out he might have been killed because his investigation might expose it."

McGonagle paused. "Any questions?" He held up his palms. "I'm kidding, we're just getting started."

"This is incredible," I muttered to Abby.

"Whadya mean?" Abby said. "Except for the alternative theory that Mrs. Bartoni was the intended target, we predicted this, or at least suspected it. You should be taking a bow instead of being amazed."

My peripheral vision told me Novello was watching, and the sly grin I had spotted earlier resurfaced.

Chapter 42

Two and half hours sped by. The growl of my stomach reminded me I had skipped lunch and it was past time for dinner. I was struck by how much of the information Abby and I had gathered found its way into McGonagle's outline of the investigation. I was also struck by the lack of specific evidence, and the growing sense of frustration that while it was clear people were lying, there was little direct evidence of what was true.

Novello believed Judge Fisher lied about Bartoni's investigation, but belief isn't proof. Kenisha was certain Monsignor Roche lied about his entanglements with I.RISE. I agreed, but two people being sure someone is lying is not proof of anything. McGonagle did not appear convinced of anything other than I.RISE was a mob-controlled laundry. But which mob? Did the Archdiocese know? Who killed Judge Bartoni? Why? Who killed Mrs. Bartoni? Why? Was she the intended target all along? Did the Judge die because he opened the right door at the wrong time? For most of the meeting, uncertainty hung in the air like a coastal mist. For me, the one cutting moment had been when Novello told us within the next forty-eight hours, it would all hit the fan.

The old classroom style clock on the wall showed twenty before seven. More questions rushed through my mind. How is Judge Fisher involved in all this? Is Vinnie involved?

Are we getting anything to eat?

––––––

Bobby "Shits" Morelli drove his dark green BMW Sedan along 495, carefully keeping to the speed limit. He maintained his reasonable speed – not too slow, never too fast – the entire trip from Fall River. A ritual his occupation and the weapons in the vehicle's trunk required. Simon, the seven foot tall redhead stretched across the back seat, was an additional reason for caution.

"You okay back there?" Bobby asked. He had asked the question once before since the two left Bonfiglio's office in the back room of the auto body shop.

"You'd know if I wasn't," a thick voice answered. "No need to keep askin'."

Bobby kept his eyes straight, glancing every fifteen seconds or so at the rearview mirror. Having Simon behind him was unnerving and stupid. Bobby saw *Godfather* and *Godfather 2* a dozen times. *Godfather 3* was a waste of time. He remembered Carlo Rizzi's legs kicking the front windshield as his taunt body was being pulled over the seat by the man garroting him from behind. Bobby knew it was unlikely to happen to him while the car was in motion. But he also knew Simon was crazy.

"How much longer?" Simon asked.

"Twenty, twenty-five minutes," Bobby said. He guided his car over the Bourne Bridge. "Welcome to Cape Cod."

———

My mouth watered and my stomach growled when three pizzas and eight bottles of water arrived at precisely six fifty-nine. Conversations ceased. We got off our chairs and filled our plastic plates with slices and grabbed bottles of water. We returned to our chairs less than a minute after leaving them.

Abby leaned into me. "Novello and Kenisha are definitely an item," Her elbow went into my side.

———

The green BMW drove along Main Street, past Liam McGuire's Pub, a furniture store and an old hotel. It turned off Main at King Street, past an auto repair and lube shop and a new fire station on the right. "Not too far from here," Bobby said to the Redhead, sprawled across the back seat. "We're clear on this, right? This is my gig. I'll handle McNeill. You just be there if anything unexpected pops up."

The Redhead remained silent, his eyes taking in the small houses, most of which were dark. "Anybody live around here?" He said.

"McNeill does, and he's the only one we care about," Bobby said. The car turned onto a street and cruised to a stop in front of number 30. The house was dark and the driveway empty.

"Wait here," Bobby said. "Gonna check the garage." He got out of the car, hitched up his sweatpants, walked down the driveway, and peered into a small garage door window. He walked back to the car. "There's a car in the garage, but Mr. B said they had two. McNeill must still be in Boston."

"So," Redhead said.

Bobby started the car and backed it into the driveway of the dark house across the street. "We wait."

———

By eight-thirty, Abby and I were fourteen miles from the Bourne Bridge and Cape Cod. Traffic was light and I easily maintained a speed of sixty-eight as 495 morphed into 25. Anything higher attracts the attention of unmarked cruisers and the detectors fashioned to the dashboards of gray and dark blue state police SUVs parked in the median strip separating the north and south bound lanes.

We had pretty much exhausted our review of the meeting. What was said, who said it, and who agreed or questioned what was said. Abby and I had spoken little, preferring to take notes and watch the investigative process at work. "Surprised Judge Fisher was the only name mentioned," I said, trying to keep the conversation going. "Novello's focus seems to be on him. Got to hand it to Freddy, he was suspicious of Fisher from the beginning."

"Novello's primary focus is on Kenisha Williams," Abby said around a short laugh.

"Jealous are we?"

Abby laughed. "My affair with Novello is just a casual fling. Nothing serious. We agreed we could see others."

"Same arrangement I have with Cindy Crawford," I said. I sped into the darkness of Route 25, fat insects and road pebbles whacking the windshield like popcorn.

Thirty-five minutes later, I turned onto Triumph Street. I noticed a car backed into the driveway across from our house. The property was owned by three sisters. One was named McNeill, the other two were anonymous to me. "One of the sisters got a new car," I said to Abby as I turned into our driveway.

"BMW," Abby said. "Nice."

We got out of our car and walked towards the back door. I glanced over my shoulder at the car and the dark house. The darkness and quiet bothered me, and I quickened my pace to the safety of home.

———

"Give them a few minutes to get settled," Bobby said.

"Better to hit them while they're getting settled," Simon said. He opened the back door. The interior lights of the car had been disabled so it remained dark.

"Hold on Simon, this is my operation," Bobby said. He got out of the car just as lights came on in O'Neill's house. The two began a slow walk across the street.

Bobby felt the vibration and fished his phone from the pocket of his pants. He recognized the number and signaled Simon to stop. The two walked back to the car. "Mr. B," Bobby said. "McNeill and his wife just got home. We're ready to go in." Bobby listened for a few seconds. "Yes, Sir. We're on our way."

"What's up?" Simon said.

"Mr. B says he's got something he wants us to do. Says he knows who killed Judge Bartoni."

Chapter 43

At ten thirty, Anthony Novello and Kenisha Williams lay across the crumpled sheets in Novello's North End condominium on Richmond Street. They had arrived two hours earlier, Kenisha's first visit to his home. Twenty minutes later she took her first visit to his bed. Their initial love-making had been frantic, each anxious to explore and experience the other. The second had been a slow, tender symphony. The third had been raucous and exhausting, and had toppled a bedside lamp purchased at a charity auction.

Novello stared at the slow moving ceiling fan, his right arm draped across Kenisha's exposed left shoulders, her body turned into his. Once addicted to short thin cigars, Novello felt a nicotine craving and realized it had been a long time since he had engaged in sex. He continued to think and concluded it had been a long time since he had even kissed a woman in anything other than a perfunctory fashion. Then, it occurred to him he had never experienced the romantic stirrings he enjoyed this very instant.

"Was I snoring?' Kenisha said untangling herself from Novello's arm and a sheet damp with sweat and carrying the fragrance of her perfume. "Hope I didn't expose any of my faults."

"You weren't snoring," Novello said. "I liked everything you exposed." He grinned. "Didn't notice any faults. And, I'm a trained observer."

"Yeah, right," Kenisha said, letting the skepticism ride on her voice. She was on her side, her head propped up by her right hand. "You've never observed a naked body you didn't like." She smiled and lifted her eyebrows. "Then again, neither have I."

Novello laughed. "Hungry? I can make us omelets."

"Sounds great. Let me help." Kenisha jumped to her feet and put on a white terry cloth robe, Novello had left on a wall hook beside the bed. "Don't suppose I'm the first to wear this," she said.

"Purchased this morning," Novello said.

"Aren't you sweet? Wait a sec, you were that confident?"

"I was being prepared," Novello said. "And optimistic."

The buzz of a cell phone cut through the lightness of the mood, like turd floating in a swimming pool. They hustled over to their respective bundles of clothes to search.

"It's mine," Novello called out from across the bed. "Hey Ed, what's up?" Novello paused a moment. "Yeah, yeah, besides me."

————

We were still in our kitchen when we heard the start of the car engine across the street. I looked through the window. The car moved along Triumph Street, its headlights off and disappeared into the darkness. The house was dark. "Something's fucked up," I said to Abby.

"Maybe they were just down for the day," Abby said, doubt and skepticism wrapped around each word. "You don't think we were being watched?"

"If someone was waiting for us, why would they leave once we got here? I said. "Tomorrow, I'll check the town's tax records and get the names of the owners. Then I'll call one of them and check out the BMW. I'll be the good neighbor looking out for the owners of an empty house."

————

By ten after eleven, Novello and Kenisha were sitting at the walnut farmer's table each with a three-egg tomato, cheese and onion omelet, and a chilled glass of chardonnay. "This is great," Kenisha said. She pushed a fork full of eggs into her mouth and swallowed. "Can you tell me what Ed wanted?"

"First, I have a question for you," Novello said. "Can you get your Chief to let you in on this?"

Kenisha thought for a moment and nodded. "Both murders

occurred in Concord, and the vics lived in Concord. We certainly have a legitimate interest. I think I can get him to let me be part of this." She smiled. "You asking because you need help or because." Kenisha nodded towards the bedroom.

"Both," Novello said. "I want your help. Something's developed, and I think you'd be a good person to pursue it. Fresh eyes, that sort of thing. Ed and I may be predisposed on some things."

"But, it's the other thing as well, right?" Kenisha nodded again to the bedroom.

"Absolutely," Novello said. He lifted his glass in toast.

Kenisha lifted hers and touched his glass. She took a small sip and put it down. Okay, tell me what Ed had to say."

"You remember me telling you about Malcolm Butts, the forensic accountant," Novello said, more a statement than a question. "Well, Malcolm likes to remind us how good he is at detecting criminal activity. So he called Ed and announced the company he told us was his top pick as a shell and part of the I.RISE laundering was, in fact, a shell."

"And he discovered this how?" Kenisha said.

"He looked for companies receiving regular payments from I.RISE. Then, he asked an analyst to check out the company's financials, ownership, who they pay rent to, and other stuff."

"And he found the shell that easily? Kenisha said.

"Ed says he found two. Secure Data Technologies in Fall River, which was Malcolm's first pick, and another, Cape Business Systems in Bourne," Novello said.

"So how do we know either or both of these shells are part of a laundry operation?"

"Butts' theory is I.RISE created files for every fictitious patient or client," Novello said. "These files would have to include the kind of information you'd find in a typical patient's file. Intake forms, treatment plans and summaries, discharge statements, billing summaries, etcetera.

"Got it," Kenisha said,

"Here's the problem," Novello said. "Legitimate patient files are created over time, over the course of treatment. Since these patients don't exist, an entire file would have to be created. That's a lot of work. Butts figures I.RISE would have to use an outside source or a shell company controlled by whomever they're laundering for to create the phony files. Then I.RISE would send them regular payments under phony invoices for what would appear to be legitimate services."

"Seems too easy," Kenisha said. How'd Butts determine these companies were creating fake docs?"

"Sure you want to know?' Novello said.

"Why I asked," Kenisha said.

"Butts told us this afternoon, he'd hack the systems of any company he suspected as a shell. He figured the shells were electronically sending the fake document to I.RISE." Novello swallowed a fork full of omelet and pushed aside his plate. "Tomorrow Ed and I will visit each of these companies, find someone to brace and hopefully get enough for a seizure warrant."

"What's my job tomorrow?" Kenisha said. "You said you needed my help."

"Ed said Butts investigated these two shells. While there's more information to come, Butts gave Ed a piece of information you'll be interested in hearing. Both companies operate out of properties now owned by the Akron Realty Trust."

"Do we know the real owner?" Kenisha said.

"Not sure, but we know the person who sold both of the properties to the realty trust," Novello said.

"You gonna make me beg?' Kenisha said.

Novello took a sip of his wine and smiled. "Vincent Preskin."

Chapter 44

At seven thirty the following morning, Novello, McGonagle and Malcolm Butts sat at the same table in the Fill-A-Buster where Ed learned Win Allen was getting his ashes hauled by Chief Justice Gloria D'Alessandro. Butts and McGonagle ordered scrambled eggs, bacon and wheat toast. Novello, the three egg omelet still sitting in his stomach, had coffee.

Butts confirmed Cape Business Systems in Bourne and Secure Data Technologies in Fall River were shell companies for Anthony Bonfiglio. Both companies were privately held corporations run by known associates of the crime boss. Both operated on properties once owned by Vinnie Preskin and now owned by the Akron Enterprises Realty Trust.

"These clowns are more sophisticated than I thought they'd be," Butts said. He forked some egg onto a triangular piece of toast and carefully brought it to his mouth. "They're both emailing documents to I.RISE every four or five hours, which is no surprise. But, the docs are encrypted, which did surprise me. It's an easy code to crack, so I can tell you it's the phony patient files I predicted. We're running a bunch of the names through our data systems. We'll know more in a few hours, but I'm telling you the names and the SS numbers won't match." Butts smiled, as if waiting for an "Attaboy" or "You're amazing," from his breakfast companions.

"So we got the right companies, but we need to crack someone to get a seizure warrant," Novello said.

"True," Butts said. "Obviously, the hack wasn't legal, so it never happened, but at least you can be certain you're not hassling innocent people."

"We know anything about this Akron trust?' McGonagle said.

"Got someone good working on that," Butts said. He picked a

piece of egg off his tie. Who's this Preskin guy who sold both parcels to the trust?"

"Vincent Preskin," Novello said. "A lawyer in Falmouth. His cousin is mob connected and works for Bonfiglio. Owns a lot of property. Hard to believe he's not involved in this."

"He's the asshole who brought Judge Fisher to us," McGonagle added.

"Real estate's a nice way to launder money, and easier than having a bunch of mules running around making small cash deposits in hundreds of banks," Butts said.

"Something to look at," Novello said.

"Being done, as we speak," Butts said. "Should know more, later today."

Novello glanced at his watch. Ten before eight. "Ed, when we finish here, you head down to Fall River and pay a visit to Secure Data Technologies. I'll go to Cape Business Systems in Bourne. Call, when you're ready to go in. We want to hit these assholes at the same time." He turned to Butts. "Malcolm, you've been great. Thanks and we'll stay in touch. You know, you're good at detecting criminal activity."

Butts flashed a wide smile. "My pleasure," he said. "Actually, I'm very good at detecting criminal activity."

———

Hump Day on Falmouth Harbor. It was a few minutes past nine, on a cloudy morning that carried the hint of distant rain when I arrived at the Law Offices of Vincent C. Preskin & Associates. Last night's meeting with Anthony Novello & Associates left me too tired to respond to the alarm clock's summons at six o'clock. I slept until eight and now, as a poet might say, I was late. *The Boston Globe* on the porch told me Vinnie had not yet arrived. Vinnie is pretty loose on formalities and time schedules. As long as the work is completed and accurate billing hours are recorded, it doesn't matter to him when you arrive or leave the shingled Victorian on Falmouth Harbor. He does, however, prefer hot coffee upon his arrival, so that became my first task, after picking up *The Globe* and unlocking the door.

Vinnie had left a note on my desk saying he'd be in Hyannis most of the day. A revised "to do" list provided me research subjects that were neither daunting nor interesting. It would be an easy day. I put on the coffee and went into Vinnie's office. The golf clubs were gone, which explained Hyannis.

I went back to my desk and sat. I tossed *The Globe,* still in its delivery fold and unread, onto a side table. I leaned back in the chair, stared at the ceiling and tried to think. Yesterday's meeting hung over me like an obsessive parent. Was Vinnie a part of whatever this is? What did I really know about Vinnie? He was a Jimmy Buffett Parrot Head, who loved margaritas and golf. Who are his clients? I remembered Millie Harkins, his title examiner, kidding that Vinnie either owned or received rent from most of his clients. Had I ever met, seen or even spoke with a client over the phone? No. So what? I was a paralegal doing the grunt back room work. And I was getting paid very well for part-time relatively easy work in a stress-free, ocean harbor view environment.

What was my beef?

Francis McNulty, the Chief Probation Officer at the Falmouth District Court, told me Vinnie owned a lot of property in Falmouth; said he'd buy the ocean if he could. Jealous? Maybe. How much property did Vinnie own?

I remembered telling Novello I'd check if Vinnie owned the old Falmouth Theater block, where I.RISE once rented space for one of its OUI classes. I snapped back to an upright sitting position and turned on the computer. I went to the Town of Falmouth Website and clicked onto the link for the Board of Assessors. I bounced around several links and pages, but eventually opened an assessors' map showing the old theater block consisted of one taxable parcel. Another page told me the parcel was owned by Preskin Realty Trust. So what, I thought. McNulty said Vinnie owned property at the theater block, so if he knew, others must have. Vinnie wasn't keeping it a secret. Just as he never hid his connection with I.RISE and even invited me and Abby to play in its annual golf tournament. Were the insults Judge Fisher had hurled at him at our meeting just an act? Was Vinnie being too cute, or was he just an innocent bystander in all this?

The image of the BMW sitting in the driveway across from us floated into my head. I went back to the Tax Assessor's records and put in the address. The owner was a realty trust with a Cambridge address. Fuck. I was tired of dealing with realty trusts and got up to get some coffee. I'd deal with the BMW issue later.

After filling my cup I went into Vinnie's office and thumbed through the files scattered across his massive desk. I looked at his unopened mail, which he stored in a bright yellow flat wicker basket on the credenza behind his desk. I didn't see anything referencing Preskin Realty Trust. I pulled out from a pile of clutter a bright pink form – Vinnie's monthly client billing summary. He used an outside service to manage all of his billings and his payroll. Each month he would complete a form, which identified clients by number, the amount of billable hours and the expenses attributed to the client. He would send the form electronically to the business service and it would, in turn, send bills and manage the revenues each invoice generated. Vinnie once said to me he farmed out as many administrative duties as he could to allow more time for billable hours and golf. It all seemed a bit strange to me, but it appeared to work.

People with clutter all over their desk, always seem to know where everything is. I carefully returned the form to the place in the clutter where I had removed it. I noticed the company's name running along the bottom of the form: Cape Business Systems, Bourne, Massachusetts.

Chapter 45

Cape Business Systems was on the second floor of a long, rectangular two-story weathered shingled building with four dog house dormers, about a mile from the Bourne Bridge. The building was set back from the highway to provide a large parking lot. Cape Plumbing & Hardware Supply Co. occupied the entire ground level, and had the largest of the black letters on a white colonial sign perched on a twelve foot pole near the entrance to the lot. Two trucks, both with ladder racks and large, steel, tool boxes fashioned to the back side of the driver's compartment, were parked close to a small loading dock at one end of the building.

A new structure designed to look old, Novello thought, as he pulled into a parking spot near an outside staircase at the opposite end of the building. Novello got out of his car and pulled out his phone. "I'm outside Cape Business Systems."

On the other end of the line, Ed McGonagle told him he was five minutes from Secure Data Technologies in Fall River, the other company identified by Butts as a shell. The plan was for Novello and McGonagle to enter the two businesses at the same time to avoid one warning the other.

"Call me when you're there," Novello said. He walked towards the entrance to Cape Plumbing and Hardware Supply.

———

Ed's call came nine minutes later, as Novello was paying for a tube of industrial strength glue in hopes of repairing the lamp in his bedroom. "When I hang up, count to one hundred and go in," Novello told him.

Novello was at eight-nine when he climbed to the top step of the outside staircase. He went left and stood before a solid black wooden door with a white sign and black lettering announcing:

Cape Business Systems. Novello reached hundred in his head and pulled the door open.

He walked up to a wooden wainscoted counter of a large room and immediately began a survey. No pictures on the white plaster walls. Three rows of paired desks, each two desks deep. There were no telephones on any desk. A thirty-something, bullet-headed male with a shaved head and protruding jaw, sat at the nearest desk staring at his computer screen. At the rear of the room sat a twenty-something Asian woman glancing surreptitiously at Novello. Three windows on the back wall, thin blinds, no shades or drapes, two doors on each side wall leading to small offices, one appeared to have a coffee dispenser and a microwave. The kitchen. All appeared empty.

Bullethead blew out a breath of exasperation and rose from his chair. He sauntered slowly to his side of the counter He wore black pants and a stained, wrinkled white dress shirt.

"You need something?" He said to Novello. The twenty something Asian woman at a desk near the rear of the room never took her eyes of her computer, her fingers dancing across the keyboard.

Novello leaned into the counter. "I need to speak with you in private. It won't take long."

Bullethead gave another exasperated sigh. "What about?"

Novel flashed his badge and leaned a bit closer to the man's face. "I'm Anthony Novello, Chief of the Homicide Bureau for the Department of the Attorney General. I have all the information I need to put this operation out of business, and you in jail. So, asshole, you can either talk with me, tell me the truth, and I'll know if you're lying, or you can play tough guy, get hand cuffed and put into the system. What'll it be?"

The young man stared straight ahead. "Fuck you."

———

By eleven o'clock I had completed Vinnie's To Do List, and I was considering my options for lunch. The Boat Yard on Scranton

Avenue, directly across the harbor from the back deck of Vinnie's office was the leading contender. The phone rang. "Law Office of Vincent Preskin and Associates," I said. "This is Connor, how can I help?"

"Top of the morning to you Connor McNeill," Vincent said in what seemed to me to be an octave lower than his usual greeting.

"And the rest of the day to yourself. Vincent Preskin," I answered. What hole you on?"

"We tee off in twenty minutes," Vinnie said. "Connor tell me. Do you know a Kenisha Williams?

Tightness grabbed my stomach. In a millisecond I decided, Kenisha would not use my name in calling Vinnie. It would violate every rule Novello lived by. "No," I lied. "I don't think so." I left myself some wiggle room. "What's up?"

"She says she's with the Concord Police. Got three messages on my phone asking me to call her to set up a time to meet. Says she wants some background on a case she's working," Vinnie said,

"Want me to call Novello?' I said. "See if he knows anything?'

"What makes you think she's with Novello?' Vinnie said. Coldness crept into his voice. I had made a mistake.

"I don't know," I said. "Just thinking out loud, trying to be helpful. Bartoni was killed in Concord, so was his wife. I just assumed the police were part of the investigation. I won't call him if you'd rather I didn't. I don't want to fuck things up."

"Jesus, you're right." Vinnie said. "I didn't make the connection between Bartoni and Concord. I'll call her back and set something up for tomorrow. Maybe I can drive you into Boston, if the appointment is early enough. I'll let you know."

The usual Vinnie tone and cadence were back. He hung up.

———

Novello walked the male into one of the side offices, where he sat him on a bright orange plastic chair. "Last chance asshole, I put you in the system or you tell me everything you know about this place."

Bullethead narrowed his eyes. "Fuck you."

Novello grabbed the back of the chair and pulled it out from under him.

Bullethead landed hard on his tailbone and shouted something that sounded like, "Aaarrg."

He removed his cell phone and wallet. Questionable under the constitution, but Novello had given up on getting any cooperation from him. He fished through the wallet and found a Rhode Island driver's license with the name, Victor Nunez.

"Don't tell him a fucking thing," Nunez shouted to the Asian woman, who remained at her desk, as directed by Novello. "I'll send the Redhead if you even smile at this sonofabitch."

Novello grabbed Nunez's left hand and held his fingers to an electronic gadget about the size of his cell phone. He put the device on the table, pulled out his phone and pushed in the numbers to the Falmouth Police Chief. Novello smiled at Nunez as he waited for the connection. "Chief Davis, please. This is Anthony Novello." Novello gave Nunez another smile and a thumbs up sign. "Chief, I have a cocky, uncooperative, wiseass waste of time, sitting here with me. A Rhode Island license says he's Victor Nunez. I'm sending his digital prints to you. Could you run a check and get back to me?" He glanced again at Nunez, who was now paying attention. Novello repeated the thumbs up sign. "Even better. Thanks. And it wouldn't be a bad thing if we could lose him in processing for the next ten hours I'll leave his cell phone with whomever comes to get him." Novello hung up and assumed a catcher's position to face Nunez. "Chief's sending a car to pick you up." Novello rubbed Nunez's shaved head. "Wait here. I'll come back when your ride arrives."

Chapter 46

By eleven-thirty, Victor Nunez, his hands cuffed behind him, was bouncing in the back seat of a police car on its way to Falmouth. Two bench warrants for failing to show at court appearances in Falmouth and Barnstable made Novello's wish for losing Nunez in processing easier than expected. At the same time, Amanda "Mandy" Li was sitting comfortably in the front seat of Novello's state issued vehicle as it crossed the Bourne Bridge on its way to Boston. Her computer and the files on her desk were in the trunk.

Mandy gave Novello the information he needed within six minutes of the same spiel he gave Nunez. Novello could smell the stress rolling off, as she told him about a software program that created names, dates of birth, social security numbers and other information for I.RISE Intake forms. The program also created intake forms, diagnoses, treatment plans, discharge summaries, outpatient referral forms and other reports. Billing summaries and even phony insurance reports were created with the click of a mouse. "My job was to keep moving the cursor to the right box in the form," she said. "Mindless, but it paid my bills until I could find something else." After Novello took her computer and the files she had been working on to his car, a Falmouth police officer arrived to limit access and prevent destruction of records.

Novello kept his eyes straight and used his portable flasher to speed through light traffic along Route 25. McGonagle had succeeded in turning the only person present at Secured Data Technologies in Fall River. The plan was to meet in Boston at one o'clock, have affidavits prepared, signed and before a judge by two. McGonagle and Novello believed they had until six tonight – at most – before news of their visits to Cape Business Systems and Secure Data Technologies reached Anthony Bonfiglio.

253

"I never met Mr. Bonfiglio, although I did hear Victor mention his name to somebody on his cell phone," Mandy said. "I kept my mouth shut and did what I was told. I'm not going to jail am I?" She added, not for the first time.

"If what you've said is true and your involvement is limited to that, and you keep telling the truth and cooperating, you won't go to jail," Novello said. "Tell me about Victor Nunez."

"He was in charge of the office, and did some of the same kind of work I did. It was usually just the two of us, although sometimes a fat guy called Bobby would show up. He dressed like a slob, but Victor was always polite, called him sir, when he was around. I figured Bobby was his boss."

Novello maneuvered around a truck and headed onto Route 24. "Anyone else ever drop by?"

"I remember a woman. She was very nice and always stopped by my desk to say hello, ask how I was doing. She even remembered my name."

"You remember hers?" Novello said. He stepped it up to ninety.

"No, she only came by maybe three times in the eight months I worked there. She was very nice. You promise I won't go to jail."

"Describe this woman." Novello looked over to Mandy. "You won't go to jail."

"I'd guess she was in her late sixties, tall, thin, always well dressed. She didn't dye her hair. It was very gray, and she wore it up. I remember she didn't wear jewelry. I guess I noticed that because I don't wear much either." Mandy flexed her long white fingers as if to prove her honesty.

Carmela Bartoni, Novello thought as he sped past a Burger King and gas station.

———

Novello sat with McGonagle and Butts in the bullpen waiting for a member of Flaherty's staff to arrive with the affidavits and supporting documentation for the seizure warrants that would be requested of a "friendly" judge. "That wiseass at Cape Business Systems, Victor Nunez?" Novello said to the others. "He's the kind of asshole who gives crime a bad name. Lucky for us, Mandy was there."

Mandy was eating sandwiches in another room with Julio Santiago, the employee at Secure Data Technologies McGonagle flipped at its Fall River office.

"Santiago not a bad kid," McGonagle said. "Just naïve and dumb as lettuce. He spilled his guts as soon as I showed the badge."

"His face looks like he was a goalie in a dart game," Butts said. "Kid never had a chance. Hard not to feel sorry for him."

"His testimony will get us Monsignor Roche and maybe the Archdiocese of Boston," Novello said. "Far as I'm concerned, Mandy and Santiago should get the keys to the city."

———

I skipped lunch and decided on a jog from Vinnie's front door to the finish line of the Falmouth Road Race and back, a little more than two miles. The phone was ringing when I entered the office at two o'clock. I picked up and delivered the usual greeting. It was Vinnie.

"Hi Connor, I've got a meeting with Kenisha Williams tomorrow morning in Boston at eleven. I'm wondering if you can shift your schedule around and cover the office tomorrow instead of Friday."

"That won't be a problem, I said.

"Great," Vinnie said. Thanks for doing this. See you tomorrow when I get back from Boston." He sounded rushed.

"You want your messages? There's only a few, phones have been quiet."

"I have a tee shot coming up," Vinnie said and clicked off.

———

At two thirty-six, Novello's cell phone hummed. He pulled it from the inside pocket of his suitcoat, which was draped across the back of his chair. "Novello," he said and listened for a moment. He showed a fist pump to Butts and McGonagle. "That's great. Get them served ASAP. There's been no activity at either CBS or Data Technologies, so give the others priority, but make sure everybody's hit no later than four o'clock." He slid the phone into his pants pocket. "We got our warrants. The shit starts hitting the fan no later than four o'clock."

After a round of high fives and shoulder slaps, they sat down. Novello turned to Butts. "Kenisha's meeting with Vinnie Preskin tomorrow. Talk to me about him."

Chapter 47

"Preskin has more property than the Vatican," Butts said. "His law practice brings in over four million a year, and he doesn't have a secretary? Just Vinnie and your friend the paralegal?" Butts squinted skepticism and shook his head.

"You think he's dirty," Novello said.

"He's a lawyer and his cousin's a mobster," McGonagle said. "Ya think?"

"I think Preskin's taking cash, buying property, setting up trusts and LLCs and it's all part of a laundry operation," Butts said. "I'd bet on it."

"Is this when you remind us you're good at detecting criminal activity?" McGonagle said.

Butts smiled. "Just listen for a second. I'll admit Preskin's connection to Bobby Morelli is an influence. But so is the fact two Bonfiglio shell companies pay rent to a realty trust that acquired its property from Preskin." Butts paused and absorbed the silence. He had their attention. "Real estate is a great way to launder money. You pay three hundred thousand in cash for property. You can leverage it to get a mortgage and clean money. And, while the property is appreciating in value, you can use it. You can live in it, use it as an office, or rent it out, collecting more clean money. And then," Butts said in a triumphant tone, "sell it in three years for say three hundred fifty thousand. A profit and all of it clean money. You can hide your interest in the property with realty trusts and LLCs. Christ in some states, you can set up LLCs without listing the owner."

"How much of this can we prove?" Novello said.

"If I'm right, and you know I am, then everything will start to unravel when the seizure warrants are served."

———

Nelson Decker, the clinical director of I.RISE, sat at his sleek, aluminum and glass table desk. Decker wore a pale green short-sleeve dress shirt with no tie. An ugly maroon and gray plaid double knit sports jacket hung on the back of his chair. Twice divorced with no prospects, he dressed in double knit jackets and slacks because they didn't need ironing. Decker stared at his computer screen and moved the five of diamonds to the next column under the six of spades.

A voice from the intercom on his desk shattered his concentration. "Dr. Decker, there are several gentlemen to see you."

Decker recognized the receptionist's voice and pushed a button on the intercom. "I'm in the middle of something important, Phyllis. Do they have an appointment?"

"No Dr. Decker, but they have badges and search warrants."

———

Novello, McGonagle and Butts were still in the Bullpen. Ten minutes earlier, Attorney General Flaherty provided Mandy Li and Julio Santiago protective details and each was driven home by a state police officer.

"Ever read Agatha Christie's *Murder on the Orient Express?* Or see the movie versions?" Butts asked. He didn't wait for an answer. "Of course you have. Everybody has." He stood up, the energy of the moment taking over. "This case is like that. Everybody is guilty of something. Some more serious than others, but everyone's involved. This isn't just a case of some guy running around killing people. You've wandered into a network of criminal activity, woven around and over a bunch of organizations like the wool in one of those fucking Irish fisherman sweaters. You pull on I.RISE, and it brings you to the EZ DUZ IT Realty Trust and Carmela Bartoni. You pull on Cape Business Systems and Data Technologies and all of a sudden you have I.RISE, Anthony Bonfiglio, Bobby Morelli, the Archdiocese of Boston and Monsignor Roche. Keep pulling and Preskin will pop up like the clown in a jack in the box. You wait and see."

"Nice to be sure," Novello said. "I'd like to have more facts."

"They'll come. Just keep pulling on what you have."

———

Monsignor Roche, armed with papers and reports, walked the carpeted corridor between his office and the corner suite occupied by Philip Cardinal Mulcahy. He stopped at the closed door, quietly knocked and opened it.

"Yes, Monsignor, how can I help you?" Carolyn Tomei, the Cardinal's executive assistant, said.

Roche stepped inside. "I have papers for the Cardinal to sign, and a few reports I want to review with him. He's not in?"

"No, his Eminence left for New York an hour ago. He'll be back tomorrow afternoon. You can leave those with me." Tomei reached for the papers.

Roche pulled the papers closer to his chest. "He didn't mention New York to me." He immediately regretted the comment. Any sign of ignorance or worse insignificance, was heresy. Regret morphed into anger when the smile on Tomei's thin face grew. "Never mind, I'll catch up with Philip tomorrow," he said." Roche smiled inwardly when Tomei flinched at his use of the Cardinal's Christian name. He put his back to her and walked out.

Roche was a few steps from the door to his office when he sensed the approaching herd. He turned. Four uniformed police officers had come up the large staircase from the lobby. They approached him with grim faces and strident walks. The lead officer held up several pieces of paper.

———

Novello, McGonagle and Butts stood in front of the bank of elevators at One Ashburton Place.

"You'll call me as soon as you hear anything," Butts said.

"Absolutely," Novello said. He pushed the button and the three stood in silence.

Butts held up a finger, a signal he had another thought. He looked towards Novello. "Your friend Connor McNeill said Vinnie told him he sponsors a hole in a fund raising golf tournament for I.RISE. Yet I.RISE doesn't list Vinnie as a financial supporter in its annual report. Right?"

"Right," Novello said.

"I'll bet you a hundred bucks, the golf tournament is phony. All part of getting more dirty money to I.RISE and getting it cleaned." Butts stepped away from the elevator door and leaned toward Novello. "Let's say each hole is sponsored for five thousand dollars. Eighteen holes, that's ninety thousand. I.RISE is a fucking for-profit company. Who the hell contributes to a for-profit?" Butts paused to add some drama. "No one. The money doesn't come from the so-called sponsors, it comes from the mob. We originally suspected Salamanca, but now we know it's Bonfiglio. I.RISE funnels the money to members of its board of directors, and to shell companies, and pays Cape Business Systems to make them phony patient files. Wouldn't surprise me if the whole I.RISE enterprise is owned by Bonfiglio." He smiled shifting his head from Novello to McGonagle. "When those warrants hit and you've got computers and files, just keep pulling. Preskin will fall out of his tree. You could get Bonfiglio and the whole kit and caboodle.

"I thought Preskin was in the jack in the box," McGonagle said.

"People still say 'kit and caboodle?" Novello said.

The elevator doors opened and Butts stepped inside.

———

"These files contain highly sensitive information and are confidential," said Nelson Decker, his face and neck heart attack red. He was standing in the reception area surrounded by four police officers with white cardboard boxes. Susan Landry, the executive director of I.RISE, had arrived, but stood a respectful distance away. She was not going to be dragged into this.

"This is a seizure order, Doctor Decker." The uniformed officer pointed to the paper crumpled in Decker's hand. "No one is reading anything. We'll put the files into boxes, seal them and turn them over to the judge and the grand jury."

"I need to speak with counsel," Decker said. "Wait here."

"You can speak with anyone you want. That paper says we don't have to wait and we're not. We're also taking the computers."

Decker looked over to Landry. "For chrissakes, you're the CEO, do something.

"You're in charge of clinical records, Doctor," she said. "Not my place to interfere. I suggest you call Vinnie Preskin."

———

"Who let you people up here? Monsignor Roche growled at the officers. "You need to get back to the reception area on the first floor." Roche saw Tomei entering the corridor and waved her away. "I'll handle this, Carolyn."

An officer handed Roche some paper. "That is a seizure warrant," he said.

Roche glanced down to the sheet of paper.

The officer continued talking. "We are taking, under seal, all records pertaining to any referrals by the Archdiocese of Boston to the Institute for Recovery, Independence and Self-empowerment, also known as I.RISE. This includes all billing statements, reports, assessments, or other communications between I.RISE and the Archdiocese." His eyes moved up and met Roche's. "We're also authorized to seize your computer."

"The records aren't here you idiot, they're in Braintree and other locations," Roche said, staring through the officer.

"As are other teams with similar warrants," the officer said. "Step aside so I can take the computer and whatever files are here."

Roche looked over towards the Cardinal's suite. Carolyn Tomei was still there, an amused look on her face. "For God's sake, don't stand there like a potted plant," Roche shouted. "Call Win Allen."

———

At nine o'clock that evening, Archie sat, eyes closed, on a high back upholstered chair in his living room and listened to soft strands of Mozart emanating from the black cylinder that played whatever he asked. He still marveled at the device given to him five years ago by a friend. Archie was seconds from sleep when a soft knock at the door snapped him to attention.

"Who the fuck is this?" he said as he walked across the floor. He peered through the eyehole and groaned. What do you want, at this time of night?" Archie said as he pulled open the door.

A massive hand grabbed him by the neck and lifted him into the air.

The world went black.

Chapter 48

Freed from the drudgery of the five-forty morning bus to Boston, I ate a leisurely breakfast with Abby and walked to Vinnie's office. It was the kind of day you dream about in January. Blue sunny skies and mild breezes. I walked the two miles to the office in about thirty-three minutes, arriving just before eight-thirty. I picked *The Globe* off the front porch, unlocked the door and stepped inside.

The odor hit me immediately. An animal, trapped in the office, had died. I opened the windows in the front room and went into Vinnie's office. On the floor, his head and both arms twisted in grotesque and unnatural directions lay Judge Tobias Fisher.

———

By eight forty-two, Falmouth Police officers, crime scene technicians and one enterprising reporter from the aptly named *Falmouth Enterprise* were inside and around Vinnie Preskin's law office. The reporter had been assigned a spot outside the yellow strip and across the street. When I was a state representative I never avoided reporters. I often fed them information because I thought they worked hard, for little pay and deserved at least the morsels I could provide. Of course, until I was indicted, reporters rarely sought me out.

I wandered over to the reporter, who appeared to be in her mid-twenties. She was typing madly into her phone. I waited until she sensed my presence and stopped. She looked up and gave her best I'm-your-friend-you-can-trust-me smile. "What's going on?" She said.

"On background only," I said. "No name just a person familiar with the scene or investigation?" I added for clarity.

Her smile dissolved. "Fine."

I gave her my first-hand account of what had happened. It took less than a minute. Because she was a good reporter, she immediately started firing question I did not want to answer.

"Where was the body? Was there any blood? Is Mr. Preskin here? Who are you and what were you doing here?

"Look," I said. "You can call your editor and report the body of Judge Tobias Fisher was found dead at the Law Offices of Vincent Preskin. That'll put you ahead of *The Globe*, the *Herald* and *The Cape Cod Times*. You'll even beat the TV stations. You can get more details from the police or at the inevitable news conference. Don't waste your time trying to get information from me."

"I've already alerted my editor and fed a tip to Channel 4. I'll be the person at the scene for a telephonic news feed in less than two minutes." She smiled. "Don't try to tell me how to do my fuckin' job."

I shrugged. "Well played, Lois Lane." I scurried back across the street and assumed a perch on the front steps. Since I had called 911, an ambulance and a fire engine also responded. After giving my statement to two different officers, I sent texts and left messages with Novello and McGonagle. Then I called Abby to let her know. I debated calling Vinnie. He would be on his way to the meeting with Kenisha. Something told me not to call. Probably Novello's jealous guard of information. I decided I'd rather Vinnie's anger at my not calling him, than be subjected to Novello's rage at my sharing information with a person on the way to an interview with one of his colleagues.

Five minutes passed. I felt remarkably calm, as if watching a movie. The fire engine left a few minutes after arrival, but the ambulance remained. I knew (because of TV) the body would not be removed until the arrival of the medical examiner, or coroner.

I sat on the steps at an angle with a view of the harbor waking up and which allowed me to hear the sounds of a police force commencing a murder investigation. Two concerns began gnawing my stomach. One, I hoped Novello or McGonagle would arrive before I was asked additional questions. I didn't know how much I could tell them about what I had heard at yesterday's meeting, and I didn't want to be evasive or worse lie to cops investigating a murder. My second concern; did Vinnie do this?

———

Ten minutes later, I was still on the steps. The Falmouth Police Chief's car pulled up and a chunky white-haired man, just under six feet, got out and approached me with a wide smile on his face. His face had that look you see when a person suddenly stops wearing glasses. Something looked off. In the middle of his face was a nose that had been hit more than twice. He extended his hand. "Brad Davis, friend of Anthony Novello. You Connor McNeill?"

I stood and grabbed his hand. "I am. Nice to meet you Chief. I called Novello and left a message, after I called 911."

Davis nodded. "He's on his way." He glanced at his watch. "Should be here within an hour. You give a statement to anyone?"

"Yeah, the first guy on the scene after I called. He was in uniform. Then a few minutes later to a guy in plainclothes. Don't remember any names. Guess I was pretty shook up."

"Don't worry about it," Davis said. "You'll be answering questions most of the morning. You know where Preskin is?"

"Yesterday, Vinnie told me he had an eleven o'clock meeting this morning in Boston. He asked me to cover the office. I don't usually work Thursdays. Vinnie said he'd be here later today, but didn't specify a time. I arrived just after eight-thirty. Nobody here except Judge Fisher. I backed out of the office and called 911 on my cell." I silently prayed he wouldn't ask any more questions. He did.

"You know who the meeting was with and where?"

I decided not to lie. "Kenisha Williams, a Concord Police Officer. She's working with Novello. I don't know the location."

The Chief smiled. "Okay, look I've got business inside. You

should go home and meet me at the station say about ten thirty. Novello should be there by then."

Abby's car pulled up across the street.

"My wife just arrived. Maybe we'll walk to the Dunkin' and get some coffee."

The Chief stared at me. "Connor, this place is going to be a three ring circus in less than five minutes. I need you and your wife to get yourselves out of here and meet me back at the station at ten-thirty. Okay?"

I waved Abby off. "Ten-thirty it is." I headed down the short path to her car.

———

At ten-thirty-six, Abby and I were in a small room at the Falmouth Police Station sipping something the Chief assured us was coffee from large white plastic cups. We sat on the same side of a gray table facing a large mirror. "We're being observed," I muttered to Abby with a nod towards the mirror.

"I'll try to keep my hands off you," Abby said. She pushed her cup to the other side of the table.

"Didn't have to make it sound so easy," I said. I took a small sip. Horrible.

The door swung open at ten forty. Novello came in carrying a small cardboard carrier with three large white Dunkin' cups of steaming coffee. The space for a fourth cup was filled with packets of sugar and three small plastic containers of cream. Novello held the container with straightened arms to keep it away from his dark blue suit, French blue starched shirt and pale gold tie. He placed the carrier on the table. "Thought you might need this," he said.

"No donuts?" I said.

"Ed's on the way with a dozen plain," Novello said.

'I was kidding." I took one of the cups and handed it to Abby.

"So was I," Novello said. "Tell me what you've told our friends on the other side of the glass."

"The truth," I said. "Got to the office about eight-thirty. Picked up *The Globe*, and unlocked the place. As soon as I stepped in, I could smell what I thought was a dead animal. Went into Vinnie's office and saw Judge Fisher. Knew he was dead. Head spun around like a ventriloquist's dummy. His arms and legs were broken and twisted into unnatural positions. I backed out of the room, dialed 911 and stepped out on the porch and waited. I left messages with you and McGonagle while I waited for the Falmouth Police." I took a sip of coffee. "Oh, Chief Davis asked if I knew where Vinnie was. I told him Vinnie said he had a meeting scheduled with Kenisha this morning. I told him she was a cop and worked with you. That's everything."

"When did Preskin tell you he was meeting with Kenisha?"

"There were two calls," I said. I lowered my voice. "Vinnie called abut eleven yesterday and asked me if I knew Kenisha Williams. He told me she had left messages with him identifying herself as Concord Police and she wanted to meet to get background on a case."

"What'd you tell him?" Novello said.

"I lied and said I didn't know her. I suggested she might be working with you since both the judge and his wife were killed in Concord." I lowered my voice to a whisper. "I didn't mention that call to Chief Davis."

Novello's eyes locked on mine. "You said Vinnie called twice."

"He called again around two o'clock. Said he was meeting with Kenisha at eleven this morning and asked me to cover the office, which is why I was there at eight-thirty to see Fisher."

Novello nodded. "Good." He pulled out his phone and pushed a button. "Kenisha, it's me. Has Preskin shown up?' He glanced at his watch. "Give it 'til ten after eleven and call me whether he shows or not." He placed the phone on the table. "Christ, I didn't see this coming. We had a soft tail on Fisher, but it ended about nine last night. They thought he was in for the night."

"Are we in danger?' Abby said. "What if Connor had been early for work and was in the office when this happened."

"Judge Fisher wasn't killed at Preskin's office," Novello said. "He was killed in the basement of his home sometime after nine last night. Coroner estimates his body was moved to the law office around midnight."

"Someone wanted to send a message to Vinnie," I said.

"Or to you," Novello said.

"I wasn't supposed to be there," I said.

Novello nodded. "Look, I have something I have to do. I'll be back in less than five and fill you in on everything." He picked up his phone and walked out. He left his coffee on the table.

I turned to Abby. "I feel bad. Earlier, I wondered if Vinnie killed Fisher. Couldn't have done it. No way would he move a dead body to his own office."

Abby shrugged. "Why would someone go to the trouble to move a dead body to his office? Vinnie must have pissed someone off." She leaned into me. "Did you notice Novello has Kenisha on speed dial."

Chapter 49

"Who the hell are these people?" Monsignor Roche raged. "They think they can just come into my office, hurl around a bunch of baseless accusations, and then leave with my computer and files?"

They didn't just think it, Monsignor, they did it, Win Allen thought, but didn't say. Instead, he waited patiently, for Roche's rant, now nearing the three minute mark, to end. It was almost eleven o'clock. The two were in Roche's small, paneled office at the Chancery on Beacon Street. Allen sat in a tall leather chair, across from Roche who was sitting behind a large desk, covered with folders, magazines and scattered pieces of paper. *How'd they get that desk through the door? Must have come through in pieces.*

Allen had learned of the warrants yesterday in a late afternoon call from Carolyn Tomei. He sprang into action immediately, fearing this was tied to his illicit relationship with the Chief Justice. Using charm, influence, and a vague promise of future remuneration, Allen was allowed to read, but not copy, the affidavits and supporting documents used to obtain the seizure warrants. Now, giddy with delight the raid had nothing to do with either D'Alessandro or him, Allen allowed his mind to wander as Roche's rant went into its fourth minute.

"I swear to God, that idiot Flaherty, and whoever authorized him to do this, will wish they'd never been born." Roche's red face leaned towards Win Allen. "How soon can you get this resolved? I want everything returned before His Eminence is back from New York."

Chair's comfortable, but way too big for the office, Allen thought. *I suppose it would fit better if his desk wasn't the size of Kansas. Egos must be fed.*

"Are you listening?" Roche said.

Allen smiled reassurance and crossed his legs, carefully adjusting the trouser legs to avoid wrinkles. "Monsignor, we are both experienced, men of the world. We have known each other for more than a few years, and we respect each other. We have both triumphed over adversity, and I think it's fair to say, each of us in his own way has enjoyed the fruits of his labor and the rewards of success."

Roche leaned back in his chair. "I have full confidence in you, Win. I'm looking forward to kicking the asses of these bastards."

"I'm sure you do," Allen said. "But let me be frank and honest."

"Of course," Roche said, extending his arm. A signal to proceed.

"I have seen and read the affidavits for every warrant served yesterday and the documentation supporting every application for a warrant. And, Monsignor, you need to know I'm not just talking about the warrant served on you yesterday, but also the warrants served at the Archdiocese's offices in Braintree, and a few other places. And, I am also talking about warrants served yesterday at the offices of the Rothwell Foundation, I.RISE, and two companies. Just a moment." Allen removed a piece of paper from the inside of his suit jacket. "Two companies, Cape Business Systems, and Secure Data Technology."

Roche brought his swivel chair upright. "What's going on?" He said in a voice dulled with apprehension and doubt.

"Monsignor, you are in a boat load of trouble. You don't need me. You need the best criminal lawyer the Archdiocese can afford."

———

I had finished my coffee. I was thinking of taking Novello's cup when he came back into the room. Over the next ten minutes, he told Abby and me about the seizure warrants, and Malcolm Butts' assessments of Vinnie's law practice. Novello told me Butts was confident Vinnie was involved and it would soon become clear as the records seized in the warrants were examined.

"I'm sorry," Novello said. "I know you considered him a friend."

"He never showed for his meeting with Kenisha?" I said.

"No, Novello said. He could be running, or maybe he's suffered the same fate as Fisher."

"What was Fisher's role in all this?" Abby asked. The fear of asking him questions suspended by the day's events.

"I thought I knew," Novello said. "I've got to look at everything with a different perspective. Maybe Butts is right. Everything will fall into place when we start reviewing all the documents and computers."

"What's next?' I said. "Can we leave?"

"The law office will be off limits for several days," Novello said. "We're getting someone appointed to go over all the files, records and Vinnie's computer to make an inventory, and protect confidentiality of his clients. The ones that are real." He lightly touched my shoulder. "We'll be taking your computer, as well."

"Christ, I hope I don't find out I've been working for clients that don't exist," I said.

Abby squeezed my arm, "Who else would hire you?"

We all had a good laugh at my expense. Abby said she was heading to a meeting at a health care insurer in Braintree. Novello gave her an air kiss and said he was heading back to Boston.

"I'm going home," I said.

"I'll drive you," Abby said.

"I want to walk. I need to clear my head. Can't believe I've been working with a guy involved in a massive criminal enterprise. Feel like a fuckin' fool." I shrugged at Abby. "I'll have to think about my next move. Pretty sure my days at Preskin and Associates are over."

"I can help,' Novello said. He paused and looked at me. "I want to help." He left.

"You think he means it?" Abby said.

"Hope so," I said. "I don't know any fake law firms and clients that'll hire me."

We hugged and I followed her out the door.

Chapter 50

"It was that bastard Vinnie Preskin who set up the whole thing," Monsignor Roche said. "He assured me everything was legal. Even told me he had a retired judge as a partner. He invited me to the opening day ceremonies. I played in one of his fucking golf tournaments. This'll tell you the kind of guy Preskin is. He knew I was a former pro, and he still snuck me into his foursome. Preskin's the sleaze ball, I'm a victim."

But you played, didn't you? Win Allen thought. "Monsignor, you knew it wasn't legal," he said in a soft voice. He didn't want another rant.

"Vinnie called them referral fees," Roche said. "Said lawyers do it all the time." Roche huffed and shifted in his chair. "Now, all of a sudden it's illegal for me? Is it because I'm a priest? Because we're talking about pedophilia? Let's not mince words. This is discrimination."

Allen leaned in toward Roche. "It's illegal because if the affidavits are true, and the supporting documents tell me they are, the church was charged for services that were never rendered. I.RISE placed the priests in cheap hotels, or one-room motels, did a few counseling sessions a week and billed the church three thousand a month."

"So we're victims," Roche interrupted. "We can push that. I can testify against Preskin if I get immunity."

Allen smiled. "The church – the Archdiocese of Boston – was *the* victim. You, maybe others, knew about it and took an active role." Allen held his hands up. "Look, Monsignor, we need to be honest with each other. I'm telling you what the documents I saw allege. The Archdiocese received invoices for three thousand, which you forwarded on for payment. However, I.RISE received both the

Archdiocese's check for three and another three thousand dollars in cash, making it a total of six thousand. Then, I.RISE, or someone, sent you five hundred dollars."

"A referral fee," Roche said. "And there's nothing that shows I knew about the three thousand in cash."

"It's not a referral fee, it's what we call a 'kickback' for the initial referral of the priest for services."

"Semantics," Roche said. "Good lawyer could win this case."

"Five hundred dollars every month on every referral is not a one-time referral fee. It's an illegal kickback. Your name is also on referral forms and intake forms for priest that do not even exist. Phony patient records established by a company called Secure Data Technologies as part of a money laundering operation." Win paused and took a breath. "Fortunately, for you, Monsignor, the church was not billed for these ghost priests, but you did receive two or three hundred a month for each of them."

"It was two hundred," Roche said. His shoulders sagged and he fell back into his chair. "What kind of a deal can I get if I agree to spill the beans on that prick Preskin?" He sprung up in the chair with another thought. "What if I can implicate the Cardinal in all of this?"

The phone rang. Roche pushed a button and placed the phone on speaker. "Carolyn, I said no calls or interruptions. Was I unclear?"

"Sorry, Monsignor," Carolyn Tomei's voice echoed from the old device. "It's a Scott McCabe from *The Boston Globe,* calling for Mr. Allen."

"Fucking vultures," Roche whispered to Allen. "How'd they find out about this so soon?"

"Shit happens," Allen said. He leaned towards the speaker. Please put him through. He glanced at Roche. "You can leave it on speaker. Here's where I earn my fee." The sound of the connection filled the room. "Yes, Mr. McCabe, what can I do for you?"

"Thank you for taking my call," McCabe said. "We're going to publish a story this afternoon on our website and in tomorrow's morning edition that a petition for rehearing in the *Sheehan versus Archdiocese of Boston* case has been filed by Attorney Mitchell Garofalo. The petition alleges improper conduct between you and Chief Justice D'Alessandro, specifically the two of you had a sexual relationship, and she should have recused herself from the case. It further states she may have leaked important information about the Court's deliberations to help you and the Archdioceses advance your legal position in the case. Would you care to comment?"

"Those are the rantings of a lawyer hopelessly over his head and now using slander and libelous allegations in a desperate effort to win a case he has already lost. Any such petition ought to have been sealed, and if you publish those allegations, you and *The Globe* will join Mr. Garofalo as defendants in the largest defamation suit you could ever imagine." Allen terminated the call and fell back into his chair. "Christ."

"Shit happens," Roche said.

———

It was almost eleven–thirty, when I turned the corner onto my street. I was excited at the prospects of Novello helping me find a job. Would it require us to move to Boston? I liked Falmouth, but employment possibilities were limited. Lobbying was a possibility. Could I go full-time at the Clean Environment Campaign?

Unlikely.

I knew I didn't want to lobby for multiple clients. That was too much like practicing law. Balancing the time and demands of several companies was not something I was good at or interested in doing for the next twenty years. Maybe a large non-profit that had enough work to support a full-time lobbyist/paralegal. Too bad I.RISE was going out of business.

I turned into our driveway and around the car I use for travel to the bus station on the days I go to Boston. The bus station is only a bit longer than the walk to Vinnie's office, but parking is free and driving allows me to leave home at five after five for the five-twenty bus. Walking would require me to leave no later than four-forty. Beyond waking up and showering, there is only so much early morning activity I can take.

I slid the key into the door and stepped into our kitchen. Not sure why, but I sensed the presence of others. I turned and looked into the living area. Sitting on a low tan bucket-swivel chair was Vinnie Preskin, the long barrel of a gun pointed at me. Its hole looked like the business end of a cannon. Behind Vinnie, his hands on the top back of the chair as if posing for a picture, was a giant with flaming red hair. He had to be over seven feet. On the couch was a fat guy in sweats, with a bandage on his nose and a large patch over his left eye.

"Top of the morning to you, Connor McNeill, Vinnie said."

Chapter 51

I stared at Vinnie for several seconds as a cold finger went down my spine.

The Redhead standing behind him was a like a statue, his dark eyes lifeless as those of the fat haddock on ice at the grocery story. Instinct and habit took over. "And the rest of the day to yourself, Vincent Preskin."

Vinnie laughed, but it was not the friendly laugh I knew. It wasn't malicious. It sounded a bit nervous. "We need to talk, Connor. And no bullshit like telling me you didn't know Kenisha Williams. Paul Roche called me after you, Abby and Kenisha grilled him about I.RISE earlier this week."

"Can I sit down?' I said. "Can you stop pointing that at me? All I have are my house keys."

Vinnie lowered the gun. I felt the relief a condemned man must feel with news of a reprieve. Instantly, I felt things were going to work out. Crazy, but I remember hearing feelings have no morality or sensibilities. They just are. I walked slowly past the back of a wooden Windsor chair and to the matching bucket swivel chair, diagonally across the room from Vinnie. It made it a longer shot for Vinnie and got me closer to the stairs and second floor. Vinnie didn't seem to be watching. He appeared more focused on a spot on the rug only he could see.

"Sorry about lying to you," I said. "I felt I had to. Roche thought it was a grilling?"

'Not his word,' Vinnie said. "He felt the meeting went well. I knew it was a grilling, since there'd be no other reason for you and Kenisha to meet with the sonofabitch."

Vinnie seem to relax a bit, his body not as straight and taut as when I came in. "Roche and I played together at a Pro-Am charity golf tournament a long time ago. I liked him, and when Judge Fisher and I started I.RISE, I invited him to the opening. We kept in touch. When he was assigned to Chancery, he called me and said he was in a position to refer priests for treatment, and asked if I.RISE was interested." He shrugged, shifting the gun to his left hand.

Good sign I thought.

"Well, of course it was interested. I.RISE was a wholesale laundry and wanted as many real patients coming in as possible. But, the SOB wanted a fee for every referral and a piece of every monthly bill. We worked something out, but for a guy with a Roman collar, he's as greedy as they come."

Vinnie leaned towards me, still holding the gun, but allowing it to rest on his knee. "I'll tell you what kind of guy Roche is. He begged me to let him play in a foursome I was putting together for the I.RISE golf tournament. Begged me. The guy's a former pro and he wants in on a Mickey Mouse event for a charity – well supposed charity. Well, I let him play, and he brings his A game and we win the tournament. Then the SOB tells me he'd like to play the next year. By the time next year came, the mob had taken over the tournament and it really wasn't a fund raiser."

"Novello has a forensic accountant who suspected that," I said. "At least that's what he told me this morning.

"What else do you and Novello know? No bullshit."

"Novello thinks Fisher killed Judge Bartoni because he was investigating something to do with I.RISE. At first, he believed Fisher's story about Bartoni investigating Win Allen and the Chief Justice. They even interviewed D'Alessandro and Win Allen. When Mrs. Bartoni was killed after she took a duffel bag her husband kept in a locker at his gym, Novello decided Fisher had been lying to him. Novello thought Mrs. Bartoni never would have taken the duffel bag unless she thought something in it implicated her and the person she was turning it over to. Novello figured it was Fisher since he started the original lie about what Bartoni was investigating." My throat felt like sandpaper and just as dry. "I could use some water."

"He's right about Fisher killing the Judge and Carmela," Preskin said, ignoring my request for water. "But, it was a mistake. Judge wasn't supposed to be home, but he answered the door. Fisher panicked and shot him."

"Mrs. Bartoni was the target all along?" I said. "Why?"

"She provided funds for I.RISE when Fisher and I were doing the planning. Then, when Bonfiglio saw its potential as a laundry, she stayed in and even used her foundation to launder money. She liked the cash and felt like a big shot. When her husband got suspicious, she got antsy and wanted out. She threatened to expose all of us. We could have dealt with it. It wasn't a big issue." Preskin shook his head in exasperation. "Neither of them needed to be killed," he said.

"Wasn't she suspicious when her husband got killed?" I said.

"Fisher told her it was a mob hit, because her husband was going to expose the money laundering."

"She believed that?" I said.

"She believed it enough to meet one more time with Fisher" Vinnie said.

"D'Alessandro and Win Allen. Where'd that come from?" I said.

Vinnie shifted the gun back to his right hand.

My stomach tightened.

"Bartoni once told Fisher he'd seen Win Allen and the CJ together, and thought it was odd. So Fisher used that and made up the story he told Novello. He told Carmela to confirm her husband was investigating something involving the church. Fucking Fisher thought he'd put the fear of God in her by saying it was a mob hit. Thought that was brilliant. Neither of them had to be killed."

It seemed to me he was going to sob, and he looked away briefly.

His face turned back to me. "Fisher thought he was the boss. That he was in charge. Fucking idiot never got permission or even discussed killing anyone. He just did it. And, he blew up the whole operation."

"Why you found Archie twisted like a pretzel this morning," the fat guy on the couch said.

"Archie?" I said.

"Archibald," Vinnie said. "Fisher's middle name. He sometimes referred to himself as Archie. Usually when he thought he was being particularly devious or whatever." Vinnie shook his head. "Such an asshole. Ruined a brilliant scheme. Nobody needed t get hurt or killed. Asshole."

"Novello knows Fisher was killed in his home. Said the body was moved to your office. As a message," I said.

"He's right again" Fat Guy said. He turned towards Vinnie. "Sorry cuz. But you knew the score when you brought that asshole into this."

Bobby Morelli, I thought, but didn't say.

"What else does Novello know?" Vinnie said,

"He got seizure warrants served on I.RISE, the Rothwell Foundation, the Archdiocese of Boston and two companies he believes are shells for Anthony Bonfiglio. Cape Business Systems, which I know you use, and some company in Fall River called Secure Data Technologies or something like that. Novello figures he'll know the whole story once he gets a look at the records and computers they seized."

Vinnie was weighing his options. I'd seen the look many times. "One other thing," I said. "Novello believes your law practice has been laundering money for Bonfiglio."

"Vinnie's laundering for me," Morelli said. "Part of our deal when he got the nice house on the harbor."

Vinnie shrugged. He looked to me. "Most of the matters you worked on were for real clients. Sorry, to put you in the middle of this. About ten years ago, when Bonfiglio learned I was doing some cleaning for Bobby, he wanted in and it kept growing and getting more profitable for me. There was more money than I could hide."

"Made you a better golfer," Morelli said around a laugh as if we were good old boys enjoying a beer.

"Can I say something?" I said to Vinnie.

"Go ahead."

I knew it was risky saying anything in front of Morelli and the redheaded giant, but the only gun I saw was in Vinnie's hand. I decided to ignore them and talk with him.

"In the next day or so, Novello will know everything there is to know. And we can make him see you got caught up in something that kept growing and got out of control. You didn't kill anyone, and you didn't ask that anyone be killed. You're a lawyer, you know this can only get worse if you use that gun, or if you don't end your involvement now."

"The fuck you up to?" Morelli said. He pulled a baseball bat from behind the couch. Better than if he had pulled a gun, I thought.

Behind Vinnie, the Redhead shifted his feet.

"Let's all relax and not act like the assholes we are," Vinnie said. He glanced at Morelli and then tilted his head up towards the giant behind him. "We got the information we came for. We gain nothing killing Connor."

Vinnie shifted in the chair. "We have at best one day, at worst less than 12 hours, before the entire law enforcement network, federal and state descend on us. Airports, bus and train stations, toll roads and every street camera will be searching for us. Our pictures will be on TV more often than that asshole selling gutters. So, you both need to move quickly. You need to call Bonfiglio give him a polite heads up. He won't thank you or offer any help, but it's the right thing to do. Then you need to get the fuck out of Dodge."

"What about you and this asshole?" Morelli said, with a nod toward me

Vinnie gave me a this-is-what-I-have-to-deal-with shrug. "I am going to stay here with Connor and do nothing for four or five hours. Let you guys get out of here and put some miles between us.

Then, I am going to the Falmouth Police station tell them I never went to Boston because I didn't want to speak with Kenisha Williams. I panicked. I'll tell him I've been riding around and hiding, and have finally come to my senses. I will assert attorney-client privilege or take the Fifth on all other questions. I am taking my chances in an arena I know – the law.

Vinnie shifted his attention to Bobby. "I don't want to be a fugitive the rest of my life. Looking over my shoulder, jumping every time somebody farts. Fuck that. That's your world. I think you and Simon should get the hell out of Dodge."

I thought about making a run for the stairs, but I didn't want to spook Vinnie. He still had the gun

"This fucker will talk," the Redhead said. He nodded toward me. "He'll tell them everything."

"Simon, they already know everything," Vinnie shouted. "Haven't you been listening? Get you head out of your ass and get going. It's over."

The Redhead shifted. He was faster than he looked. He grabbed Vinnie's head with his huge hands. An ugly snap filled the stale air. Morelli jumped off the couch, and went towards Vinnie, now slumped in the chair.

I ran up the stairs.

Chapter 52

I raced into our upstairs office/den and pushed one of the recliners against the door. I heard footsteps coming up the steps. I went over to the window near Abby's work space and opened it. My heart was racing and I felt sweat rolling down my face. I pushed open the screen and dove out the window, scrambling and kicking my legs to get fully out and onto the small portion of the roof below. The window was part of a three-quarter dormer, which gave me a place to land and shortened the distance to the ground below. Behind me the recliner scraped the floor as someone pushed the door open. I grabbed the gutter and let myself slide off the roof. I hit the ground on both feet and started running to my left towards a neighbor's yard and away from the nine foot hedges that lined the property to my right.

A man with a huge gun came around the corner of the house almost running into me.

Freddy.

He pushed me aside and aimed at the window I had just left. Morelli, his arms, head and part of a shoulder hung out the window. He had the baseball bat in his right hand.

Freddy fired.

The sound was deafening. I looked up. Most of Morelli's head splattered the black roof shingles. His baseball bat rolled off the roof and into a small shrub.

Freddy grabbed my arm. I turned back to him to see Redhead step up from behind, put him in a bear hug, and lift his feet off the ground. He turned and carried Freddy towards the hedges and an old wooden picnic table. I searched for Freddy's gun. I couldn't see it. Only the back of the behemoth and Freddy's legs and arms swinging at air.

I gave up on the gun and grabbed Morelli's baseball ball bat out of the shrub and ran towards Redhead. I jumped onto the picnic table, which provided me the perfect height to take a home run swing to the back of the Redhead's skull. It was like hitting the largest melon on Cape Cod. Bones cracked and blood spurted. Redhead's arms dropped, and Freddy fell to the ground, gasping for breath. Redhead stood tall for what seemed a full minute. Later I learned it was just a few seconds. I was winding up for a second swing when he fell forward, hitting the ground face first with a thud. Freddy had rolled just far enough away to avoid being crushed.

Seconds later, Freddy and I, both running on adrenalin, yet sweaty and struggling to suck up oxygen sat on the picnic table, taking deep breaths, smiles and relief on our faces.

"How'd you suddenly show up? I said. "Happy you did, but how'd that happen?"

"The man I work for thought something was going to happen. He got a call from Bonfiglio asking about you. He called me."

"Salamanca?" I said.

Freddy just stared. The sound of distant sirens filtered through the shrubs and into the yard.

"You staying?" I asked Freddy.

"Too much trouble for you if I leave," he said. "I'll be okay."

"So tell me, how'd you end up here?"

"I followed you to Preskin's law office this morning, and then back here when Abby picked you up. Then, I followed you to the police station. When Abby left in her car I followed you on foot back here. My car's still in the lot behind the station. These assholes must have come here while we were all at the police. An obvious weakness to a one-man security detail," he said.

"You were here the whole time?" I said. "Jesus, I could've been killed in there, while you were out here."

"Another weakness," Freddy said. "I could hear most of the conversation. I was pretty sure Preskin wasn't a killer, and it looked as if he had the only gun. I figured it would come outside at some point. Didn't figure on Simon – the Redhead – killing Preskin, and you going upstairs instead of out the front door, where I was waiting. My plan was to ring the doorbell if things got dicey. Then come in guns blazing when the door opened.

"Doorbell's broken," I said.

Freddy shrugged. "Yet another weakness."

The sirens got louder. We got up to look for his gun.

Chapter 53

I never felt a second of remorse for what I had done, or sympathy for Simon, the Redhead, who died after being in a comma for six days. Bobby "Shits" Morelli died stuck in the window of our upstairs office/den. Novello and Flaherty were instrumental in convincing the grand jury not to indict me or the hombre known Freddy.

The grand jury learned Freddy's true name, but Novello and Flaherty have refused to disclose it to me. I believe Freddy is back in the wind. He left without leaving me a call, a text, or a two headed quarter.

Abby and I never moved back into our Falmouth home. It was cleaned, and the contents stored until we sold it. We moved to a community north of Boston. True to his promise, Anthony Novello interceded on my behalf and I'm now a special assistant and investigator in an office under contract with the Federal Bureau of Investigation, and headed by Malcolm Butts. He's a character, but we get along. I'm not exactly a person with marketable skills who can command competing employers. I gave up my part-time lobbying gig. I haven't been in "The Building" for nearly a year.

Abby never missed a beat. She works from our new upstairs office/den and still makes more in three days than I do in five.

Monsignor Roche got the best criminal defense attorney the Archdiocese of Boston could buy. He pled guilty to a single count of conspiracy and received a four-year suspended sentence. He was reassigned to an affluent parish in Vermont, which I'm told is within walking distance of a Bobby Jones designed golf course.

Cardinal Mulcahy mouthed the usual expressions of "horror and regret" at his friend's "malfeasance." He said he would pray for Roche's redemption. The Cardinal is no longer considered a strong favorite to become the first American Pope.

Chief Justice Gloria D'Alessandro resigned from the Supreme Judicial Court just hours before a scheduled impeachment trial before a joint session of the Massachusetts Senate and the House of Representatives. She was also disbarred. No criminal charges were ever filed. She's now a cable TV judge presiding over cases on a show called: *GLORIA!*

No criminal charges were filed against Win Allen. He was disbarred from the practice of law. I read he sold his townhouse on Marlborough Street for ten million dollars and is now living in Paris.

Mitchell Garofalo's petition for rehearing was allowed, and after several months of negotiations, Danny Sheehan and six other plaintiffs received a settlement of twenty-eight million dollars. As frosting on the cake (or salt in the wound), Governor Concanon nominated Garafalo to fill the vacant seat on the Supreme Judicial Court caused by D'Alessandro's resignation.

I.RISE was, in fact, a money laundering operation and shell for Anthony Bonfiglio. Susan Landry, the nice lady with even better legs, flipped on Nelson Decker, I.RISE's clinical director, and its board of directors. They pled guilty to multiple counts of conspiracy, criminal fraud, larceny and tax evasion. Each received sentences ranging from fifteen to thirty-six months.

A federal RICO (Racketeer Influenced and Corrupt Organizations Act) investigation is ongoing. The reported targets of the probe are Anthony Bonfiglio, the Rothwell Foundation, Cape Business Systems and Secure Data Technologies. The US Attorney has said the Archdiocese of Boston is not a target.

Vinnie Preskin was cremated. I wanted to, but did not attend the memorial service. Later, I learned there were more television and print media outside the church than mourners. It seems Vinnie had even fewer friends than he had legitimate clients.

Novello told me he heard Vinnie's ashes were entrusted to Millie Harkins, his title examiner. She reportedly has told friends his remains are part of at least one bunker on every golf course he ever played on Cape Cod.

Each day, I offer a quick prayer or light a candle for Vinnie. He was good to me, and I don't believe he would have shot me, or let Simon or Bobby hurt me. I think that's why he held the gun and not either of them. Besides, good people – like Mother Theresa – don't need my prayers.

Vinnie does.